Organ Symphony

A Leon Cazador Thriller

Nik Morton

ROUGH
EDGES
PRESS

Organ Symphony
Paperback Edition
Copyright © 2022 Nik Morton

Rough Edges Press
An Imprint of Wolfpack Publishing
5130 S. Fort Apache Rd. 215-380
Las Vegas, NV 89148

roughedgespress.com

Paperback ISBN 978-1-68549-146-8
eBook ISBN 978-1-68549-145-1
LCCN 2022942383

With love to Jennifer, friend, wife and first editor; and to our daughter Hannah whose name was used for the first incarnation of Sister Cristina many years ago; and to our son-in-law Farhad ('Harry') and our grandchildren Darius and Suri.

My thanks to James Reasoner, Mike Bray, and Jake Bray for believing in the character, Leon Cazador.

ORGAN SYMPHONY

PART ONE

SILENCED IN DARKNESS

CHAPTER 1

HEART SOLD

August 2016
Lazzaretto Piccolo, Laguna Veneto, Italy

GHO JUN CHUCKLED BENEATH HIS SURGICAL MASK and in his high-pitched voice joked, "Soon our rich client will be heartless, no?"

Nobody in attendance responded; they were all used to his dark humor; he was considered eccentric but he was also a brilliant transplant surgeon. Not unduly bothered at the lack of banter in his colleagues, Gho made an eight-inch long incision down the middle of fifty-two-year-old Kenneth Carswell's chest. The wealthy British entrepreneur under the scalpel was twenty-four years older than Gho, and now in a deep sleep, courtesy of a tube inserted down his throat which was attached to a ventilator; this maintained Carswell's breathing while he was anesthetized. His body temperature had already been lowered to around twenty-eight degrees Centigrade which would reduce the cell activity—preventing damage to his cells when blood flow halted. Earlier, the thinner heparin had been introduced to Carswell's blood to prevent it from clotting. All the man's blood was rerouted through the nearby heart-lung bypass machine, which would add oxygen and remove carbon dioxide and sustain blood circulation throughout the body and, most importantly, the brain and other organs.

The flesh had been peeled back and clamped by Theater Sister Li Jing to reveal the breastbone. Now, wholly professional, Gho said, "I'm about to crack the chest." He lifted the hand-held sternum saw, placing its blade on the exposed area and began cutting the breastbone down the center. "This is the fun part!" Well, not entirely professional: he enjoyed this bit particularly; the sound clearly grated on Nurse Weng Tao but it was music to his ears.

On the stainless steel trolley nearby were sterile packs of metal plates and screws, Gho's preferred method when finally fixing the sternum halves together as they provided more rigid fixation than wire and improved bone healing.

All of this was standard procedure in Gho's considerable experience. He'd been a trainee surgeon in Queensland in 2006 when Australia banned further joint research with China regarding transplantations because China wouldn't guarantee prisoners were not being used in transplant operations. He was twenty-two then. Undeterred, he continued his work in China, harvesting organs from Falun Gong practitioners and Uighurs in their confinement camps. He learned a great deal and became highly proficient, but he felt his hard work was not duly recognized by the authorities. And he certainly was not receiving an adequate financial reward. So he left China to join the Black Foundation Clinic run by Aiden Black, based here. And he hadn't looked back since.

Sister Li spread the ribcage and applied clamps on the sternum to keep the chest open and allow the surgeon access to Carswell's dysfunctional heart.

"Clamps," Gho said and Nurse Weng handed him the tools one at a time. He speedily clamped off all the major blood vessels to the client's heart and then disconnected them in readiness for receiving the replacement organ.

Now he lifted out the useless heart and placed it indelicately in a bucket at his feet. "That won't be needed again," he said. "Where is our $300,000 replacement?"

"Right here, Jun." Surgeon Kwan Yow and Sister Li presented him with the "donated" heart.

The two surgeons made a good team. Kwan had worked at the Nangfang hospital in Canton, a leading transplant hospital with a special wing for foreigners. It frequently used criminals' organs. As the hospital's chief surgeon at the time had said, "Why ask for consent when they're going to be executed?" Enticed by Gho, Kwan also defected to the west and was recruited by Black. When he could be spared, his other place of work was in the Black Clinic in Córdoba, Spain.

"Almost there," Gho said, beginning to connect the blood vessels to the replacement heart.

Nurse Weng swabbed his brow.

———

The Black Foundation Administration Offices, Venice, Italy

THIS WAS A MARVELOUS COUP, Aiden Black thought, as the Chinese professor, an expert in immunology, was escorted into the palatial room with its vaulted ceiling, marble floor and tall windows that overlooked the Grand Canal.

Yu Wei had been poached from the Wuhan Institute of Virology. "Welcome to ACM, Professor," Black said, his lips curving in a generous welcoming smile. His voice carried deep cultured African-American tones and echoed slightly in this room. Black stood up from his plush leather seat behind the imposing teak desk. The height of a basketball player, with musculature to match, he had buzz-cut black hair, broad nostrils, a high forehead and gleaming black eyes. Today he wore a crisp yellow short-sleeved shirt open at the neck to reveal a gold pendant, dark blue chinos, and a deep brown leather belt. He was far from being vain, but preferred bright colors to contrast against his ebony complexion.

A half-dozen framed certificates hung on one wall, most from the Salk Institute, San Diego.

He walked round the desk to greet the newcomer.

Yu bowed. "Thank you." He spoke good English, which made life easier all round. His flat features did not convey any emotion, yet his darting gimlet eyes seemed to take in everything. Yu was in his mid-forties, probably only a couple of years older than Black, though he conceded that it was often difficult to gauge the age of Orientals. Yu wore a Westernized suit in dark blue, a crisp white shirt with a bow-tie.

The two men shook hands; the professor's grip was firm and dry.

Black gestured at two ornate gold and mahogany armchairs facing across a low-level coffee table. The two men sat opposite each other.

Aware that at the outset he should not be too direct as it was frowned upon by Chinese, Black began, "I trust the flight was pleasant?"

"It was. The journey from the airport was an eye-opener too. No amount of exposure through books and film can prepare you for the real thing. Venice is truly unique. The boat trip here was a pleasure also. We in China have attempted to duplicate aspects of the city, but we have clearly failed."

"I believe you will enjoy working in this environment, Professor. I confess I like it here very much, it's a far cry from my previous residence in Washington DC."

"Indeed, I have no doubt it will be conducive to my research. It is good to be working with an open-minded scientist like yourself, Mr. Black."

When the overtures were first made to Yu, the feedback had been positive. The professor had become disillusioned with Dr. Shi Zhengli's cavalier attitude to containment. Apparently, she was obsessed with her damned bats, but lax in ensuring that basic safety procedures were followed. "To be honest, I am glad to be getting out," Yu had revealed. "I fear there will be another outbreak—perhaps worse than the SARS incident."

Which didn't bear thinking about, Black mused. The last he had learned Yu was involved in creating new biological weapons to destroy without trace the body's immune system. Black was happy if the immunology research could reduce tissue and organ rejection. "Their loss is our gain," Black had opined.

As the transplant coordinator of the charity *All Colors Matter*, Black wielded considerable power and had at his disposal almost limitless funds, which he utilized to scour the globe for suitable surgeons to do his bidding in several clinics. The charity purported to save the lives of the poor and neglected with organ transplantation, which they did accomplish, though only five percent of the operations were for individuals from deprived families. The remaining operations were performed on rich, criminal and influential patients, all of whom paid very well indeed.

Although he was a self-made man, Black had inherited vast sums of money from his father, who had died of a sudden heart-attack. Black had been frustrated that even with all the money at his disposal the doctors had been unable to save his father's life. Grief emboldened him and he lost himself in his work, buying and selling property, fostering scientific start-ups, constantly increasing his wealth, and garnering expertise in medical and technical research. Even so, he found time for affairs of the heart with a string of available women—until he fell for young Flavia De Santis. After a whirlwind romance, they married and nine months later she gave birth to a beautiful boy, Adriano Byron. Those days and years were bliss, a mixture of luxury travel, dedicated work and family get-togethers. Then, when Byron was ten Flavia was diagnosed with an inoperable brain tumor and died six months later. Byron was sent off to boarding school while Black buried his heartache and redirected his energies into financing medical research and establishing the Black

Foundation and a number of worthy charities, including ACM. He had no wish to die like his father and wife; he intended to live long and prosper, and would employ any means to achieve that aim.

"Would you like to be given a tour of the city before you begin your work?"

"No, thank you." The professor bowed politely. "The free time you have allotted to me in the contract will permit me to sight-see in due course. I am most anxious to see the laboratory facilities you promised and continue with my work."

"Good. It's only a short boat ride to the island. I will arrange it. Dr. Godsafe will accompany you."

———

January 2017
Charleston, South Carolina

HE RAN AS if his life depended upon it. The boy's breath was strained because he was bodily weak, partly from malnutrition but also from the after-effects of the operation. He'd made good his escape and he hoped the night would envelop him, hide him from pursuit.

He darted among shadows and hurried between the parked huge semi-trailers. He wheezed, clasping his side. A dull throb stabbed at his vitals. Yet the ache could not rid him of how terrible he felt, abandoning the others. He would get help, he would, truly!

The smell of oil, grease and burnt rubber from overworked tires filled his nostrils.

At the end of the alleyway formed by trucks he glimpsed the lights of a gas station and a diner.

Help was there for the asking! His heart leaped at the prospect. A heart that, he reminded himself, had already been sold.

"Yo, boy!" the hateful man shouted from behind him.

He shouldn't have but he could not avoid reacting; he stopped, hesitated and looked back.

Legs splayed apart, the tail of his checkered shirt hanging loose, the man grated, "You come back here, kid!"

"No way!" the boy snapped and turned and started running again.

Until massive pain hammered between his shoulder-blades and he found himself on the ground, lying in a puddle of oil. Now his breathing was really difficult. Waves of pain washed over him.

He had failed. He thought that, after all, his life really had depended on him running away.

Then blackness deeper than night overwhelmed him and took away all the pain.

CHAPTER 2

UNGAINLY PUPPETS

JANUARY MORNING SUNLIGHT SLANTED THROUGH the jalousies of the window. Sister Cristina flung aside the sheet, swung her legs out of the narrow bed and sat for a moment in contemplation, her breathing steady and relaxed, welcoming a new day, another day in her life as a nun in the Order of Missionary Sisters of the Mother of Christ.

She removed her lightweight linen pajamas and plucked from its hook on the otherwise empty wall her gray tracksuit, its back emblazoned with ST. PAUL'S HOSTEL FOR THE HOMELESS. She put it on, then tied with a twirl gizmo her long curling auburn hair at the nape, and finally fastened the laces of her trainers. All set, she opened her room's door and stepped into the lobby of the hostel.

Their old handy-man Marco glanced up, his lazy eye following shortly after the good one. He waved "good morning" and she signed back.

She exited through the front entrance doorway. Above was the plaque: "Then will the rags of the poor shine with splendor, and the gorgeous raiment become tarnished." She descended the steps and breathed in the air—grateful for its freshness before the day's traffic built up.

As she jogged toward the Battery, she called "Hi, Al" to the newsvendor on the intersection of Market Street. Somewhere she could hear gospel singing, probably from Georgia cleaning the steps of the Pentecostal church on Bay. At the last count there were roughly twenty-five denominations in the city.

After a while, Sister Cristina rested for a short spell in the gardens of White Point, leaning against an old cannon. Here, in the shade of palmetto and oak trees, she caught her breath. She breathed in deeply, the air crisp and invigorating. She let out a gasp, watched her breath float in front of her. Seagulls squawked over the confluence of the rivers Ashley and Cooper, which created the Atlantic, if Charlestonians could be believed. God, it was good to be alive!

The low-profile skyline of Charleston was bathed in the orange glow of the sunrise, punctuated with over 180 steeples or spires. The white spire of St. Michael's boasted a four-faced clock. A beautiful city with its antebellum homes, it had suffered hurricane, fire, earthquake, epidemics and bombardment during the Civil War—that "Late Unpleasantness" as the older fraternity preferred to call it. There seemed to be more Civil War commemorative plaques than black-eyed peas. But now it was a vibrant exciting and beautiful city again.

She spent half an hour at old Rich's Gym, mainly on weights, and then returned to the hostel, ready for another day.

Showered and dressed, she donned the scapula—the yoke of the Lord, the wimple and veil—the helmet of salvation, which restricted vision the better to avoid distractions from prayer and good works, and tied the black cord about her waist with three knots to signify the three vows she took almost five years ago; some other Orders insisted on twelve knots, for the Stations of the Cross; she thought that was a mite excessive. She tied the rosary to the cord belt and kissed her crucifix and then knelt down on the prayer stool and thanked God she had found new meaning in her life.

No sooner had she entered the hostel office than the telephone rang, breaking into her thoughts.

It was Leon Cazador. Her heart missed a beat to hear his mellifluous voice. "Hello, Leon. It's lovely to hear you—but why such an early call?"

"I'm afraid it's bad news, Maggie. I'm with Armando."

Before taking her vows she'd been named Maggie. Their friendship had been intermittent since he left the States in 2001. Her profession then had been a private investigator working in New York. That's where they'd first met. They'd grown fond of each other, but neither committed. When she got the call to the Order and took the religious name of Cristina, he insisted on calling her by her old name; it was less formal, he argued, and besides that's how he'd always known her. Usually, he only did so in private.

Armando Salinas was FBI, attached to the Charleston office with Leon temporarily in tow by agreement with the Spanish authorities. Had to be serious if the Feds were involved.

"Not one of my people, surely?" she said. "They were all accounted for last night."

"No, this entails a visit to the morgue."

———

THE AUTOPSY ROOM WAS CHILLY, the air conditioning units venting cold air. Dr. Sally Marshall, the brunette medical examiner, was dressed in her green scrubs. She was overweight, buxom, with perpetually flushed chubby cheeks and mesmerizing hazel eyes. Her once-sterile latex gloves were blood-spattered.

Sister Cristina had attended several autopsies as a cop before becoming a P.I., but the experience never failed to upset her. Supervising was Special Agent Armando Salinas and their mutual friend Leon.

Taller than average for a Spaniard, Leon had dark brown hair edged with hints of grey, and a powerful broad-shoul-dered build that suggested he was younger than his fifty-four years. Whenever she watched him, his movements gave the impression of being nonchalant but measured, yet she knew from experience there was the subtle hint of a coiled spring in his demeanor. His mouth was thin, his chin firm, and his complexion tanned. Lines in his face suggested a hard weathered life.

"This poor kid's brought back bad memories, Sister," Leon said, standing to one side.

She nodded. Years ago they'd teamed up briefly and tracked down a serial child-killer.

On the stainless steel table lay the corpse of a boy of no more than ten years, his torso already slit with a 'Y' incision. Liquid made a swirling sound as it spilled through the table's drainage holes into the tank below. The boy's organs were stacked on the small dissection table at his tagged feet.

Salinas had a pockmarked sallow complexion and a scar down the left side of face, which he claimed tended to endear him to the criminal fraternity. He turned his chestnut brown eyes on her, ran a hand through his wavy black hair, and cleared his throat. "Dr. Marshall says one of his kidneys was harvested no more than two weeks ago. Not particularly well excised, either."

Harvested. Such an innocuous, almost bucolic term, Sister Cristina thought.

The port-wine stain blemish over the child's forehead and down the left cheek sent a sudden horrible shiver down Sister Cristina's spine, and the sensation had nothing to do with the chill atmosphere in here. She stepped closer, and her heart sank.

"Oh, Rafael," she said in a hushed voice, her tone one of puzzlement. She leaned over, now oblivious of the blood or the gaping cavity in the child's body.

Even with his eyes shut—eyes that were once mischievous and bright with life—she recognized him. *How did you come to be here?* She stroked his face, a finger lingering over the edge of the prominent birthmark.

She briefly signed the cross on the boy's forehead then

took a pace back. "I'm sorry, doctor," she said softly, "I didn't mean to touch him..."

"That's alright," said Dr. Marshall.

"Do you know this boy?" Salinas asked.

"Yes, I knew him."

Leon gently touched her arm. "Was he with one of your homeless?"

She shook her head.

It was times like this when she was grateful for the traditional "custody of the eyes". She looked down at her hands as they tightly clasped her rosary. The overhead lights briefly flashed on her gold ring. "It is really puzzling. There were three children. They went missing from our village in Peru only days before I was due to leave the mission..." She gazed at the ceiling, calculated. "I returned from there three weeks ago."

"Strange, for him to be found dead here," Salinas said.

"It is... I can't comprehend why."

"Are you sure it's him, Sister?" asked Dr. Marshall, ever the probing scientist.

"Yes. You've seen the birthmark. That's Rafael alright. The other two were Claudia and Paco, brother and sister." She eyed the M.E. "What happened to him?"

"Gun wound in the back," Dr. Marshall said. "I can only surmise he was running away and someone shot him."

"There was no sign of the slug that exited his front," Salinas said.

"Presumably he was reluctant to lose his second kidney," Leon observed coldly.

Somberly, Cristina asked, "Can I make the burial arrangements when you release Rafael's body?"

"Of course."

———

LATER, Salinas sat with Cristina and Leon over the remains of a crabmeat casserole in a small restaurant in the bay area.

Salinas explained. "Couple of years back, I was on the trail of a guy named De Souza." He pulled out his billfold, removed and spread a crinkled photograph on the table. A zoom lens pictured a stout, balding man with a mustache leaning forward slightly as he was about to get into a limousine. "That's him."

"Surveillance camera?"

He nodded. "We wanted it water-tight. He'd walked on several minor counts. This time we wanted it to stick. Leon agreed to go undercover and work for him..."

Leon took up the story. "We didn't realize he knew we were getting close, oh so close..." His voice thickened; a break in the inflection. "He knew, alright..."

She touched his fingers. "Do you want to go on? You should only let painful memories out if you're sure you can cope with them." She hated seeing him hurt. Because, she admitted warily, worriedly even, she loved Leon. Not on the physical plane; this was something else, destined perhaps yet denied, as if forged in the crucible of fire from both their pasts.

"It hurts, Maggie. My friend Patricia—we'd just come back from a pal's wedding..."

Leon remembered:

He had pulled the Oldsmobile into the drive. "God, I feel old," he said, switching the engine off.

Pat unfastened the seatbelt, her lovely thick lips curving. "Weddings do that, you know, but don't worry, I'm not the marrying kind." She leaned over and pecked his cheek. "But I imagine that once we get upstairs you'll find you've got renewed vigor, hmm?" And she pressed his thigh in promise.

At that moment he noticed a movement in the rear-view mirror.

A Chevy pickup coasted to a silent stop, blocking their drive. There were two figures inside, wearing white coveralls.

The old sixth sense clicked in and he snapped, "Get down!" at the same instant as a hail of lead slammed into the Olds.

"Leon!" Pat shrieked.

Grabbing his .44 Magnum from the glove-compartment, he unlatched and shoulder-barged the door.

Falling onto the hard concrete driveway with a jarring thud that sent his bones and insides rattling in complaint, the smell of engine oil and cordite thick in his nostrils, he fired two rounds and rolled away onto the lawn, drawing the fire from the car and Pat.

The gunmen were amateurs, standing in plain view, too cocky with their Uzi machine-guns. Leon rested on his elbows and through narrowed eyes took careful unhurried aim as the Uzi bullets spat sparks from rockery inches from his face. The Magnum slugs lifted them both off the ground and they jumped like ungainly puppets and slammed into the fender of the Chevy.

He got up and ran over to the bodies. Only then did he feel the lancing pain of a flesh wound on his forehead and cheek. And there was a dull ache in his chest. He'd not been wearing a bullet-proof vest—not de rigueur at weddings, strangely enough.

Wiping the blood from his eyes, he hurried over to Pat.

The two cops in the squad car, called out on a 10-13—shots fired—found Leon Cazador sitting in the drive, cradling his girlfriend in his arms, his jaw clamped tight. If he hadn't gone undercover, if he'd let some young bloods take on the De Souza investigation, if he'd been a ballet dancer... If...

Leon ended fatalistically, "You can't fill your life with 'ifs' and 'maybes'—you've got to live it as it comes."

"Call the shots. Take the shots..." Salinas said unhelpfully. "What the hell."

Sister Cristina clasped Leon's hand, squeezed it gently. "I'm so sorry, Leon..." She brushed her finger against his brow. There was no sign of any facial scar now. Salinas politely averted his eyes. Their booth was secluded, but she didn't care anyway. Her action was a genuine act of tenderness, and God knows she had contained any old sensual feelings regarding Leon since taking her vows.

Leon held up a zippo lighter, its case badly dented. "This was Pat's birthday gift to me—it sounds damned corny, but it saved my life..."

"I've never seen you smoke, Leon."

"Gave it up that same day. Long before I met you..."

"This De Souza," she said, finger tapping the photograph. "He had something to do with Pat's death?"

"Oh," said Salinas, "he sure as hell did, Sister. Rumors were rife. A lot in the underworld didn't like the attempt on an FBI agent's life—even if he was only temporary..."

"But rumors don't convict," she said. "There's never been any proof against him?"

"No."

"What was his racket?" she asked.

"He had his dirty fingers in plenty of pies," Salinas said. "Child prostitution, pornography, and drugs of course..."

"And you couldn't get anything on him?"

"Annoyingly, no. That's why we welcomed Leon's contribution."

"Then," Leon said, "we had a tip-off about two weeks after Pat's funeral."

It had been a dark night, no moon, just how they liked it. The SWAT and FBI squads were dressed in black, night-sights scanning the compound and warehouses. Special Agent in Charge Conway was grim, his square chin firm, his piercing blue eyes determined. Besides body-armor, he wore a black cap that covered his blond crewcut hair, pulled down over his high forehead.

Reports came back: no sign of any movement.

They went in, SAC Conway with Salinas by his side and Leon Cazador along for the ride.

The bolt-cutters sliced into the gate's chain, snapped at the night's silence. Weapons were cocked. Feet padded across the Tarmac. Warehouse doors clanged open, flashlights beamed in every direction. Shouts. Warnings. Exclamations.

Empty.

"The bastards had gone," Salinas explained.

All that was left were partitioned cubicles, each with truckle beds or gurneys with the occasional blood-stain. The FBI forensic pathologists would sift over these tiny clues but resolve nothing, except that the apparatus suggested they were harvesting organs. De Souza's prints were all over the place.

Dead end.

De Souza had vanished.

"Until now, I hope," Leon said. "Little Rafael might give us some clues..."

"What do you reckon De Souza's been up to?" she asked.

"Baby farming," Leon replied. "Dealing in organs and babies."

"Baby farming. The new frontier of crime," Salinas growled. "They predict it'll be as big as drugs are now..."

"Mafia?"

"Some of it. Cartels. Even surgical specialists. But there are plenty of bodies to go round. Life's cheap to these guys."

"Third World children?"

"Some. Others from India...though most of their organs end up in the Middle East or Europe. Maybe China's doing it—one way to get rid of unwanted girl-babies..."

"What about the safeguards, the doctors' ethics?"

Salinas held up a hand, palm out. "Hey, ninety-five percent are good overworked doctors, doing a great job in a lousy situation. But there's plenty of the other sort to get sucked into this racket. It pays well, apparently. A pancreas or a liver can fetch $150,000, a single kidney $130,000, and a heart is the really big money—$325,000 all on the illegal market."

Leon said, "I wouldn't have thought any medic is so underpaid they need to resort to this criminal activity." He shook his head. "Those poor kids..."

"You want De Souza badly, don't you?" she said.

He gazed distantly into his past where nobody should

enter. "The patrol found me there in the drive, cradling Pat in my arms," he said, reliving the moment. "A stray bullet ricocheted, severed her wind-pipe... The doctor got there too late..."

Sister Cristina leaned over and rested her hand on his, feeling oddly like a soul-mate. She wanted to share her recent past with him, unburden herself, and show him her own terrible cicatrices that hastened her conversion to the Order, all concealed beneath her robes and the wimple, but that smacked of pride. A few more Hail Marys tonight, she thought, and smiled to herself. "I'm sorry, Leon."

It was no secret to either that there was still an attraction, but both knew it was now impossible. Sister Cristina made her vows and she was determined to stick to them. Leon Cazador was content to enjoy her presence whenever he was in the States, to look on her wonderful smile of mouth and startling big blue eyes. Not for the first time, he envied her hostel's inmates: with minor exceptions, such as a snatched lunch, she gave the hostel homeless her undivided attention. Besides, he had a growing gumshoe business in Spain to run. What he needed was an assistant.

Leon dug inside his breast pocket and unfolded a creased glossy sheet of paper torn from a magazine. "Don't get mad at me for bringing this up," he said, "but I've got a reason."

"Oh, Leon!" It was about six months old, a TIME article about the homeless hostel, complete with a color photograph of Sister Cristina. Scrawled in felt tip over the white of the wimple was the hostel telephone number.

"Did Rafael call you?" Leon asked.

"No. I only wish he had..." She picked up the sheet. "You found this on his body?"

"Yeah," Salinas replied. "Doc Marshall's done all the tests on it. Reckons there's not much to glean. She was a little surprised to see it, though, after your encounter this morning."

"You think he was trying to get in touch with me when he was shot?"

"It's possible." Leon pocketed the clipping.

"I haven't much to go on," Salinas said, "but it's likely."

Leon said, "Don't know where that gets us, though."

"I'd say at the point where we decide who's paying for the check," Salinas replied.

She attempted to object but Salinas held up a hand. "Expenses, Sister."

"The least we can do," Leon said, "since you're helping us with enquiries."

She said, "I don't think you've a deceitful bone in your body, Leon, so I'll go along with that suggestion. But let's not make a habit of it."

"No pun intended, eh?" Leon smiled. "Has the Abbess been saying anything about our friendship?"

She pursed her lips, eyed both men. "Dear Abbess Ursula sees things in black and white and wouldn't impugn your professional standing at any time, Leon. And that goes for you too, Armando."

Salinas nodded. "Sounds like a 'yes' to me..."

"Well?" Leon prompted.

"Oh, yes, she has mentioned it—once or twice..."

And today was no exception.

Immediately after leaving Leon and Armando, she had endured another interview under Abbess Ursula's icy cold stare. The Abbey was a converted mansion off the bay area, bequeathed by its owner in the hope that divine providence might protect it against any future incursions from nature, such as hurricanes and floods. The building was in the double-galleried colonial style, with splendid wrought iron fence, gate and balconies.

Sister Bernadette, the Abbess's secretary, let her in, and the signs were not good for she seemed agitated which usually meant the great lady was in a foul mood.

The large hall was dominated by the portrait of the Order's foundress, Mother Lucrezia Camigliano, with the dates 1800-1902 carved in the gold leaf frame. She'd been born in Sienna and travelled to New York in 1857 to set up several convent houses for her Order of the Missionary Sisters of the Mother of Christ. The sisterhood had followed her main precepts since that time: if someone needs help, then help them. There were off-shoots, such as Sister Cristina's own hostel for the homeless, which catered only for women and their children. Locally, the place was now known as Sister Cristina's—another sore point for the Abbess to worry over: "beware of the cult of personality, my dear."

Entering the Abbess's room, she exchanged the usual ritual *Deo Gratias* and knelt to kiss the lady's amethyst ring.

"Welcome, Sister Cristina. I hear you have been busy helping the police again?" The pale face was lined, with crows'-feet and deep troughs from nostril to the corners of her mouth, and yet for all the Abbess's stern appearance and manner, Sister Cristina found something endearing, something unfathomable about her. She had worked for quite a few superiors, male and female, in her life before becoming a nun, and while she respected most, none affected her as greatly as Abbess Ursula.

"Yes, Mother." At times like this she had learned to maintain a monosyllabic response where possible. It prevented her digging herself deeper into the mire. And whatever you do, maintain the custody of the eyes. Eyes are the window to the soul and now that she had taken her vows only God should have access through that window.

"You are not letting your past affect your calling, I hope?"

"No, Mother."

"We must be impartial when dealing with the needy, the sick and the homeless, my child."

"Yes, Mother."

"If you are seen—shall we say, regularly meeting?—with male officers of the law, then you may be jeopardizing that trust you have built up—most commendably, I might add."

"Thank you, Mother."

"I do not give it any credence, but there is talk that you are seeing rather too much of the man named Cazador."

"It's possible, Mother."

"What is possible, my dear?"

"Talk. Rumor. It happens."

"Yes, but we must be above that, must we not?"

"I am a dutiful nun, Mother, and I try very hard to obey my vows. I don't take them lightly." Obedience was the hard one, she had to admit. Celibacy—"the little crucifixion"— was difficult at certain times of the month, but the yearning could be contained or released in the solitude of her room at the cost of confession and twenty-five Hail Marys. Poverty was fairly easy, as she had handed over her money to the Order, though she wondered about the poverty of the spirit: there, too, she might be wanting. She tended to "go at things" without thinking about the consequences—spiritedly, in fact. Still, "know thy faults" is a start.

"I am sure you are exemplary, my child. I do not mention this to criticize, only to guard you against putting yourself and our Order into an invidious position."

"I understand, Mother. But my visit was necessary this morning."

"Will you tell me about it?"

Sister Cristina lifted her eyes. "I regret I had to visit the morgue—there was a child, Rafael, someone I knew at the mission..."

That was the end of the audience, really. Once the Peruvian mission was mentioned, then Sister Cristina could do no wrong, because she had gained a remarkable reputation for getting things done down there in the Andes, creating a tremendous bond between the villagers and the mission nuns which no terrorists could influence, a bond which no Government bureaucrats or edicts could sever.

"I am truly sorry to hear about the boy Rafael, Sister. Please keep me informed of any developments, will you?"

"I will, Mother. I will." She genuflected and left.

———

Massachusetts

THE CONVOY of three trucks and a pickup pulled into an all-night diner off the turnpike.

Moose, the lead driver jumped down from his cabin, circled the vehicle and kicked the tires as he did so. Not because there was anything wrong. It was his mental state which caused him concern.

Throughout the drive from South Carolina he'd tussled with his conscience. Doubts had been there from the beginning, but had gotten worse since that brat escaped and Yancy shot him in the back. You could convince yourself it was for their own good—they'd end up in homes where they were wanted, loved—*not like me*, he thought sullenly. But killing seemed on the extreme side, even for a redneck bastard like Yancy.

There was something more to it than fake adoptions, he reckoned. But the money was good. With that kind of money he could set up his own haulage firm in about six months. So Moose turned a blind eye.

But the whispers started to insinuate themselves into his soul. He'd read of the Nazi experiments in concentration camps and believed that if even a fraction of what he'd heard was true with this crowd, then he was no better than the bastards in Buchenwald and places like that.

Out of the corner of his eye he spotted a checkered shirt. Yancy strolled up to him while Moose was reaching up for the padlock on the truck door. "Yo, Moose, whatcha doin', boy?"

Moose was tall and thick-set and could take on Yancy in a fair fight any day. But Yancy had an automatic pistol tucked inside his reefer jacket. That made them even. "Just checkin', don't want no more runaways, do we?" In truth, he didn't know why he'd come round the back—to check on the kids, see they were okay? Maybe.

"Mighty industrious of you, boy." Yancy's well-worn features, puffy round the eyes and cheeks pitted with acne should be a turn-off for women, yet he scored more times than most guys. Go figure.

Sarcasm from Yancy was a rarity. *Tread real careful*, Moose told himself. "A bite to eat, y'reckon?" he said, thumbing the diner.

"Sure. We ain't gotta be at the site afore midnight..."

Inside Yancy's truck it was pitch black. But Paco knew the layout from memory when they'd opened up in daylight. There were now five of them: Claudia, Joaquin, Fernando, Maria, and him. They'd started out with Rafael as well but he was stupid; he got caught and shot for his trouble.

Each of them was tied by legs and torso to a metal bed: there were triple tiers on each side. At the end of the central aisle was a fixed trolley with drawers containing drugs, hypodermics and food. Toilet facilities consisted of a hole in the floor too small to squeeze through. Their guard was an uneducated hood from Chicago called Frankie: he never spoke. Frankie was there simply to release any of the children should they want to relieve their bladders or bowels, and only one at a time. Frankie let them "jabber" as he referred to it, partly because he couldn't understand them and partly because he didn't care so long as he could sit and listen to country and western tracks on his personal CD player.

"Claudia, are you awake?" Paco whispered hoarsely. His sister was on the bed below him; he occupied the top one in his tier.

"Yes." Her voice was faint, and she was still frightened.

"You're not to worry, you hear?" he said forcefully, in his big-brother voice.

Tremulously, she replied, "No, Paco. I won't worry. I promise."

"We'll get out of this somehow."

Paco blamed himself for getting them into the mess. Rafael had argued against going off with the American "tourist" for ice cream, but he'd sneered and dragged them along with him. When the so-called tourist led them into the trap it was too late. He smiled momentarily, recalling the shout of anger and pain expelled from one of the men who'd received Paco's foot in the groin. The cuffed ear could have been worse but the American growled, "Go easy on them, they're valuable merchandise!"

Sister Cristina taught all the children well in his village. He understood enough English to realize that with these people he was no longer considered a human being, a child of God, but a commodity, to be bartered.

The nightmare started in the hold of the ship, during a terrible storm. They were all seasick and wanted to die. One of the stolen children did die, choking on his vomit; he was taken out and they never saw him again. "Consigned to the deep blue," he'd heard Yancy say afterwards. Then they were secretly landed in the belly of Florida, and divided up into transports. By chance all three stayed together, and were trucked to South Carolina. Here, Rafael was taken away—it must have been about two weeks ago—and returned with a bandage wrapped round his body. One of the older kids showed his own operation scar, proudly displaying it as a badge of honor, and said, "They start on the bits we've got two of—like kidneys, eyes, lungs..." The rest was left unsaid.

Over the weeks, they were transported five times. In that period Paco had gained odd snippets of information and lost a kidney. He knew the man responsible for his continuing nightmare was named De Souza, he knew that his "charges" as he called them were to be moved often, to avoid suspicion or detection.

During their time in the baby farms they were given periodicals to read and stolen computer games from various heists to play. There were three copies of the *TIME* issue which featured an article on the dispossessed of North America. A colored box highlighted the St. Paul's Hostel for the Homeless in Charleston, South Carolina, with a sidebar photograph of Sister Cristina.

The three children were so excited to see her face, the radiant smile, the bright blue eyes, the smooth complexion, all captured within the confines of her wimple, veil and scapula.

A minder, a young Philippine girl, sauntered over, said, "What's all the commotion for?"

Thinking quickly, Paco replied, "We reckoned it funny that the United States has so many homeless—just like our own Third World country!"

The irony was lost on the Filipina. "Yeah. Well, keep the noise down, we've got babies asleep here."

Babies were snatched, too. Some for organ transplanting, others for illegal adoption. The Filipina was impregnated by one of the guards; she had given birth twice already and was only sixteen. She was one of De Souza's prized "breeders."

Because the children were a "valuable commodity," De Souza insisted on his doctors giving them and their minders regular checkups. Any who didn't meet a clean bill of health were consigned to the spare parts convoy and literally put on ice.

It was during one of these medical examination sessions while they were still in the South Carolina baby farm—God knows where—Paco hit upon a strategy to get more information. He complained of stomach cramps and fell about in paroxysms of pain. The Filipina panicked and fetched Dr. Keitel. The doctor diagnosed food poisoning which was not far off the mark: Paco had eaten a chunk of moldy bread he'd stashed for this purpose. They rushed him to the Memorial Hospital where he was treated with professional care. Appearing totally dedicated to their charge, the Filipina and Dr. Keitel hardly ever left his side and he never had a chance to speak to any nurse. But he did slip out of the lavatories once and used the Ward Sister's telephone to call Directory Assistance. He scribbled down the telephone number of Sister Cristina's hostel for the homeless.

When he was returned to the baby farm he smiled triumphantly at his sister and Rafael. Immediately, they wrote down the number on the torn-out page with Sister Cristina's photo.

Now, in the dark, Paco felt the crumpled sheet bristle against his new pubic hair, a forlorn hope hidden in his underpants. Rafael had hoped to get away, call Sister Cristina for help, but he'd failed, making his break too soon.

Paco would bide his time. He had faith in Sister Cristina. He was sure that if she knew, she would help. Besides, he'd promised Claudia.

CHAPTER 3

STOCKBRIDGE MOTHERHOUSE

WITH THE DARK CAME A LIGHT OF SORTS. MOOSE reckoned the money wasn't worth it.

He waited until the convoy was well along the Massachusetts Turnpike. Sleet and snow started about an hour back. The mesmerizing thud of the wiper blades beat home his guilt: Child-killer, child-killer... He began to sweat. Jeezus, what was he thinking of? Money, he answered miserably. Plenty of money... Not so's they'd do that to kids—it didn't matter if they were foreign kids, poor kids—no kid should go through that!

The white slush on the windscreen collected in the corners, and Moose remembered Yancy's unprepossessing features as he sneeringly laughed and said, "Yo, you're wonderin' what we're really doin', Moose ol' son?"

Moose sipped his coffee, and then said, "It kinda crossed my mind. Seems to me you wouldn't have offed that kid if it were just adoptions we're into."

Meaningfully, Yancy patted his reefer jacket. "This pistol and me have been buddies all of fifteen years now."

"Yeah." Moose wondered if he could take the son-of-a-bitch before he could draw the weapon. At that moment, Rickard, the other truck driver and Wesley, the driver of the pickup, joined them at the table. He noted that Frankie, the guard for his kids, plus two others, kept to themselves at a table near the toilets.

"Be glad when we can put our feet up at the farm," said Wesley. He was thin and resembled a weasel. But according to Yancy he was De Souza's favorite.

"Me, I'm looking forward to getting that new Cuban nurse into the sack." Rickard made a lewd gesture and Wesley chortled.

"I'll settle for the Chicana," said Yancy.

Frankie and the others watched without speaking.

"Yeah." Moose was out of his league, it seemed. He'd been taken on at the last minute when a driver hadn't turned up. Now, he wondered about the bits and pieces of information they'd all dropped, as if on purpose, toying with him. He decided to face them out. He eyed Wesley, the likeliest to talk. "Yancy here was saying I should be put in the picture about those kids. About the farms."

They exchanged knowing glances, smirked and Wesley said, "Okay, since you're in, you might as well know *what* you're in."

While Wesley told him everything Moose's blood ran cold and he felt sick to the pit of his stomach. His shirt under the windbreaker was now soaked with fear-sweat and the sensation was unpleasant.

Good God, what have I got into? And with that thought along came another: *you'll not easily get out.*

The truck radio was playing an old track, Canadian Loreena McKennitt's *The Mask and the Mirror*—the love poem of St. John of the Cross: "...shrouded by the night and by the secret star I quickly fled..."

Fled. His mind was made up. Find the right place—and flee.

Traffic was slight now. Anyone with sense was at home. Infrequent headlights glared, reflecting from the snow on the sides of the highway, blinding in contrast to the dark night.

Junction 2 signs lit up and he passed them.

Moose switched over to the CB channel, but Wesley and Yancy were only exchanging dirty stories.

Now, he thought.

At the last second he swerved off the turnpike, toward the township of Lee. If he could get help, tell the sheriff...

Tires screamed and the truck behind him continued on its journey, as did the third vehicle. The CB radio screeched: "Keep goin'!" Wesley's voice. "I'll get the bastard and bring his cargo back!"

It was treacherous here. Moose was having difficulty controlling the wheels. The blizzard was coming in thicker, heavier. He slowed. Visibility was down to a mere thirty yards or so. He wanted to brush away the white on his windshield and once, absurdly, he caught himself attempting just that!

Unexpectedly, he was thrust forward onto the wheel and dash as the truck came to an abrupt stop.

Peering through the white gauze he could see a snow-drift, spanning the entire road. This was one mother of storms!

The kids in the back! Zipping up, he grabbed the keys and opened the door. The contrast of the chilled blast hit him as he jumped down. He sank into snow up to his thighs. The air was cold, whipping all warmth from his face, almost freezing him to the bone. The wind took his breath away; he bowed into it and manfully trudged round to the back. At least here the road surface was fairly clear, only inches deep.

Fingers already numb with cold, he struggled with the padlock and finally got it open. He yanked it off and flung back the hasp.

Inside it was chaos. Frankie had been thrown from his seat and knelt on the metal floor, his head penetrated by the upright of a tier of beds; it was so cold inside there was very little blood-flow. The kids, thankfully, were still strapped in.

Moose heaved himself up inside, glad to get out of the biting icy wind.

None of the kids said a word.

Their gaze followed him, but the children were too cold to speak. Teeth chattered loudly, like demented castanets. The trolley at the rear had dislodged all its drawers. Amongst this debris Moose found a scalpel and began slicing the leather strap that secured Paco.

Once free, Paco started helping Moose release Claudia.

"My hands, they're so cold!" Claudia cried feebly. "I can hardly feel my legs..."

"Hush, we'll be free in a—"

"I think not," said Wesley. He stood at the entrance of the container, his automatic leveled steadily. Breath blossomed from his mouth like smoke from a gun. The scarf fell from his face. Moose thought the weasel looked too warm to be Death.

"Hey, go easy with that thing, Wesley. It might go off!" His breath erupted in wisps. Maybe some of his breath would linger after he lay dead...? His mind was seizing up, as if he was already dead. Stop this! Get a grip!

"An accident," Wesley said, "is that it?"

Grasp at straws! "Yes, Wesley, I just swerved, then it was either go on or—or—"

"Or what?" Wesley held up his billfold, adding, "Says nothing about delivering no driver in the manifest."

Moose dried up, frustrated. Another small punk with a gun, but this time, this time he wouldn't back down!

The first shot hit him in the shoulder but by then he was already in motion, propelling himself forward as in the old football days when life was uncomplicated, when there were plenty of jobs to go round. "Run, kid!" he shouted at Paco. "Run!"

Moose took the second bullet in the chest as he collided into weasel Wesley. He caught a dark movement to his right. Must be the kid. Go, go, go, get help, kid! Then he was falling in the snowdrift, trying to wrestle the weapon from Wesley.

Paco landed gently on snow.

As Moose tackled Wesley, Paco pushed past, his heart

pounding with fear as he grabbed the billfold that had fallen from Wesley's hand. Paco scurried off, holding the thick leather wallet tight to his chest.

The cold and blood loss sapped Moose's strength. The weasel man finally squirmed free and turned, dusted off his snow-covered coat. "Bad career decision, Moose," Wesley said and fired. The snow surrounding Moose's head took on a dark crimson hue.

The single shot echoed in the snowy stillness.

Paco hid under a snow-capped bush. Before the cold got him, he checked through the weasel's wallet: credit cards, hundred dollar bills, a few handwritten notes, a list of addresses, and two medical-looking order forms.

Shivering, fearful to move, Paco wanted to return for Claudia. She was terribly cold. She needed his help. He'd promised. He was tired as well. The lack of one of his kidneys probably had something to do with that. He wanted to rush the weasel-faced whoreson but that would be useless. He was a mere boy, and the weasel was a man with a gun.

Paco felt inside his crotch, glad of the warmth, and ripped out the torn page, stuffed it into his shirt pocket, next to his heart. Sister Cristina will help. Find a pay-phone.

His teeth chattered and he clamped down hard, trying to silence them.

Weasel was inside the container again. Paco thought about shutting him inside, but he hadn't the strength normally to move those heavy doors, let alone now.

One after another, three flashes came from the back of the truck and three shots rang out; at each tremendous echoing sound Paco flinched. Tears briefly warmed his cheeks while his heart felt as if it had transformed into solid ice. He was about to stand up and rush out, shouting "Kill me as well! It's my fault!" when Wesley emerged, dragging the two girls.

At sight of Claudia Paco's heart melted a little. There was still a chance; he could still save her.

Claudia and Maria struggled feebly; it was like a mime

show, as they uttered no sounds, trembling in shock at what they had just witnessed.

Wesley bundled them into the cab of his pickup and got in himself. Swiftly, he turned the vehicle round and headed the way he'd come. He only had room for two kids, and they might as well be "breeders."

———

Charleston, South Carolina

WHEN THE TELEPHONE rang in the hostel office, Sister Berenice answered, "Yes, this is St. Paul's, who is speaking, please?"

The voice was a child's, faint, tremulous. "I must speak to Sister Cristina. It's very important."

"She's busy with a class at the moment." Sister Cristina was teaching English to three Syrian waifs and their mother. Alarm bells started to ring for Sister Berenice. She didn't like the sound of the caller, he seemed desperate. Heaven forbid, he could be a suicide case! "Can I help you? Do you want to talk to me? I'm Sister Berenice, by the way."

"No! Bring her now, *puta*! I will only speak to her!" The words might have been intended to be forceful, a rude shout, but his voice was so weak they sounded more like a plea.

"Can you hold while I bring her to the phone?"

"Yes... But hurry!"

The wait must have felt like it lasted forever.

"Who is this, please?" Sister Cristina asked gently.

"It's Paco—Paco Rodríguez from your village. Sister, come for me, please!"

Her heart skipped at the news. The voice sounded strange, unlike Paco, but he was obviously in distress. Recalling Rafael, shot in the back, she said, calmly, "Are you in any immediate danger?"

"N-no—I'm hiding in a hunter's shed. But I risked the weather to phone you, Sister."

"Have you got plenty of money for the phone or do you want me to ring you back?"

"No, 's okay, I've gotta credit card." Faint though his tone was, it implied "don't ask."

The thought struck her. "The weather?"

"Snow and stuff. Lots of it."

"Where are you, Paco?"

"Near a place called Stockbridge, I guess."

Sister Cristina sat down, suddenly feeling faint herself. Near the Motherhouse? "Massachusetts?"

"Yeah. Isn't that where you come from?"

"Yes. Now, look, I'm going to give you the Motherhouse phone number. I'm going to ring them myself and forewarn them. Then you must phone them and tell them where you are. Someone will come and get you, take you to the Motherhouse—it's our main convent."

"I want you to help, Sister. Only you."

"They're all nuns, Paco. You've got nothing to fear." Then she recalled his sister, Claudia. "Is Claudia with you?"

He started crying. Between sobs he said, "No—she—they took her away—I've gotta get her back—it's all my fault…"

"Steady, Paco. I'll fly up, but that will take time. You will be safe at the convent until I can get there. Then we'll see about finding Claudia, alright?"

There was a pause. Then: "Okay, Sister. But please hurry. I'm real worried about Claudia."

———

Massachusetts

THE FLIGHT out of Charleston International was smooth until they came in over Boston. The cold front buffeted the aircraft, winds at gale force. Snow made visibility poor. No sooner had Sister Cristina landed at Logan than Sister González was in the concourse waving to her. They briefly embraced. Hardly anyone paid them any attention. Two nuns meeting after an absence; so what? The traffic was normally bad in Boston, but with the weather in blizzard mode it seemed almost impossible. The two and a half hour drive to the Stockbridge Motherhouse took them an extra hour.

Before leaving Charleston, Sister Cristina had telephoned Leon, but he was at Fort Moultrie, "since he was half-English". Apparently an English tourist had gone berserk, wanting to relive the Revolution over again and kill lots of damned Yankees. Two Americans dead, four wounded, and the shooter was holed up in the wooden barracks, shouting "Long Live King George!" She left a message, briefly outlining Paco's reappearance. Leon might want to follow it up; yet in truth it was now another state's problem—though of course as an FBI agent Armando could get involved.

"How's Sister Emily?" Sister Cristina asked.

"Chirpy, considering she's seventy-four and riddled with arthritis. She worries over not being able to polish the silver or teach German and Italian anymore."

"Oh, she's cut down to just French and Spanish, now, has she?"

Sister González laughed; a tinkling sound. "That's her, alright."

Snow-capped everywhere: trees and buildings—the Federal style houses, their hipped rooftops with balustrade-bordered widow's walk where the wives of sea-captains used to pace, waiting for their husbands' ships to re-enter harbor.

"This snow will not please Sister Polly!" As the convent gardener, Sister Polycarp was particularly remonstrative with God when the weather spoiled her horticultural arrangements. Her favorite flower was the heliotrope, because significantly it would always seek the light.

"And Joaquina?"

"Still a few beads short of a rosary, I'm afraid..."

Sister González sounded sad, and rightly so, because she

had suffered at the hands of cruel men in Central America, as had Sister Joaquina; unfortunately, Joaquina had not recovered mentally from the ordeal.

They lapsed into a companionable silence.

It was good to return to the old building. Its gray stone, bordered with white, trimmed by snow-tonsured firs, seemed to spring straight out of a picture-book. To the left was an expanse of snow-covered lawn, then the fir trees, and beyond them was the frozen lake, a large area of water resounding now to the call of a small number of late Canada geese.

Sister Cristina peeled back her voluminous sleeve: it was an hour to Compline. Always a part of her life, music meant something more here where during her first sojourn she heard the beautiful stilling voices of the choir singing Gregorian Chants.

In 1965, in moves to update the Church for twentieth century people, the Second Vatican Council (later truncated to Vatican II) gave permission for the use of languages other than Latin at the religious service. But occasionally the convent Choir mistress Sister Cecilia insisted they sang in that ancient tongue, and Sister Cristina had to admit it was glorious!

But she was brought back to reality as the station wagon scrunched to a halt in the wide drive, outside the porch and Sisters Polycarp and St. Agnes opened the great doors.

The wind had died down, but flakes still dropped serenely, threatening to block most minor roads in a matter of hours.

Between the two nuns stood the diminutive figure of Paco. After almost a month, when she'd feared him lost forever, to see him, to hold him close to her, was virtually miraculous. She knelt in front of him, reluctant to let go, and for his part he held onto her as if for dear life itself.

"Sister Cristina, I think we should go in. The cold..."

"Yes, Sister Polycarp. Of course." She stood up, holding Paco's hand. "It's lovely to see you both again," she said, bowing to the nuns. They smiled back, pleased but a little discomfited by the presence of young Paco—essentially an illegal alien.

The Mother Superior had assigned Sisters Polycarp, González and St. Agnes to assist Sister Cristina where possible; she decreed that the rest of the nuns were not to be disturbed. They assembled in the library. The whole place smelled of beeswax polish, tinted with the sweet scent of incense from the chapel thuribles.

In halting phrases Paco related the deaths of the children in Moose's truck. When the whole story was told the nuns sat stunned. Sister Polycarp wiped her eyes. Sister González hardened her features, as if unbidden atrocities were unreeling from her mind.

"But you say Claudia and Maria are alive?" pressed Sister Cristina.

Falteringly, he said, "Y—yes, I think so. I hope so"

"And do you know where they were taking you all?"

He nodded, sheepish.

"Well, Paco?"

He handed over Wesley's billfold. "I think it's the place in there. It looks like an address for this area, anyway."

All were attentive as Sister Cristina opened the billfold and displayed its contents on the small coffee table. "Paco used one of these credit cards to phone me. They can be locked away with the money when we've finished." She lifted up the slips of paper. "These documents may prove interesting."

One was a typewritten sheet with tabulated addresses. The most local was The Chesterwood Health Farm; other health farms on the itinerary seemed to be Tanglewood and Lenox. All of them were in the wooded mountainous region of the Berkshires, where the wealthy of New York and Boston had long ago built their summer mansion houses—great country estates now serving as hotels and schools—or possibly baby farms or worse. "This Chesterwood Health Farm looks a likely place, Paco."

She turned over the other sheets of paper and sensed

goosebumps on her arms. "Oh, dear..." There was no mistake, these were requisitions for organs: one heart and one heart-and-lungs, both from female child donors. And Sister Cristina shivered, as if her blood suddenly ran cold.

The organs were required tomorrow, 9pm.

Sister Cristina straightened up, folded the requisitions inside the billfold. "We must get the children out of there," she said. "Straight away."

"How?" Sister Polycarp was obviously distressed. She loved flowers and children, admittedly in that order, and the strain of this meeting was beginning to tell on her.

Sister Cristina looked around at her friends. Strange, when she first came here she thought the nuns looked very much alike, which in the old days had been the ideal—the habit was intended, after all, to subsume self and extinguish personality, the better to serve God.

But really, the habit achieved quite the opposite goal: the sameness of the garb concentrated attention on the faces. And each face held so much character; so much of life's hopes and fears, in all of them, that personality shone through far more than anyone in distracting civilian clothes.

Vatican II permitted Orders to wear secular clothing instead of the religious robes, but the Missionary Sisters of the Mother of Christ had unanimously decided to retain the wearing of the habit as an act of witness. "Besides," as Sister Bertilla observed, "people know where they are then, don't they?" The math and morality teacher for the convent, Sister Bertilla liked things orderly, in their place.

Sister Polycarp's long beaked nose sniffed and she wiped her eyes; she was in her late thirties. "The flower of youth, snipped off... Oh, God..." she murmured in despair. "Those hateful men!"

Sister St. Agnes was about forty and usually quiet. Her gentle features and large wide eyes were filled with worry. "We should call the police. They will investigate this farm place. Surely, it is their job?"

Sister González shook her head. "Not the police. I don't

trust them." She had good cause, though now quite misplaced: she'd been raped by policemen in Guatemala. "I think we should go in and kill the beasts that did these atrocities, no? An eye for an eye!"

Raising her hands, Sister Cristina said, "There will be no talk of killing. And the police *can* be trusted. I'll telephone the sheriff and visit him tomorrow morning. It's too late to travel now and the roads are very probably dangerous. We would not help Claudia by getting lost or stranded overnight in this cold." She explained all this slowly and carefully, mainly for the benefit of Paco.

He seemed to accept the wisdom of her decision. "But you will go tomorrow, Sister?"

"Yes, Paco. I will go tomorrow." She eyed her fellow sisters. "Alone." There was a groan of disappointment.

———

"HELLO," she said into the receiver, "is that the sheriff's office?"

"Yes, this is Sheriff Reeman speaking. What can I do to help, Ma'am?" He had a slightly high-pitched voice, reminiscent of Slim Pickens.

"I'm Sister Cristina from the Motherhouse at Stockbridge."

"Bit off my beat, Ma'am."

"Actually, I'm calling about the Chesterwood Health Farm. Do you know anything about it?"

"The..." He paused. "Sure, Ma'am, I know about that place. Been there meself. Helps keep the figure trim, you know? Nice place."

"Oh, good. When was it registered?"

"Lemme see, now... I'd say 'bout a year back. Yeah, twelve months gone, I reckon. Hey, are some of your lady nuns thinkin' of goin' over there? To keep fit." He said this last with a condescending chauvinist chuckle, and then Sister Cristina chided herself for being so uncharitable.

"No, but I was thinking of paying them a visit. What's the weather like up there?"

"Blowin' a real blizzard, Ma'am. Worst I've seen in many a year. Even the skiers won't be too pleased about it, I reckon."

"Well, thank you, Sheriff Reeman."

"Don't mention it, Ma'am."

She hung up and a second later the phone rang. "Hello, can I speak to Sister Cristina, please?"

His voice was a pleasure to hear. "Hello, Leon. It's me. Did you sort out that Englishman?"

"Englishman? Never mind him, Maggie! What in hell's name are you playing at now?" He was unprofessionally over-protective where she was concerned.

"Calm down, Leon," she gently berated.

"Well, okay. At least you're at the hen-house—sorry, Motherhouse."

She chuckled. "Is that what you call places like this?"

"Well," he said, his voice taking on a tone of embarrassment, "that was a slip of the tongue. But what was this message about finding Paco? Is Paco one of Rafael's pals?"

"Yes." Steadying herself, she continued, "I have news about De Souza..."

There was silence on the other end.

"Leon, are you still there?" She knew he was; she could hear paper rustling on his desk.

"Yeah, I'm still here. Go on, Maggie, where d'you reckon he is?"

She told him about the baby farm addresses, the incident leading to Paco's escape.

By the time she was finished, there was a hard edge to his voice. "You're not going anywhere near this Chesterwood Farm, are you?" He didn't wait for an answer, went on, "This is FBI business. Conway's been waiting for a break like this."

"How long will Agent Conway take to get his men ready?"

She knew it was not the same as a fast response force being on call at a moment's notice. Many of the FBI agents required for the assault team would be on other assignments; replacements would have to be found.

"Twenty-four hours max."

"They're operating on two children tomorrow evening at about 9pm."

He swore then said, "Sorry... Look, I'll see if I can put a rocket under them. Promise me you won't go up there?"

"No, I can't promise that, Leon. You know I can't. They've still got Paco's sister."

"Yeah, that's the answer I expected from Sister Stubborn Cristina. Just be careful, okay?"

She flushed at the love and tenderness those last words imparted. "I'm seeing the sheriff first thing," she said, "so I expect I won't go on up to the farm anyway. But I will be careful. That I can promise."

"God bless, Maggie."

"I pray he will, Leon."

He hung up.

———

LEON CAZADOR LOWERED the telephone onto its cradle and hunched over the cluttered desk, his head in his hands.

God, why do you do this to me? Why? He was in love with an attractive courageous witty and wonderful nun!

And she persisted in throwing herself in the path of jeopardy, as if God would protect her! Well, maybe He would.

Then again, maybe it was infatuation, a kinky male thing about women in habits. No, he knew better than that. They went far back, before she took her damnable vows...

But he had to admit that at times he was lonely.

God, was he lonely!

Not that God answered.

He sighed, leaned back as Kominski, a Japanese-Polish female agent came in to the FBI office. He shoved his hands behind his head to relieve the sudden onset of tension and said, "What's up, Komi?"

She pulled a face, which was a pity because she had pretty features. "A slice 'n' dice on Brent. DOA. The perp's got a hostage, his grandmother."

"That isn't FBI business, is it?"

"The perp is claiming diplomatic immunity. Says he's a Russian spy and wants to come in from the cold."

"More likely a nut-job. There must be someone else who can take it."

"Cable?" she suggested.

"Yeah, give it to Cable. He can do with the experience." Cable had been with the team barely two weeks. Two weeks was a long time to learn the ropes.

He lifted the receiver, dialed Conway's number. He was put straight through to the Washington DC desk, FBI Headquarters.

"Hi, Leon. What's cooking?"

"De Souza."

The utterance of that name was sufficient to transform the atmosphere across the telephone line. "He's surfaced?" Conway said.

"Reckon he has. I need a favor, old pal."

CHAPTER 4

HEALTH FARM

The Black Foundation Administration Offices, Venice, Italy

ELIJAH GODSAFE WAS ORIGINALLY FROM Savannah, Georgia, but was content to live here in this hired palazzo on Canale della Misericordia while he accrued a tidy sum with which to buy his very own Victorian mansion on Oglethorpe Avenue. And as the Foundation's chief intensive care specialist and donor purveyor, he damned well earned his high salary. Sometimes it was truly stressful. Like right now, in fact.

He gripped the telephone tightly. He dearly wished it was De Souza's neck. *I'll throttle him next time I see him!* "I've heard that your latest consignment of donors has been wasted!"

"Wasted—how?" De Souza sounded cagey. Surely he knew, kept in contact with his minions?

"I received a phone call from one of your delivery men. Only two children have survived—the rest were shot!"

"No," De Souza countered, "one of them—a boy—he's still alive. He escaped..."

"Escaped! What kind of show are you running there, De Souza? If my boss hears about it, you'll be finished, you hear?"

"But, Mr. Godsafe, we've always delivered previously."

Godsafe gnashed his teeth. "You're only as good as your last job. Remember that! You've become slipshod, De Souza. Get your people organized—or else. I don't have these problems with other suppliers!"

"Yes, sir. I'll take care of it."

"Make sure you do!" Godsafe slammed down the phone, the sound echoing in the high-ceilinged room.

———

Massachusetts

DE SOUZA REPLACED his cellphone in his breast-pocket. He sat back in his comfortable rotating padded leather chair and peered at Dr. Keitel through his rose-tinted contact lenses. He affected the color because he was dyslexic but also because he liked to view the world that way. He often joked that everything, as far as he was concerned, was rosy. Except right now it wasn't. Dr. Godsafe "the fixer" wasn't happy, and if he maintained that mood too long, then this very lucrative sideline would be shut down.

"You're sure, Doctor?"

Keitel was of modest stature, dwarfed by De Souza when they stood together. The doctor wore pince-nez to project a studious bookish look. His small gimlet eyes were very dark, and darted continuously, rapid-eye-movements without the sleep. "Yes. They e-mailed barely five minutes ago. There's no mistake. A perfect match for both girls."

Tenting his stubby fingers together, De Souza smiled, a thick-lipped moist movement of mouth that revealed artificial teeth beneath a thin black mustache. Light shone on his bald head. "Then go ahead, Doctor."

As Keitel was about to leave, De Souza cleared his throat, a deep rumble in his barrel of a chest. Keitel stopped at the door, turned.

"Weather permitting," De Souza said, "I'm popping into

town to see our sheriff friend. He has disturbing news, I'm afraid."

"They've not caught that brat yet, then?"

"No. Apparently not. We had thought he'd get in touch with the authorities." He shrugged, padded shoulders jerking in comic effect. But Keitel knew better than to even smile at De Souza.

"Perhaps he perished in the blizzard?"

"We can hope," De Souza said.

———

BRIEFLY, Sister Cristina explained the situation to the Mother Superior.

Bespectacled and wise beyond her fifty years, the matriarch of the Motherhouse said, "I think we should say a special prayer for the man Moose tonight, Sister."

"Yes—he was very brave."

"You have done the right thing by bringing the boy here, my dear."

"I hope to God I have, Reverend Mother."

"He has plans for you, my child, I am sure."

Sister Cristina blushed, knowing the Mother Superior was not referring to Paco. "He has plans for all of us, Mother."

"A careful response, my child. I suspect Abbess Ursula is finding you a bit of a handful, if I'm not mistaken!"

Looking up, she was surprised to see love and amusement glinting in the old woman's kindly eyes. "I fear you are right, Reverend Mother."

"She has spoken to me about your agent fellow... Columbo, is it?"

Fortunately she was still flushed from a minute ago; however, the possessive attribution to Leon made her redden a deeper glow. But another part of her was amused. "No, Mother, that is the television detective. The man's a Spanish special agent attached to the FBI: Leon Cazador."

"You are on first-name terms with him?" It wasn't quite a reprimand, but not far off being one.

"Sometimes. In the secular world it's a little easier on the ear for all concerned."

The Mother Superior sat back. "Yes, you're probably right. The world moves on."

That evening, after they put Paco to bed in one of the guest "cells", Sister Cristina joined the other sisters in the choir stalls.

It always gave her tremendous pleasure to come back. Some of the stalls would be empty, awaiting their occupants' return from overseas missions in Africa, Central or South America. Occasionally, a sister did not return alive but in a modest wooden box. The crypt below held nuns who were murdered in Angola and Guatemala. At least their repatriated bodies had found a final resting place in the beloved Motherhouse. The grounds, the buildings, the chapel, all conspired to be restful, to promote meditation and prayer.

But the nuns didn't only live for prayer. They hadn't renounced the world, only aspects of it. They were very much a part of the world, in all its guises. They trained in first-aid, primitive house building, driving four-tracks, and studied the geography and politics of the countries where their missions maintained a precarious foothold. That too had been the ethos handed by the foundress.

Now, Sister Cristina sang with the rest and thrived on every moment. What would Leon think if he saw her now? She knew he liked music. Then she cast aside thoughts of him and lowered her eyes, flushing guiltily. The thought was as bad as the action? Hardly. But she reddened nevertheless. Hadn't Dean Swift said something about a blush being a sign of grace? Now, in the presence of her sisterhood, she felt privileged, and yes, full of grace. She hoped it wasn't hubris waiting for a fall.

A WINTER WONDERLAND might describe the scenery, Sister Cristina reckoned as she drove the station wagon into town. Straight out of Norman Rockwell. They'd spent almost an hour fitting chains to the tires, but it proved worthwhile as the roads were treacherous in parts. The township was quaint, with white picket fences, the homes clapboard and shingle, many painted as white as the snow so that at a glance several of the red rooftops seemed suspended in the air like upturned boats.

The sky was a clear egg-shell blue. Deceptive in these regions; a squall could spring up in no time and often caught unwary tourists off-guard.

The sheriff's office was halfway down the main thoroughfare, his four-track parked slantwise against the boardwalk.

She entered and wondered about Sheriff Reeman's reliability as he stood up behind a very tidy desk, his leather holster creaking; he'd never seen a health farm, let alone inflicted one on his paunchy physique.

"Hello, Sheriff. I'm Sister Cristina. I rang you last night."

"Glad to meet you, Ma'am. What can I do for you?"

"The health farm?"

"Oh, yes. That." He sat down again, signed to a wooden chair opposite. "Now, that's a real problem right now."

"Why is that?"

"Seems there's industrial work going on up there. Extensions already, it's so popular."

"Have you had any complaints about it?"

Reeman pursed his lips, smiled. "Nary a one, Ma'am." He screwed up his eyes, his forehead wrinkling. "Have you?"

"No, I'm possibly mistaking it for somewhere else. Tanglewood perhaps."

The response to her shot in the dark was extraordinary. He gulped heavily, said, "Don't know nothin' about that— off my patrol beat. You could try Lenox."

Lenox, famous for Edith Wharton's home, The Mount, whose planning and building the author had supervised, was too distant in this unpredictable weather. His reaction implied he knew something about Tanglewood, too. That would have to be checked by the FBI.

She said, "It seems to me I've wasted my journey, then?"

"Could be, Ma'am. Sorry I can't be more help."

"Oh, you've been a great help, Sheriff. Thank you." She shook his hand, which felt damp and clammy, and she went out.

As she drove away, she glimpsed a stout figure entering the sheriff's office. Involuntarily she let out a gasp. There was no mistaking that face; she recognized it from Leon's photograph of De Souza.

God help me, she thought, *but I'm going to visit the Chesterwood Health Farm after all.*

There was a message for her when she returned to the Motherhouse. With some amusement because of the jargon and phrasing, Sister Polly read it out: Cazador was on his way. Conway was bringing the assault team up shortly after dark. Computer records showed that no health farms were registered at either Tanglewood or Chesterwood: probably phony. He couldn't be contacted until he arrived by the FBI helicopter. It was exciting, wasn't it?

"Yes," Sister Cristina replied, "but by my reckoning, that'll be too late. I've got to get those children away by 6pm. The operations are likely to be at seven, as soon as practical before the deadline of 9pm. They'll doubtless fly the organs out. Time is important in these harvesting cases."

Resolutely, the three sisters stood shoulder to shoulder and faced Sister Cristina. "If you go, we all go," said Sister González, speaking for all of them. "We can help with the children."

Reluctant as she was, she nodded. "Alright." It made sense. The mini-bus would take them all—though it depended on the number of children at the farm. If it had been open up to a year, like Sheriff Reeman said, then there could be a lot of kids inside—or perhaps only a lot of unmarked graves outside. That gave her a shudder. Best to take a back-up, the station wagon, as well.

The daylight hours dragged. It was wasted time. But they all agreed that approaching the place during the day would be foolhardy.

———

SISTER CRISTINA DROVE the convent mini-bus bought for summer outings and Sister González used the station wagon. Sisters Polycarp and St. Agnes sat on the bench seat at the rear of the bus.

Dusk settled over the snowscape as they stopped a few yards before the entrance to the long drive to the country house. There was a sign which indicated: *Chesterwood Health Farm*. The metal gates were closed.

Wearing her walking boots and gloves, Sister Cristina got out of the bus and hurried to the station wagon.

"What do we do now?" asked Sister González.

"There's only a chain and padlock. It'll only take a minute." She went round the back and opened the trunk and withdrew a set of bolt cutters. Mother Superior would be surprised at the variety of useful tools in the convent garage.

She used the cutters, glad of her training at the gym. As she swung open the gates, she was tempted to sing from Stainer's *The Crucifixion*—"Fling wide the gates!"—but thought better of it.

Once through the entrance, Sister Cristina stopped again and shut the gates after them. She was relieved to note there were no obvious security cameras. In a few more minutes it would be dark. She signaled to Sister González and they switched to side lights.

Earlier in the evening, Sister Cristina and Paco had driven up through the spruce forest, along a winding road that climbed the hill behind the Chesterwood Health Farm estate. From a cold icy outcrop she had trained a set of binoculars on the Greek Revival style building and consigned the formations to memory while Paco hastily sketched the details.

The drive at the front curved toward the entrance porch with its pillared portico and steps. The fountain was switched off and frozen over, icicles hanging from a cherub statue. The ground-floor windows were all covered in wire mesh. At either end of the building were fire-escape doors, seemingly the only concessions to modern architectural style. To the left stood an outbuilding and a double garage. At the back were three tennis courts, blanketed in thick snow. There appeared to be a track at the rear curving from the drive near the entrance gates.

The station wagon continued on up the drive while Sister Cristina turned onto the rear track. The going was slow, thanks to last night's snow-fall. At least the light from the full moon reflected off the snow and afforded reasonable visibility: she had no desire to drive into a tree trunk.

Adrenaline was pumping as she braked at the back of the mansion house, right up against the wall. She was frightened, of course: the likes of Wesley wouldn't hesitate to shoot anyone, even a nun. And there was still the nagging doubt: maybe the health farms were legitimate. Then she remembered Paco, his tear-filled eyes, his pleading to come along. No, she'd insisted, he was safer in the Motherhouse.

AT THE FRONT of the mansion Sister González braked, then drove the station wagon round, pointing its hood toward the exit drive. Then, biting her lip, she slammed her palm on the horn three times.

The double doors opened and Wesley stepped onto the porch. Light from the lobby turned the porch area a buttery color. She recognized Wesley from Paco's description. "What the hell?" Then he noticed the driver. "You have a problem, lady?" He never thought to ask how the mini-bus got past the padlocked gates; possibly too surprised at the appearance of a nun on the doorstep.

"Yes," pleaded Sister González in a good imitation of a helpless woman in distress. "I seem to be lost."

"Where'd you wanna go?"

"Chesterfield Convent," she said, unworried by the lie. She steeled herself not to hate this man. Her task was to create a distraction. "But this isn't a convent, is it?"

"No, Ma'am, it sure ain't. Can't say I've heard of it."

———

DURING THIS DIVERSION, Sister Cristina exited the driver's door and climbed up the door arch and onto the roof of the mini-bus. Once there, she leaned down and grasped Sister St. Agnes's hand, hauled her up alongside her. The breath gushed from her mouth with the exertion, white wisps in the air. Moisture froze on the white cloth round her chin and it felt uncomfortable.

From here she could just reach the lower sill of the upper window and sensed the brick's roughness through her gloved fingers. She pulled herself up, the tendons in her forearms straining, the muscles in her shoulders aching: weight training in the gym was definitely preferable.

Fortunately the window-sill was of the old wide style and she had plenty of room to lean there, resting on her forearms and chest while she regained her strength. Awkwardly fishing inside her voluminous skirts with a gloved hand, she finally pulled out a glass-cutter—last used by Sister Polly to repair the convent greenhouse.

The screech of the cutter on glass seemed to resonate throughout the backwoods. Faintly she heard the station wagon's churning engine: Sister González pretending the vehicle wouldn't start. She carefully removed the glass pane and reached inside, grabbed the handle and opened the window.

Easing through on her side, she noted the bathtub and cistern. An empty bathroom.

A short while later, Sister St. Agnes stood beside her at the bathroom door, listening. No sounds nearby. So she opened the door and peered out.

Working blind, with no real idea of the internal layout, she prayed for guidance.

She moved into the passage. Sister St. Agnes followed.

There were two heavy oak doors on either side. Bracing herself for discovery, Sister Cristina opened one. The relief at not seeing anyone was quickly dispelled when she realized this was an annex room; over on the left was a door, with a round observation window and she detected movement inside.

Cautiously, she moved to the door and peeped in. There were three medical staff in blue scrubs working around an operating table. There was a lot of equipment, machinery, and blood on the tiled floor. She spotted the small feet of a patient and turned away.

Her heart sank when she saw a table in the center of this annex. Standing on it were two fairly large streamlined containers. Careful not to be seen from the operating theater, she moved to the table. The containers were labeled *Cardiac Preservation Transport System*. Indications were that one was occupied: a continuous LED display recorded the preservation condition of the organ inside; the second wasn't occupied. Each container could easily be carried by one person. She wanted to open the "occupied" one and look inside, envisaging a cold miasma enveloping a beating human heart; but didn't want to confirm her fears.

They were too late for this so-called donor.

Clearly the medics next door were preparing to excise another heart for this second container.

Mouth set in a thin determined line she left the annex and softly closed the door and tried the next.

In this room one bed was empty and on the other was a little Mexican girl, about six years old. She was asleep.

Sister Cristina bent over and gently shook the girl. The child blinked her eyes open and seemed alarmed but some instinct or prior conditioning prevented her from screaming. Sister Cristina offered a smile. "We've come to take you away, my dear. Somewhere safe. Do you want that?"

Docilely, the girl bobbed her head in agreement.

———

OUTSIDE, Wesley was becoming annoyed. "There's nothin' wrong with this engine," he called, his head under the hood.

Without warning, Sister González released the retaining latch and the hood slammed down, trapping Wesley. He swore loudly and continuously.

The next moment, she was behind the wheel, revving the station wagon forward to the accompaniment of Wesley's screams. She drove full into the coping stone of the fountain. Wesley's dangling legs were crushed between concrete and fender. Several icicles fell to the ground.

"That'll teach you to murder innocent children!" snapped Sister González. She crossed herself with trembling fingers, whispered, "Sorry, Lord!"

She reversed the vehicle slowly, braked and got out.

Disdainfully she lifted the hood and yanked Wesley off the engine and he fell to the ground. His face was splattered with engine oil, and bloody red gouges shone through the glistening blackness. He was unconscious but breathing.

Now she steered the station wagon along the drive and pulled off, into the trees. Here, concealed, she was to wait—and to pray.

CHAPTER 5

ONLY ONE

DRAPING THE MEXICAN GIRL WITH A BLANKET, Sister Cristina led her on unsteady legs along the passage.

Once they were in the bathroom, Sister St. Agnes took over and lowered the child down to the waiting arms of Sister Polycarp who then settled her on the seat at the rear of the mini-bus.

Three other children were handed down in a similar manner; all of them appeared to be sleepy, probably drugged to keep them contained, quiet and compliant.

Sister Cristina came to the last room on this floor. She opened the door and blanched. It resembled a slaughter-house. Blood stained the operating table and glistened on the polythene-covered floor. On a bench nearby was another cardiac preservation container, its lid open. Next to this was a large metal cupboard, one door opened to reveal assorted clothing on hangers.

A masked surgeon wearing pince-nez was standing over his patient, little Maria, scalpel raised, about to slice along the incision-line drawn in black marker ink across her bare chest.

Two nurses stood on either side of the operating table; one of them looked up at the sudden intrusion, her eyes widening over her surgical mask. "Dr. Keitel!" she cried.

In that frozen instant of time, a red haze filled Sister Cristina's vision as she rushed forward, oblivious of Keitel's unoriginal muffled shout of, "Who the hell?"

Her gloved hands closed on the instrument trolley and smashed it full into Keitel's hip, unbalancing him.

He fell to one side, away from Maria, and screamed "My eyes, my eyes" over and over again. His face had hit against the operating trolley's height-adjusting lever, smashing his eyeglasses, forcing shards of the glass into his eyes.

While the humane part of her wanted to stop and administer first-aid, the pragmatic side of her turned away. One of the medics knelt down beside the surgeon.

Sister Cristina wrapped the unconscious Maria in the bloody sheet. Holding the child close to her chest, she ran through the doorway and shouted down the passage, "Sister! Go now! Tell Polly to go!"

Sister St. Agnes hesitated, then, her face twisted with a troubled frown, she turned and hurried into the bathroom.

————

TUCKING his checkered shirt into the waistband of his jeans, Yancy was pretty pleased with himself as he emerged from the garage, his jacket slung over his shoulder.

The fear in the Chicana nurse's eyes had soon changed to pleasure. She'd been more than obliging. He had that effect on women.

Shrugging on his jacket, he hissed as the cold air caught his throat and bare chest.

His leather cowboy boots crunched over the snow then stopped: he was startled to see Wesley lying in an ungainly heap near the fountain.

He rushed over.

————

SISTER CRISTINA WANTED to find Claudia. She'd promised Paco. Rushing down the stairs, she heard the mini-bus engine—no, it was something else—a helicopter! Coming for the hearts?

Half-way down, she was spotted. "Hey, what're you doing there with that kid?" barked an overweight white nurse at the foot of the stairs.

"This girl's an emergency case for the chopper!" Sister Cristina extemporized, continuing to descend.

She brushed past the nurse. "There's another girl due to be taken as well. Claudia Rodríguez. Do you know where she is?"

Big mistake. "Hey, you're a fuckin' nun!" The nurse scowled. "You ain't one of us. You're not supposed to be here!" The nurse attempted to claw at her but Sister Cristina ducked and weaved, and scurried for the front door.

It opened as she reached it and a man came in carrying the groaning crippled Wesley.

She swerved away from them, to the left, and ran down a passage, the weight of Maria beginning to tell, slowing her down.

Shouts from behind. Ignore them. Head for the fire-exit at the end of the passage.

Some of the doors were open, and she peered left and right as she passed. Partitioned rooms, beds, saline drips, chil-dren comatose, and a few startled-looking black women in hospital whites.

And then she was at the door, turning her back, slam-ming her hip painfully against the roll-bar and suddenly jarringly she was stumbling into the cold crisp night air, gulping in the freshness of it, the wonder of it.

Stars shone and the moon was full.

The station wagon screeched to a halt inches in front of her, spraying slush on her skirts.

"Get in!" barked Sister González. "Quick!"

Sister Cristina wrenched open the rear door, bundled herself and little Maria onto the back seat and an instant later the vehicle shot forward, bucking over the frozen snow ruts, following in the wake of the blue-gray exhaust left by the mini-bus.

She glanced behind. People, most of them in medical garb, were gathering on the drive, their fists raised in impotent anger.

A shot sounded, faintly.

Above the mansion rooftop a yellow-and-red helicopter hovered, the down-draft from the rotors dusting off powder-snow from eaves and chimney stacks.

Sister Cristina removed a glove and felt for Maria's neck pulse and offered a prayer of thanks: it was weak, but at least she was alive.

She hugged the little girl to her and tears trailed down her cheeks. She had failed Paco. Claudia could have been any one of the children in those rooms she dashed past. She recalled the words of Sister Veronica long ago: "Jesus failed, yet out of that failure came the Resurrection." It wouldn't seem much consolation to Paco, though.

Claudia's only hope now was the FBI and Leon.

_____

Cape Cod, Massachusetts

THE BELL-407 HELICOPTER with its distinctive yellow-and-red livery skirted Boston. Night-flying wasn't difficult for the pilot as he'd done this journey many times. And the full moon helped. His radio announced that there were threatening snow-clouds massing to the west—where he'd been, not where he was headed, thankfully. He followed the Old King's Highway, glimpsing the ghostly headlights of traffic piercing the darkness below. Through the port window he spotted Provincetown's floodlit Pilgrim Monument. Now he approached Yarmouth low, the Cape Cod Hospital on his starboard side.

Then directly ahead he saw the landing lights on the roof

of the three-story Black Foundation Clinic. With precision accuracy he landed the craft and switched off the motor.

He never had the time on arrival, but he could linger before departure; usually the view from here was splendid, overlooking Lewis Bay and its brown coastal waters merging into deep blue, the countless expensive private boats moored on jetties or anchored in the bay itself. The large waterfront properties, the spacious gardens, all reminded him this was the playground of the uber-rich, something he could never aspire to. He shrugged it off; he'd never hankered after owning a sail-boat; the sky was his playground. Not much to see at night, however—just haphazard lights of variegated colors.

Once the rotors had ceased beating, the pilot unbuckled and picked up the gray cardiac preservation lightweight container. After very many similar journeys he was familiar with this storage system which preserved the donated heart by using hypothermic, oxygenated nutrient perfusion from the time the organ was procured and throughout its journey until its eventual transplantation into the recipient. He climbed down onto the hardtop, normally proud to be doing this, bringing new life to someone at risk of dying. Yet tonight had been completely different. There'd been chaos at the health farm and he'd heard what sounded like at least one shot from a gun. As he was handed the container, he'd asked what was happening and received a garbled response. "Don't delay!" he was told so he took off, confused and slightly concerned.

He crossed the clinic's roof in a measured pace and then his steps faltered. He was surprised to see waiting for him at the lit-up elevator door the stern-faced Chinese surgeon, Teng Sya. She stood on a decontamination pad in the doorway.

"You're late," she said. She was already dressed in oper-ating theater scrubs, including glossy white rubber clogs. She held out her hand. "I'll take it. Bring the other one."

"There's only the one," he said.

Her small dark eyes glared at him. "Truly?"

"There was trouble at Chesterwood..."

She sighed. "Tell me as we go down."

They entered the elevator and the doors closed. She pressed "2—Theater" and the pilot began to explain in a hurried breathless manner.

Teng Sya was in her late twenties, yet vastly experienced in transplant surgery. She had perfected her skills transplanting the hearts of executed prisoners into wealthy politicians in her homeland. Until she decided capitalism favored her more than hypocritical Communism and defected to join the Black Foundation.

The elevator reached her floor and the doors opened. Fuming inside, she pressed the button for the ground floor. "Get something to eat," she told the pilot. And then she exited before the doors shut.

The pilot's tale had unnerved her. Her hand was clammy on the handle of the container.

She hurried along the corridor to the operating theater suite.

Above the large double door a light-box flashed the words: *Unauthorized entry forbidden.* The doors swung silently open at her touch and then closed after her. Within, light was muted; sound was deadened by sound-absorbing composition flooring and ceiling baffling.

Two vacant operating tables waited and two medics in scrubs hovered expectantly.

Teng handed the container to Yip, her senior consultant, and bit her lip.

Yip gripped the container and her brow furrowed; there was an unspoken question in her eyes.

Teng glanced at the far end of the room where two unconscious children lay on gurneys, each with an IV drip attached.

"Only one heart has been delivered."

Yip nodded.

"Make the preparations," Teng instructed. "We will operate on Magda. The deposit for Ivana's op will have to be returned."

Yip bobbed her head. "It will be done, Doctor."

"While you're doing that, I must go and inform Ivana's mother." Teng pivoted on her rubber heels and left the theater. She would allow herself twenty minutes. Then she must get back and perform the transplant.

She passed guest room "B" and opened the door to room "A". There were two other guest rooms, all of them occupied when the team was especially busy performing domino transplants.

The attractive Russian woman got to her feet agitatedly as Teng stepped inside and closed the door.

"Is it alright?" Mrs. Tomich said. Worry had drained the blood from her features. Only her bright red lipstick held any color; even her eyes seemed washed-out blue. She wore Siberian furs and sported glistening jewelry, advertising her husband's wealth.

"I am sorry, but the heart did not arrive," Teng said in formal tones. No room for sentiment here. This was a job. A supply-chain issue, nothing more.

Mrs. Tomich shook her head in bewilderment, her corn blonde hair shimmering at her shoulders. "What does that *mean*?"

"It means the Black Foundation Clinic will return your deposit. We are unable to perform the scheduled transplant on Ivana."

Wringing her hands, Mrs. Tomich said, "Won't there be another soon? Another heart?"

Mindful of what the pilot had told her, Teng suspected there would be a dearth for the foreseeable future. "There is always a shortage of viable donated organs." Between the lines, what she was saying was that people on the list, like this woman's daughter, would die before a transplant could be performed.

Clenching her fists, Mrs. Tomich screamed, her features turning ugly: "You can't do this! Ivana has only weeks to live if she doesn't get a heart. You know that. We can't wait! She means the world to me. She should be your priority!" Tears erupted and blue-black mascara trailed down her cheeks. "My husband is important and rich. He will pay *anything*!"

Teng pursed her lips. Grigori Tomich was indeed a powerful underworld kingpin in Moscow. But then again so was Anton Minsky, Magda's father. It had been a balancing act, but Teng determined that physically Magda was the stronger of the pair and had a better chance of post-op survival. "I am sorry, but there is nothing more I can say or do." She pressed a call-button by the door.

Her eyes mere slits, Mrs. Tomich stood like a statue, the only movement her clenching and unclenching fists. Fists she would doubtless like to use on the messenger who brought such devastating news.

Within seconds a blond white-garbed orderly appeared in the doorway.

"Please escort Mrs. Tomich to the reception area. Her daughter will be brought to her shortly."

The orderly nodded and moved toward Mrs. Tomich.

Teng turned and strode hurriedly from the room. The dam broke, she realized as she heard a mother's hysterical screams.

———

SISTER GONZÁLEZ DROVE LIKE A HELLION. Headlights on full beam, the two vehicles bounced and skidded along the narrow winding road, occasionally scraping first one fender then the other against high snow-drifts on either side.

Gears grated and tires squealed.

The heaters in the mini-bus and station wagon strained as they belted out warm air.

Sister Cristina kept searching the starlit sky, but there was no sign of any winking aircraft lights, no FBI task force.

Ominous dark gray clouds were forming.

Come on, Leon, where are you?

And then, as if from nowhere, the blizzard dropped on the entire Berkshires area.

CHAPTER 6

MEXICAN STANDOFF

The Black Foundation Administration Offices, Venice, Italy

THE PHONE BY AIDEN BLACK'S BED RANG insistently and woke him. He reached for it. The connection was encrypted so he could speak freely. He was instantly fully awake as he noted with some surprise that the caller was Dr. Teng Sya, the Massachusetts transplant doctor at the clinic in Cape Cod. "It is good to hear from you, Doc," he said, though puzzled.

"There has been considerably serious trouble over here with the donors, Mr. Black," said Teng.

"Why are you contacting me instead of Dr. Keitel?" After all, Keitel was her area's donor coordinator.

"He has been incapacitated, sir."

"Spill, Doc."

"The latest delivery was interrupted, sir. Only half the consignment was flown to the clinic."

That's not good news. "If I recall, your patients were both Russian?"

"Yes. I chose the stronger daughter to benefit. I have arranged for the return of the deposit to the other, Mr. Tomich."

"What are the chances we can find a suitable donor for the Tomich girl?"

"Poor, sir. The disturbance at Chesterwood is liable to shut down any more donor work from there for the foreseeable."

"I see. That *is* troubling. You had better make Dr. Godsafe aware of the situation. This will put added pressure on the other clinics."

"Yes, sir, of course." She sounded crestfallen; she needed encouragement, he thought.

"How did the operation go?"

"It was successful. I believe the girl Magda will make a full recovery."

"That's good news. Well done, Dr. Teng. And thank you for using your initiative. You had better tell me in detail what has happened."

———

Massachusetts

WITH DISTINCTIVE FBI MARKINGS, three twin-engine helicopters powered by Pratt & Whitney main rotors were crossing over the beautiful snow-capped Otis Ridge when the bad weather hit.

Visibility plummeted to zero in seconds.

To Leon Cazador's chagrin, they had to turn back. "These squalls blow over, sir," the navigator advised.

Clearly a half-full glass kind of guy; the best sort to have as a pilot, Leon supposed.

The pilot added, "After about an hour or so, we'll try again."

"Thanks." Leon exchanged an anxious glance with Conway.

He wondered where Maggie was.

———

DE SOUZA SAW the gray blanket descend on the area and said to Rickard behind the sedan's wheel, "You might as well pull in. We ain't going to get through that!"

Rickard braked the vehicle alongside a signpost: *Interstate Highway 90—2 miles*.

Comfortable in the back of the sedan, De Souza clicked open the brown leather briefcase and smiled at the sight of the bricks of hundred dollar bills. Another successful conclusion at Tanglewood. He lifted the encrypted cellphone from his inside jacket pocket and dialed Chesterwood.

At the second ring, Yancy answered.

"Yancy, this is Mr. De Souza. I want to know if the shipment got air-lifted before the storm closed in on you over there. Put Dr. Keitel on the line."

Yancy hesitated and noisily cleared his throat.

"Yancy. Did you hear what–?"

"Sir, the doc's not well. We think he's kinda blinded. This nun, see, she..."

Nun? Reddening, feeling the throb of the pulse in his broad neck, De Souza snarled, "What the hell are you babbling about, man? Put Dr. Keitel on the phone!"

"I—I can't do that, sir."

"Why—what's this nonsense about being blinded? Don't tell me he's drunk!"

"No, sir. It was nuns, sir. They broke in and escaped with some of the kids."

"What!" His head started to pound, he could feel the throb, throb. Any minute now his contact lenses would pop out... *Get hold of yourself*, he thought. "Say that again?"

"Wesley's got both his legs broke, sir. And Doc Keitel's blinded with glass in his eyes."

"Jeezus. I don't believe this. And you say nuns did it? Nuns, for God's sake!"

"Yes, sir. And they took the girl before the doc could do his last op. The chopper took off with only the one heart."

"Well, that's better than nothing, I guess." That wasn't how Dr. Godsafe would see it.

"Yes, sir. When're you due back, sir?"

"I don't think it'll be for a while. Rickard and I are going to pay that Motherhouse place a visit."

"Yeah, kick some nun's ass. That sounds like a good idea, sir."

"Well, I *am* the ideas man, Yancy. Here's another idea. I suggest you get rid of both Wesley and Keitel, if you get my drift?"

Hesitation. "Er, you mean..."

"Yes, precisely."

"Oh...okay, sir."

"Good man."

De Souza disconnected the call. He turned to Rickard then stared out at the wall of snow-cloud ahead. "When you see a break in the weather, head for the Motherhouse." Idly, he fingered the bank notes. "You know where it is?"

"Yes, sir."

He remembered his conversation with Sheriff Reeman. The interfering nun's name was Sister Cristina. "Yes," he mused aloud, "Sister Cristina, I think it's time you met your Maker."

————

ONE INSTANT the road was clear, the next there was nothing—no road, no trees. It was a complete whiteout.

Sister St. Agnes gently braked, trying to remember the road ahead, but they were on a curve and she was skidding, going straight on, and all of a sudden everyone was thrust forward against their seatbelts as the mini-bus crashed into the bole of a spruce. An almighty rataplan sounded on the roof as the tree disgorged its entire contents of snow.

Seconds later, the station wagon crashed into the back, the torque buckling the doors. The children screamed. Sister Polly gave an uncharacteristic yelp.

Sister González was winded by the steering-wheel but

otherwise alright. Sister Cristina bruised her back as she lay over Maria and protected her before impact.

A radiator hissed outside. Metal groaned in protest.

Easing herself up, Sister Cristina said, "Does the engine still work?"

Sister González tried the ignition but all she got was an ominous clunking sound.

"Then we've got to get over to the mini-bus, see if that's okay. If we don't have a functioning heater, we'll not last long in these tin cans..."

The doors operated with a little stiffness. The front one brushed against heaped snow and stuck half-open but the gap was narrow enough for Sister González to squeeze through.

Sister Cristina followed, carrying Maria. She stumbled once, knees painfully hitting a boulder below the surface of snow. The wind and powdery snow dashed against her face, icy spicules stinging. The color drained from Maria's face in an instant.

Breath was hard labor and uncomfortable, each gasp filling mouths with cold air and frozen flakes that quickly chilled the throat and stomach. The short distance to the mini-bus felt like a mile.

They clambered into the front passenger side, shivering and huddling together with Sister St. Agnes to regain some measure of warmth. Maria was ghostly pale in Sister Cristina's arms.

Then she realized the engine was running, the heater was on, and murmured a prayer of thanks. Her cheeks flushed redly and stung, her gloved fingers tingled painfully, but it didn't matter. None of the pain mattered, because they would live. Pain was an affirmation of life.

YANCY POCKETED his cellphone and then went into the operating theater.

Lying on the two operating tables were the unconscious forms of Dr. Keitel and Wesley.

He recognized the Chicana nurse from earlier. She stood at the doctor's side and lowered a hypodermic into a metal dish. She looked up. "Oh, it's you…"

"How are they?"

"I've given them injections to relieve their pain… Anesthetic."

His mouth was exceedingly dry. *Get my drift,* De Souza had said. Yeh, I got it alright. He fingered the automatic pistol in his reefer-jacket pocket.

The Chicana walked round the table and approached him, her hips sashaying. "The jab should help them—until they can be medically evacuated."

He licked his dry lips and rasped, "I have a better idea."

In a startlingly swift motion he lunged for her, and with one arm pressed her against his chest, her breath on his neck, while his free hand pulled free the automatic pistol.

The distance wasn't great.

He fired two shots into each head. The explosions reverberated in his mind. Drift is got, Mr. De Souza.

The nurse gasped, her chest heaving against his own.

———

THE BLIZZARD LASTED a little over an hour. Then it eased to a heavy continuous snowfall. Another hour passed before the engine ran out of fuel. It sputtered and died and the warmth from the heater fan rapidly diminished.

"We'll have to go the rest of the way on foot," Sister Cristina advised. "We'll freeze here waiting for rescue."

So the four nuns wrapped the five children in the bedding from the baby farm and clambered out into the cold air. The white world was silent, ominously so. Snow blurred their vision.

The biggest child was carried piggyback by Sister González, while Sister St. Agnes carried a young boy and

Sister Polycarp carried the Mexican girl. Sister Cristina had one girl strapped to her back and held Maria in her arms. She stopped every few hundred yards to regain her breath. But none of the children wore shoes so there was no alternative. She would not leave any behind in the mini-bus.

It was an awful, back-breaking trek that lasted almost an hour.

When, finally, the snow stopped they were amazed to see the Motherhouse directly ahead, gleaming white, the windows glowing with yellow electric light, a welcoming warmth.

———

DE SOUZA OPENED his heavy-lidded eyes. "I think it has passed over."

Rickard put down his copy of *Playboy* magazine. "Yes, sir."

"Now, take me to that place with the nest of nuns!"

"At once, sir." Rickard steered the sedan onto the road.

De Souza removed the automatic from his briefcase and reassured himself that the clip of ammunition was full.

He scowled, because these days he rarely did his own dirty work. But this time he would make an exception. This was different: it was personal.

———

PACO WAS DISTRAUGHT. "BUT YOU PROMISED!" He'd been betrayed. "You promised to get her!"

Nothing Sister Cristina could say or do would mollify him. "The FBI will be there soon, Paco, then we'll get her out. Or maybe they took her someplace else, perhaps to Tanglewood..."

Drying his eyes, he said, "You're just saying that. Because you know you broke your promise!" He ran from the library all the way to his Spartan room where he flung himself on the bed and cried and cried.

Later that same evening, Paco fished out of his pocket the scrap of paper on which he had jotted down the numbers from details in Wesley's billfold.

All was quiet and still. It was 8.30pm; the nuns were off singing in the chapel, Combine or something like that.

He slunk into the library. The other children were in bed, the convent nurse, Sister Joan of Arc, administering to them.

He picked up the telephone and dialed the number on the scrap of paper.

It rang once, and then a voice said, "De Souza. Who is this?"

Paco's mouth suddenly felt very dry. "Hel—hello," he croaked.

"I said *who is this*?"

"Paco. Mr. De Souza, it is Paco Rodriguez. I was one of your merchandise with my sister Claudia..."

"Oh, really," came the smooth reply. "What do you want, Paco?"

"My sister. Claudia."

"Yes? What about your sister?"

"If you let her go, I'll help you..."

"How can you help me, young man?"

"I—I know..." The words seemed to stick in his throat. He flushed with conflicting emotions: anger and guilt.

"Know what?" De Souza persisted.

His lower lip trembled. It must be admitted. Sister Cristina had failed. This was the only way. He couldn't wait for some FBI goons to go in shooting, they might even shoot Claudia! "I'm ringing you from the convent. The nuns are all here. The one who brung back the children, Sister Cristina, she's here."

A pause on the other end.

"Mr. De Souza?"

"Yes, boy, I'm thinking."

"Nobody knows I'm ringing you, sir... I don't want to get caught."

"No, of course not. You will help me, Paco, won't you?"

"And if I do you will let Claudia and me go away from here?"

"Oh, yes, Paco. That's a promise. This is what I want you to do for me, Paco..."

————

RETURNING from the chapel after Compline, the nuns talked excitedly about the news that had typically spread throughout the Motherhouse, though Sister Alfreda tried and failed to put a damper on the subject by bemoaning the wreckage of two valuable vehicles.

Flakes fell on their black habits like blessings and lent a ghostly aura to their appearance.

Halfway across the snow-laden quadrangle between the chapel and the main building, Sister Cristina stopped, paused, oddly struck by an unfathomable presentiment.

Sister Polycarp bumped into her. "Oh, sorry!"

"That's alright, no problem." Sister Cristina scanned the night sky through the steady downfall of snow. "I hope the FBI get to Chesterwood soon. I'd like Paco to get good news for a change..."

Sister Polly touched her arm. "Let's go inside. It's cold."

About twenty minutes later, Sister Alfreda commented dryly, "It seems the snow's finally cut down the telephone lines!"

"Oh?" queried Sister Cristina.

"Yes. I was due to telephone my next chess move to Sister Connie in Chicago. But the line's dead."

Sister Cristina was crestfallen. That meant Leon wouldn't be able to get in touch. None of the nuns used cell-phones. It was highly unlikely he would consider visiting in this adverse weather. Was this the cause of her earlier presentiment? Then, niggling, scratching at her consciousness like one of those dreadful Peruvian chiggers that burrow under the flesh, an unpleasant thought formed. Without a moment's hesitation, she said, "Excuse me, sisters!" And she rushed out the room.

While Mother Superior believed the preparations were excessive, she agreed it would be prudent to take Sister Cristina's advice. The telephone line could have been deliberately cut, after all.

So within fifteen minutes all the nuns and the children were gathered in the Motherhouse crypt. Candles were lit and two nuns struggled down the old stairs with an oil-heater.

Sister Cristina waited until the Mother Superior had locked the door from the inside, then she climbed back up.

In the entrance lobby she removed her shoes and put on the walking boots which were thankfully dry again. She wrapped a white woolen scarf round her neck and it protected her mouth and nostrils from the cold. She pulled on white woolen gloves then opened the door.

A sudden gust of cold air swept frenetically dancing snow-flakes into the lobby. She braced herself, stepped onto the porch, and slammed the door shut. The vibration sent clods of snow falling from the nearest eaves. The sound seemed to echo across the white landscape.

The snow-fall stopped. And an eerie silence descended. Where once there was the almost indistinct whispering soft sound of snow-flakes piling on top of each other, now there was only stillness. At any other time she would have regarded this as a blessed stillness. Now, she wasn't so sure.

Her intention was to get across country, only about a mile, and try her luck on the turnpike. There, she might be able to flag down someone with a cellphone or find a highway patrol or even a roadside telephone that worked.

The soles of her boots were soon caked with soft snow that slowed her down. She tried breaking into a loping run, but the six-inch deep drifts soon caused her to break into a sweat instead.

After about ten minutes trudging at a reasonably fast pace, she topped a rise and stood between two birch trees, their branches stark and lifeless.

Below her stretched the lake. Her heart skipped. It was worth a try. A few winters ago the lake froze over and most of the younger nuns had great fun tobogganing across its glassy surface. Crossing it would certainly save time.

Unsteadily she descended sideways down the slope, arresting her headlong rush by grabbing the odd branch or tree trunk.

Within a short while snow had worked its way into her boots and her toes were wet and cold.

———

Two FBI helicopters swooped down out of the snow-laden night toward the Chesterwood Health Farm and a third veered off, headed for Tanglewood.

Spotlights illuminated the whole building. One aircraft hovered while the second—with Leon, Salinas and Conway aboard—landed on the drive a short distance from the fountain.

Snow flurried against the front of the building, the down-draft making little snow-drifts on window-ledges and in the porch.

In quick order two black-clad armed men jumped out and moved forward in a crouching run, their M-16 carbines ready. Snow slanted in the light beams, reflecting, a strangely peaceful counterpoint to the black FBI shapes coiled like springs, prepared for deadly violence.

Conway switched on the portable loud-hailer as the rotors were reduced to a slow swishing motion. "This is the FBI!" he announced. "Everybody is advised to leave the building quietly with their hands held high! We have an armed task force waiting outside. If you do not comply with this request in five minutes, the task force will be deployed!"

Leon sat in the helicopter alongside Conway and smiled

thinly with satisfaction as the front and fire-exit doors opened and about twelve adults stepped into the glare of lights. But his lips slowly straightened as he scanned the faces. He nudged Conway's arm. "De Souza hasn't come out..."

"Damn the man!" Conway spoke briefly into a microphone he was holding and moments later the second helicopter landed to the left and debouched two more FBI men: they headed straight for the doors, each man familiar with the photograph of De Souza.

Leon climbed down and trudged into the snow and the cold took his breath away. He hunched inside the fur-lined parka and walked toward the shivering civilians who huddled together in front of the building. Their faces showed worry and guilt in equal measure. This little operation would fill the newspapers and television channels for months.

He hurried past them and climbed the entrance steps of the mansion. This time the bird hadn't flown, he told himself. This time they had the bastard dead to rights.

An armed task force man stood in the doorway, acknowledged Leon, then spoke into his small radio mike clipped over his peaked cap: "No sign of De Souza, Mr. Conway. All rooms and outbuildings checked. Two bodies in the operating theater."

Fuming inside, Leon passed the trooper and entered the lobby. He had a feeling he wasn't going to like what he would see in the operating theater.

———

"IT's a mite grisly in there, sir," said an armed FBI man standing at the door of the operating theater.

Leon nodded and opened the door and walked in.

The guy wasn't wrong.

There were splatters of blood all over the polythene-covered floor; most of it had dried, but small pools of blood and brain hadn't quite congealed yet. Still tacky underfoot in places.

A corpse occupied each operating table; both male, with most of their heads blasted away.

One of them was wearing a medic's coat. He wondered if he'd been involved in excising organs. Well, he wouldn't be doing that anymore.

Some of the blood smears on the floor were quite interesting.

Leon withdrew the Astra A-100 from his shoulder-holster and then called to the guy on the door: "Have you thoroughly searched here yet?"

"Not much to search, sir. But no, I've been tasked with watching over the bodies till the clean-up party gets here."

Leon stealthily stepped up to the large metal cupboard. At the base of the doors bloody scuff marks appeared fresh. Sensing his pulse begin to race, he held his breath and put his left hand on the handle, yanked it down and swung the door open.

He aimed his automatic at the man inside and the man aimed his pistol at Leon.

Mexican standoff.

Apt, since the guy had his forearm round the neck of a Mexican-American nurse. Her eyes bulged with fear.

"I was hoping to hide here till y'all left," the man said. He possessed well-worn features, puffy round the eyes, cheeks pitted with acne.

"Let the nurse go," Leon said levelly, not moving his aim in the slightest.

"Sorry. No can do. She's my ticket out of here."

Leon decided to try another tack. "Where's De Souza?"

"If I tell you, will you let me go?"

"No. But if you tell me I might let you live."

The guy scowled. "That's no kind of deal!"

Leon shrugged. "It's the best you'll get from me."

"I'll kill her."

"If you do, you'll have thrown away your ticket to freedom."

"Alright. De Souza's gone to the Motherhouse, whatever that is."

Deep in his core, Leon sensed a numbness encroaching, seeping into his chest, clamping onto his heart. "Maybe he's entering second childhood," Leon suggested.

"Oh, yeah, funny."

The guy's grin froze as Leon shot him in his left eye.

The Chicana screamed as her captor let go of her and slumped inside the cupboard accompanied by the sound of coat-hangers clattering.

Leon turned as the FBI sentry rushed in. "Look after her!" Leon ordered and raced outside.

He hollered to Conway, "I need a chopper! De Souza's gone to the Motherhouse!"

"I've got my hands full clearing up this mess," Conway said. He pointed to Salinas. "You go with him. Good luck!"

Leon and Salinas sprinted toward the helicopter.

CHAPTER 7

SOLEMN PROMISE

ON THE OTHER SIDE OF THE LAKE, WITHIN A STAND of snow-covered fir trees, the black sedan was parked under a thin layer of snow.

"You're sure that's Sister Cristina?" De Souza demanded of Paco.

Hesitantly, the boy nodded and handed back the binoculars.

"Good boy." De Souza then said to Rickard, "I'll take care of her. I want you to go and set fire to that place. Burn all those damned witches to hell!"

Paco gasped. "But, Mr. De Souza, the children, they're inside as well! And the nuns, they were good to me..."

De Souza smiled. "Rickard'll spare the children, alright?" He winked at Rickard but Paco missed it.

"Sure thing, sir." Rickard zipped up his jacket and climbed out of the sedan.

When Rickard had gone, Paco said, "You will let Claudia go, sir, won't you?"

"Of course, Paco. Of course." And he too climbed from the car, the heavy weight of his automatic against his thigh, snug in his astrakhan fur coat's pocket.

Paco jumped out and hurried after him. "You promise?"

"Yes. You've got my solemn promise."

"Good." Paco was satisfied.

They both descended slowly, occasionally holding hands as they negotiated the slight incline of snow and mud.

———

SISTER CRISTINA TESTED the thickness of the ice and believed it was quite solid. It glistened in the moonlight. The highway was barely two hundred yards beyond the lake's far shoreline.

She broke into a steady trot and the compacted snow on her soles broke free as she trod the ice, dispersing a spray of slush at each step.

Under the light of the full moon, she hurried across the wide expanse of frozen water, streamers of breath and white scarf trailing behind her.

———

ABOUT HALF-WAY DOWN, De Souza stopped for a moment to catch his breath.

The boy was lagging behind, but he didn't care. It might be better if the kid didn't see what was going to happen. Not that Paco's future was rosy, either. His organs were still marketable.

He stared across the lake and experienced a strange shiver down his spine.

From here, in the eerie moonlight it looked as though the nun was running over water.

He snorted, dismissing the thought as fanciful.

———

WITH ABOUT TWENTY feet to go, Sister Cristina slowed to a fast walk, ready for the arduous energy-sapping climb up the bank ahead.

Her cheeks were flushed with the exertion, her lungs

ached with the cold air and she felt weary. She remembered old Rich in the Charleston Gym urging her on to pump more iron and reckoned he would laugh to see her now.

Her fears were probably groundless anyway. De Souza would either get caught by the FBI or he would vanish like the last time. He would be a fool to expose himself by considering any kind of vendetta against the Motherhouse or the nuns. And yet the downed phone line bothered her.

Movement caught her eye and her heart seemed to pitch itself against her ribcage.

De Souza trudged out from behind some snowy bushes. He tentatively trod on the ice directly in front of her.

He was no more than five feet away.

And he was pointing an automatic pistol at her.

———

RICKARD CURSED HIGH-AND-MIGHTY DE SOUZA. It would've taken barely five minutes to drive the sedan round to the Motherhouse, but no, he was left to slog through the snow!

Now, finally, he arrived. There were lights on, but he couldn't see any movement. The garage was over to the right. Should be generator- or engine-fuel in there.

The garage door was unlocked. He eased it open and it creaked on rusting hinges. Enough light reflected from the snow outside to enable him to see what was here.

Inside was a large lawnmower but no other vehicles.

Then he spotted two cans of gasoline. Just what Mr. De Souza ordered!

———

"DON'T TAKE ANOTHER STEP, Sister Cristina," warned De Souza. "You've caused me no amount of trouble. Now it's time to be rid of you."

Young Paco hesitantly plodded from the snowy bushes

and Sister Cristina made to move forward, stopped herself, and said instead, "Are you alright, Paco? He hasn't hurt you?"

"Y-yes, I'm fine."

"He's a smart boy," De Souza said and chuckled. "He made a deal with me."

She gasped. "No!" Not Paco, no, he wouldn't.

Standing slightly behind De Souza, Paco said, "Mr. De Souza's promised to let Claudia go! I helped him cut the phone lines. I had to—for the sake of Claudia! He's going to give me Claudia!"

Nodding, Sister Cristina lowered her eyes. "I understand, Paco. I understand." She would face death. What had Sister Emily called it? Death, the Call to Glory.

———

RICKARD FINISHED SPRAYING the front window frames with fuel and slopped the last on the front door. He discarded the empty cans; they landed with a hollow clang.

He flapped his arms and stamped his feet to bring back circulation into his body. It would soon be warm enough, he thought with amusement. Oh, yes!

In the background he heard the chomping sound he recognized as a helicopter; odd, there wasn't another transaction due for two days.

He took out a cigarette and lit it, heaved in a mentholated gulp of smoke and grinned as his lungs filled. Blowing on the tip until it was bright red, he stepped back and flicked the cigarette at the glistening rainbow-reflection of fuel by the front door of the Motherhouse.

———

DE SOUZA LAUGHED. "Mind you, Paco, I'll have to dig up Claudia first—she was put in a quicklime pit this afternoon.

Her heart wasn't in it, though." He chuckled, a ghastly grating sound. "I sold that."

Sister Cristina raised her eyes, shocked wide at this revelation.

Paco shrieked, "No! No!" And he leaped onto De Souza's back, smashing his small fists ineffectually against the bald head.

De Souza attempted to retaliate with a fist. But the sudden additional weight was too much for the ice to support and De Souza's feet broke through into a wet choppy blackness. Frantically he fired a shot, his arms outstretched to save himself.

Man and boy went under.

CHAPTER 8

BREAKING HEART

FROM HIS VANTAGE-POINT IN THE FBI HELICOPTER, Leon spotted the figures on the iced-over lake. *Maggie!* "That's Sister Cristina!" he shouted above the noise of the rotors. "Take me down!"

"Sure thing!" the pilot replied.

At that moment there was an eruption of flame far to their left. "That's the Motherhouse!" Salinas exclaimed.

"Drop me on the lake," Leon said. "Then you go investigate."

"Okay."

Seconds later, the aircraft hovered about a foot above the ice.

Leon jumped out and landed firmly and then slipped and had to right himself. He exhaled thankfully: the ice beneath his feet held.

The chopper veered off.

Leon's heart lurched as he saw a young boy leap onto De Souza's back and they then both sank through a hole in the icy lake.

———

As THE CHOPPER APPROACHED, Salinas watched in puzzlement as the matchstick figure backed away from the front door of the Motherhouse. Alarmingly a whooshing sound, even detectable above the noise of the rotors and engine, accompanied the blue and yellow flames that engulfed the entire porch area.

The figure turned now, laughing—until he noticed the FBI emblem on the side of the aircraft. He unzipped his jacket, reached inside.

Salinas leaned out and fired his .44 Magnum twice. The first shot shattered the man's leg, the second hit his chest and lifted him backwards, to fall into the flames.

The down-draft of the blades extinguished some of the fire.

Salinas grabbed an extinguisher from the cockpit and jumped from the aircraft as the pilot landed. He bathed the remaining flames in white fluffy foam, just as though it were snow on snow.

———

"PACO!" Sister Cristina knelt by the edge of the black hole, the water churning with little pieces of ice. Her heart hammered against her rib-cage. Sweat collected in the small of her back, cold and uncomfortable. She trembled, as if with a fever. Probably fear, fear for the boy. She wanted to jump in, fish him out, but that would be foolish. She must keep dry, conserve her body heat; she'd need it for Paco.

Abruptly a hand rose out of the churning water—a man's hand. It grasped Sister Cristina's wrist and tugged. De Souza's head surfaced, mouth spluttering. He was pulling her toward the gaping hole, his lips trembling, teeth chattering. His other hand lifted the automatic pistol from his sodden coat.

Oh, God, where was Paco?

An explosion sounded near her ear. She jerked in shock as De Souza's face was obliterated by the shot. His grip on her wrist relaxed, the hand fell away, and the body sank from sight. The water churned red.

There! Something pale, moving underwater.

She reached into the bloody water, soaking her gloved hand and the forearm of her sleeve. The cold was a sudden shock. Even as she realized her hand was becoming numb she felt something, a thin wrist, and gripped tightly. Paco was struggling, and she was at risk of falling forward, into the hole.

Then strong arms encircled her waist and tugged her to her feet. "I've got you, Maggie!" Leon said.

She leaned back against him and heaved, her shoulder making a cracking noise with the effort. She wasn't going to let go, she had him! Spluttering, shivering, coughing up water, Paco emerged from the black hole in the ice.

She hauled Paco entirely out of the water and no sooner had she clutched his soaked body to her than Leon pulled them both away from the hole.

Then Leon let her go and she tentatively stood straight, hoping their combined weight wouldn't plunge them in here. The ice under them held.

Still in her grasp, Paco gulped in air and coughed, wheezing.

"Let's get to the edge!" Leon said, holding her again.

Between them they carried Paco over the slippery surface to the shoreline.

At last she stepped on to firm snow and relief flowed through her.

A quotation from the *Book of Samuel* sprang to mind: "He will guard the feet of his saints, but the wicked shall be silenced in darkness"—from Hannah's Prayer. De Souza was silenced in darkness. And guiltily she had no regrets over his loss of life.

She wanted to hold Leon, thank him for being there for her. But her first concern was for Paco. She drew the boy to her, tears in her eyes, tears for Claudia: it must have been his sister's heart she'd seen in that container... Oh, God—*why*?

"Paco, Paco, you're alright?" she asked, hugging him to her, wrapping the great sleeves round his wet shivering frame.

Teeth chattering, Paco nodded, mumbling "I'm sorry" over and over again.

Reaction set in: she felt weak at the knees.

Then Leon held her and she gained strength from his presence.

The FBI helicopter hovered over the trees, brushing snow from branches. The black water in the hole in the ice sent out small eddies.

Salinas leaned through the aircraft's door and waved, relief etched on his features.

———

LEON CAZADOR RETURNED to Charleston the day after the silent dark death of De Souza, leaving Sister Cristina to make arrangements with the coroner for the funeral of Claudia and the other children. A few days after the funeral Paco was flown home to Peru.

On the following Friday, a week later, Leon drove back to the Motherhouse to collect Sister Cristina.

The Mother Superior had been impressed with Leon as he'd helped her out of the crypt with Conway looking on in amusement. It was quite a sight, the nuns with their pale faces smudged with candle-smoke, emerging from that candle-lit sepulchral place, followed by the children wrapped in woolen blankets. "So you're this mysterious Special Agent Cazador," she said in greeting. Leon looked nonplussed.

The Abbess, having been apprised by the Mother Superior of the trauma Sister Cristina had witnessed and undergone, sanctioned three days leave to travel south at a leisurely pace.

They booked two rooms at the Oakwood Inn in Raleigh, North Carolina. The proprietors were at pains to explain the building was one of the oldest in the area, built in 1871, and may have been the first to be electrified. As it happened, there were no other guests so the dining room was theirs for breakfast; a Temptation urn stood on the mantel and there was a needlepoint firescreen by the Victorian credenza.

For sheer devilment, they elected to try some typical North Carolina food at a nearby restaurant they found which boasted exposed oak beams, a roaring fire in a delightful inglenook fireplace and a flagstone floor: deviled eggs, shrimp and grits and fried green tomatoes topped with pimento cheese. "It's similar to choices of tapas in Spain," he suggested. They were quite used to people staring at him accompanied by a nun in full regalia.

Leon said, "These three days being with you have been wonderful, Maggie...I feared I'd lose you on that frozen lake..."

The look in his dark brown eyes almost broke her heart.

She stood up. "Let's skip the dessert trolley tonight, hmm?"

They returned to their bed and breakfast inn in silence, the tension between them so strong neither wanted to risk touching the other.

At her door he said, "Well, good-night, Maggie."

She opened the door and stepped inside.

He stood, waiting for her reply, a puzzled frown on his brow.

Without warning, she tugged at his arm and with his pulse singing and his heart pounding he crossed her threshold. She swiftly shut the door and embraced him.

It seemed odd to feel the soft serge of her head-dress instead of hair. Her mouth lifted to his and they kissed.

The kiss lasted a very long time.

When they surfaced for air, Leon said, "Are you sure this is what you want, Maggie?"

She nodded, eyes studying his face. In slow measured actions she peeled the helmet of salvation away from its Velcro fastenings and finally allowed her auburn hair to cascade free to the white shoulders of her scapula. "Yes, Leon, I'm sure. I'm frightened, but I'm sure."

They kissed again, and it tasted sweeter, better. This time he ran his fingers through her hair.

He then carried her towards the birdseye maple cannonball bed, the scent of her filling his nostrils.

———

SHE FELT like an adolescent again as she tingled to the touch of Leon.

"God, how I want you!" he whispered in her ear.

An unfortunate choice of words, bringing God into it, she thought. And a shadow flitted across her brow. But she said, truthfully, "Me, too!"

On the nearby rosewood chair lay discarded garments, a mixture of the secular and sacred: his jacket, tie and shirt; her wimple, veil, scapula and habit.

Leon couldn't bring himself to remove any of her clothes. As she stood before him in her white sleeveless shift a trick of the light glinted on the silver crucifix around her neck and made Leon blink.

Abruptly he moved back a pace.

"What's the matter?" Her heart was trembling. With need or fear?

The smile of her eyes and mouth was no longer present; it only seemed to radiate from her when she wore the habit, Leon realized. No, he was being stupid, superstitious! But in his bones he knew something was amiss.

"This isn't right, Maggie. You know it. I know it."

"I thought you wanted this, Leon. I love you."

"But you're supposed to love God, not a man. That's how it works, that's the vow you took."

"I don't love God any less for loving you."

He stroked her hair. He so wanted to embrace her, to make love.

Leon shook his head. "You're doing this for me, aren't you?"

She held his hand against her soft smooth cheek, kissed the pads of his fingers. "Yes. I know it's wrong, but I love you."

"Are you always this willful?" He laughed but there was no humor in the sound. "No need to answer that! I know you are!"

She couldn't return his laugh; there was emptiness inside her, an aching void waiting for God, or Leon? Frighteningly, she wondered what she would do if Leon could not salve the ache; where would that leave her and God?

He withdrew his hand, leaned forward and kissed her forehead. "I'll ask you one more time, Maggie. Is this what you really want? And the consequences?"

She eyed him and for an instant the shining mischievous sparkle was there and he expected her to nod her head, but instead she said, "No, Leon."

And his heart tumbled.

Tears fell. She reached for the black habit, wiped her eyes with it. "I want you so much, Leon. I ache for you..."

She held up the garment in a strong grip, the tendons in her forearm standing out. "But I want this, too!"

Sister Cristina buried her face in the black serge material and sobbed her heart out.

Leon put on his shirt and then hugged her to him.

"You've made the right decision, Maggie." His voice felt rough, not his own. "Neither of us would have forgiven each other if we'd gone ahead."

Between sobs, she said, "My vows, Leon. It's my vows. I can't break them... I made them before God."

Her vows were intact, he realized sadly and, a little self-ishly, believed his heart was breaking.

SISTER CRISTINA SAT before the bishop, her hands nervously twirling the knotted cord. She had asked for this meeting, this confession, and she hated herself for being so weak now.

Bishop Anthony MacDonald possessed kindly features, his small pale blue eyes suggesting a shrewd mind at work.

"It is most unusual for such an interview, my dear," he began, "but considering the strange affairs you have been involved in, I can quite understand if you want to speak to me rather than your usual confessor."

"Thank you, Your Excellency..."

He chuckled. "Let's forget the formality, shall we?"

She studied him, head to one side, confused.

"Call me Bishop Anthony. I'll call you Sister Cristina. Alright?"

"Yes, Bishop Anthony."

Then it all came pouring out, her love for Leon conflicting with her love of God; her desire to remain in the Order.

She sank to her knees and confessed, heart and soul, asking for guidance and forgiveness.

"Nothing happened, Bishop, we saw sense in time, but it frightened us. Our love seems so intense!"

"Love is a powerful and blessed emotion, my child."

"Bless me, Bishop Anthony..."

He took firm hold of her arms and raised her up, and she was surprised to see moisture in the corners of his eyes.

His voice caught. He said, "It is you who should be blessing me, my dear."

Her brow wrinkled, eyes searching his for the meaning of his words. Was he playing with her?

He said, "You maintained your vows, didn't you?"

"Yes, I did." She flushed, sensing she said that with a hint of pride.

"Sometimes we should entertain pride, my dear. I am proud of you, of your work for the Church and your Order." He smiled and gently made the sign of the cross on her forehead. "If my parish and many of my clergymen were filled with such strength of will and devotion as you, I suspect we would be in Heaven already!"

Embarrassed now, she said, "But what must I do, Bishop Anthony?"

He took her hands in his. "Follow your heart, Sister Cristina. Follow your heart. And all your troubles will be silenced in darkness."

PART TWO

DAY OF WRATH

CHAPTER 9

MOSQUE-CATHEDRAL

August 2022
Spain

Tuesday

SITTING AT HIS DESK, LEON CAZADOR CLEANED HIS Astra A-100 automatic; he hated being idle. As it was the time of year when many companies shut down for the summer holidays—arguing it was too hot to work, which it was, even in air-conditioned offices—the private investigating business was not so much slow as moribund. Yet for over two years there had been enforced absence from workplaces, thanks to the Covid-19 pandemic. It didn't help that the authorities only waived compulsory wearing of facemasks in April—a mere four months ago. You'd think that firms would try to catch up on lost time and forego lengthy holidays, he mused, but no, tradition was engrained.

To pass the time, Carlota busied herself sorting the filing system yet again.

Then the silence of aimless industry was disturbed; Carlota's phone rang and she limped hurriedly to her desk and breathlessly answered it. "Leon Cazador, Private Investigator's office. How can I help you?"

Leon stopped what he was doing and lowered the weapon onto a sheet of the *El Pais* newspaper.

"Leon," she called through the interconnecting office door, not bothering with the intercom, "there's a Pureza Rabadán on the line. Do you want to—"

"Yes, I'll take it. An old friend; long before your time. Haven't seen her or her son in quite a few years." He switched the phone to speaker mode.

"Leon?" Her voice was soft, mellow and yet she injected urgency into his name.

"Yes, Puri?"

"Can you get away, come and visit us some time soon, please?"

"You sound distraught. Is Geraldo alright?"

"He's well... but you must be psychic as it is about him I wish to discuss."

She'd been too young to be widowed with a son. He was now eighteen, Leon recalled.

"In fact," she added, "he needs a stern talking to."

"What makes you so concerned?"

She took a deep breath then said, "Well, when I collected his dirty washing from his room yesterday, I saw documents and drawings under the bed. Maybe I shouldn't have, but I was curious..." She paused, cleared her throat. "I picked them up, and found under them colorful pamphlets..." Another dramatic pause.

"Go on," he urged gently.

"The—the writer was calling for a *jihad*. Urging people to rise up to reclaim the Lost Caliphate *here in Spain!*"

Islamist radicalization... Not good. "Of course I'll come."

"He just needs a man to talk sense into him, I think."

"My car's in for its service, but I can leave later tomorrow, is that alright?"

"Yes. But there's no rush."

No urgency, after all. He'd been mistaken about her tone, then. "In that case I'll take a leisurely drive, behave like a tourist." Carlota appeared at the interconnecting doorway

and thumbed her chest imploringly, mouthing *me, me, me*!
He grinned and nodded. "I'll bring along Carlota as well. She
can do with a break from the office. Show her the sights. See
you the day after tomorrow."

Carlota beamed and bobbed her head vigorously.

Puri added, "That will be nice. I haven't met her yet.
Look, I'll be working until eight, as usual." She was a private
secretary in an accountant's office situated on the northern
side of Córdoba's *Plaza de las Tendillas*. Some firms didn't
close for August. "See you both in the plaza the evening after
tomorrow, then? Just after eight?"

"I look forward to it, Puri. We also have reminiscing
to do."

"Yes, I'd like that. Adiós!" She hung up.

He put the phone down.

"I've never been to Córdoba before," Carlota said,
coming up to him.

He wasn't too surprised. Even these days a good number
of Spaniards were unadventurous and even incurious about
their own country. Quite a number simply holidayed in the
next town or the nearest coastal resort.

"You'll love it. So rich in history." He pointed to the
print on the wall: *Oranges and Lemons* by Julio Romero de
Torres. "He was born in Córdoba. We might have time to
visit the museum and see a selection of his paintings. I must
admit, of all our cities I've been to, Córdoba's my favorite."

The Islamic rule permitted the worship of other religions, so Jews, Christians and Moors lived and worked cheek
by jowl. A far cry from the intolerance of the Spanish Queen
Isabella and King Ferdinand who threw out of Spain not
only the Arabs but also the Jews in 1492.

"A break from the daily grind?" She leaned down and
kissed him. "I can't wait to pack!"

"And don't forget your passport," he said.

"Passport? We're only going to Andalusia!"

"Remember what we said after our visit to Malta—we
found ourselves in Tangier without passports."

She grinned, eyes wide with excitement. "You think we might end up somewhere outside the European Union?"

"No, not really. But my motto is 'be prepared'."

"I understood that it was the Scouts' motto."

"It is—but still valid whoever or whatever you are."

She gave him a mock salute. "Right. Will do."

————

Wednesday

THAT FIRST NIGHT he and Carlota stayed at a two-star hotel, the Guadalquivir in Cazorla, an attractive small town on the edge of the National Park; many of its shops sold hunting apparel and other outdoors gear.

Later, they strolled along the crooked streets between the Plaza de la Corredera and the appealing Plaza Santa María. The ruined church of St. María formed a picturesque backdrop. Above stood the imposing Moorish Castillo de la Yedra.

They entered a restaurant of old wood and marble, with dozens of framed photographs of hunters with their slaughtered prey, many of them in monochrome.

"You must try the wild boar in red wine sauce," he suggested, pointing to the mock-antiquated menu. "It's the area's specialty."

"I've never had it before, so I'm game—no pun intended."

It was the first time he'd eaten the animal since he'd encountered a sounder of them during his escape with Daraja four years ago. It was tender and tasty and happily left no after-taste of that confrontation.

————

Thursday

NEXT MORNING, waking with Carlota lying beside him, like every morning since they'd consummated their relationship on their boat journey from Tangier, he marveled at his good fortune. She was still asleep, her head to one side, features relaxed, strawberry blonde hair splayed on the pillow like a halo. She was roughly thirty-two years younger, yet she was content. He wondered how he had deserved her love, which he was only too happy to reciprocate wholeheartedly. He'd had several flings with desirable and darling women after he'd left Sister Cristina to her devotions, but he had not been able to commit to any of them. He knew it was his fault, not theirs. He found that it was only Carlota who had the generosity of spirit and unconditional love to mend his damaged heart.

Normally on weekdays they would exercise after waking. With Carlota sitting enticingly on his ankles, he would perform seventy sit-up crunches, alternate elbow to alternate knee, followed by seventy press-ups. Carlota did the same, though she was faster than him—but then again she was younger. After breaking a sweat, they would shower. At the weekend they would refrain and instead perform tai chi in a convenient park for a complete change.

But he'd vowed that on this mini-holiday they would give that form of physical exercise a miss. "Only that form of exercise?" she queried mischievously.

"Quite," he answered straight-faced.

After a light breakfast, they set out on the road again. He drove through the *Parque Natural*; they passed the dominating castle ruins of La Iruela, the fortress perched on top of a rocky spur.

Carlota was anxious to see some wild boar but was disappointed. A sudden sighting made up for the lack of the tuskers: "Oh, look there, deer!"

"Yes, dear," he quipped and received an elbow in the ribs, but the fond jab didn't affect his driving.

Finally, he turned on to the N322 and headed for

Córdoba and an anxious mother who feared her son was being radicalized by Islamic extremists.

DRIVING and parking in the city was no fun, so he had booked a room in the hotel Hesperia on the Avenida de la Confederación, situated on the southern riverfront. As it was August and hot, there were plenty of rooms available; most holiday-makers escaped to the seaside resorts or the mountains.

They arrived at about midday and registered at the reception desk.

Their room was on the top floor; modern, light and airy. The balcony overlooked the river and the old bridge that spanned the Guadalquivir, its broad arches still supported on the original Roman foundations. On the other side, on the right of the bridge entrance he could see the bell tower, the Mezquita and the Cathedral, like conjoined religious twins.

They unpacked their cases and showered, dried and dressed.

He wore blue Calvin Klein boxer shorts, a light blue short-sleeved shirt with an open neck, slim blue jeans and a suede jacket that would conceal his shoulder holster. "My blue period," he joked.

"That joke's a bit rusty by now," she countered, donning a lacy rust-colored bra and matching Brazilian briefs. She chose a black scooped T-shirt, and a three-quarter length sleeve jacket in light purple and pants to match.

Sitting on the balcony they sipped Amontillado sherry and he gave her an itinerary: "I think we'll visit the Patios de Leyenda, the Mosque-Cathedral, the Courtyards of Viana, and then I'll drive you to Medinat al-Zahra, the remains of a fabulous tenth century city built by the Caliph Abd al-Rahmán III."

"I'll be exhausted after all that!" she exclaimed.

"Not too exhausted, I hope?"

She leaned over and kissed him full on the lips then pulled free. "No, never too exhausted for that..."

When they'd finished—their sherry—they left the hotel and strolled across the Roman Bridge alongside a small number of tourists and passed the Mosque-Cathedral on their right. "Don't worry, we'll be back to tour the place," he promised her.

A handful of elderly folk in the streets wore face-masks, but the majority didn't; the pandemic, by all accounts, was finally on the wane. "About time, too!" Carlota said. "I blame the Chinese!"

A couple of narrow streets later, they found a restaurant that catered for early diners; the majority of the locals didn't begin eating until 2pm. Here they enjoyed simple food: delicious cool gazpacho, paella with rabbit and smoky chorizo and golden rice flavored with rosemary and saffron. Dessert was tempting, especially the leche frita but they were interrupted. Leon received a call on his cellphone. "Puri?"

"Oh, Leon. Have you arrived yet?"

"Yes. We're in the city now."

"Oh, praise be!"

"What's the matter?"

"I found something this morning, in the wastebasket in Geraldo's room before I left for work. I've been at my wit's end, fearing, wondering... Leon, can I see you in the plaza *now*? It can't wait!"

"Of course." He checked his Omega: it was 1:35. "Give us about fifteen minutes."

"I'll be waiting."

He closed the call and hailed the waiter, paid and they left.

The pedestrian square Plaza de las Tendillas was bordered by a number of restaurants and cafés. The floor of the square was paved in decorative flagstones.

Leon and Carlota selected a vacant stone bench under a tree, glad of the shade. People crossed the huge expanse, hurrying to a dinner date, work or perhaps a secret assignation. Again, few bothered wearing masks. A man dressed in a clown's outfit and a black hat was whirling round with a large plastic hoop. Having dipped it in a big bucket of soap solution, he created huge bubbles to entice watching children and adults alike. A troupe of very young children dressed in smart uniforms snaked across the square in single file, led by a matronly woman. As schools were on holiday perhaps these were orphans, or they belonged to a club.

One section of the square was devoted to several trick fountains that gushed from the paving at erratic times, dousing curious children and unsuspecting tourists.

The imposing equestrian statue representing El Gran Capitán stood out, surrounded by small fountains and a low wall where people sat, ate and chatted. And high on the sixth or seventh story of an imposing corner building was the Tendillas Clock which has been striking the quarter-hour for sixty years.

He recognized her as she strode across the square. Pureza Rabadán was in her late thirties, stout and short, wearing a bright yellow blouse, a flower-patterned skirt, and a multi-colored silk scarf round her neck. Her black-and-white leather shoes matched the purse she carried. She disliked colors which she considered appropriate for the elderly, not "a woman in the prime of life", and had eschewed the traditional black two weeks after her husband's funeral. "I have a life to live and a son to bring up," she'd argued with anyone who deplored her lack of respect for the dead. "I respect the living—which is me!" He got to know her shortly before Geraldo's birth eighteen years ago. She'd always been forthright.

Both he and Carlota stood to greet her. He joined hands with her briefly, cool to the touch.

Puri was distinctive in her looks, with prominent cheekbones, a long nose, thick black eyebrows and short black hair. Her thin lips trembled slightly and her big chestnut-brown eyes glistened. "It is good to see you, Leon."

"Likewise." He clasped a hand round Carlota's shoulders, drew her nearer. "And this is—"

"*Encantada!*" the two women said in unison.

They all sat on the stone bench.

"You made good time." She glanced anxiously at her fine thin gold wristwatch. "I'm sorry to drag you all the way here."

"You know Córdoba's my favorite city." He swept a hand to encompass the plaza.

"I had hoped to go and stop him, but I'm so afraid. Lately, I barely know my son. I've hardly concentrated on my work all morning." She lowered her eyes, stared at her purse. "I'm a mess..."

"Then you'd better tell us all about Geraldo."

She leveled her gaze on him, deadly serious. "We will have to be quick. There is not much time." She fished in her purse and gave him a small snapshot of her son. "It was taken last year... before... Well, it is recent, anyway." Geraldo had grown since Leon last saw him: perhaps a little stockier now, and taller than his mother, who stood beside him in the photo. He had her cheekbones, thick brown eyebrows, and long nose; but he'd been bequeathed his late father's thick lips, dark brown curly hair and prominent chin.

"Did you question him about the pamphlets?"

"Yes. But he would not answer me."

"Have you been to the police?"

"Until this morning, I did not think there was any need for urgency. I know I should contact them... But I fear they will take him away, they might even put him in prison for terrorism offences..."

"But," Carlota said, "there is a real risk that he might harm other people—or himself..."

She paled at that valid observation and then thrust a sheet of slightly crumpled paper into Leon's hand. "This is what I found this morning."

It read: *Cathedral. 3pm.* The date was today. The big clock across the plaza struck 2:15pm.

Leon swore under his breath. "If we're going to find him, it would help if I knew what he's wearing."

"He is boring, typical for his age, I suppose. The same style all the time," she said in exasperation. "A white T-shirt and of course fashionably torn jeans. In my day only poor people wore ripped clothes. We'd be ashamed to be seen outside like that." She shrugged away the memories and shook her head. "I don't know how he affords them on a barista's wages, but he wears Nike sneakers."

He stood and handed the sheet to her. "Return to the office. Call the Guardia. Tell them what you've told me. Get them to go straight to the Cathedral."

"But—what are you going to do?"

"Pray—in the cathedral." He clasped Carlota's hand and, Carlota limping alongside him, they hurried away.

Puri crossed herself and murmured a heartfelt prayer.

———

THEY ENTERED the Mosque-Cathedral through the Door of Forgiveness, to the left of the bell tower. "A minaret was constructed in the courtyard," Leon told her, "but this is now embedded in the tower, its name still signifying its origins: Torre del Alminár."

Once inside, Leon purchased tickets. The bell tower overshadowed the patio of orange trees which long ago replaced the original palms; here the faithful used to wash before prayer. Now, rather than the faithful, the patio was frequented by tourists of all shapes, colors, sizes and nationalities, predominantly Japanese; many of them carried rucksacks and other travel paraphernalia, including video cameras and smart phones. Here, too, apart from some elderly people, the majority did not wear face-masks. There still seemed a tendency to socially distance, however. The dreaded Covid skulked about even now.

Moving around the patio area, Leon scanned the individuals but couldn't spot Geraldo. He must be inside.

Leon and Carlota joined the throng queuing to enter the mosque. He checked his watch: 2:30.

The movement of the queue was constant and they were swiftly processed.

What Leon immediately noticed was that the staff member stationed at the door was not fastidious about searching hand-baggage or backpacks. Carlota's purse wasn't even considered worthy of attention.

The subdued lighting, the echoing of many hushed voices resonated with him. No matter how many times he came here, he was overcome by the uniqueness of the place. Something ineffable.

He glanced sideways at Carlota. She stared in awe. "I've seen pictures of it," she whispered, "but they don't convey the grandeur."

Hundreds of red-and-ochre Islamic arches in serried ranks, a crisscrossing of alleys, the pillars supporting two tiers of striped arches that add height and create a remarkable feeling of space. Seventeen aisles of granite, jasper and marble, combined to create a dazzling effect. "Over 850 columns," Leon said.

"It takes your breath away. It's like a forest."

"A holy jungle, maybe," he suggested.

The mihrab—a prayer recess—was situated along the wall that faced Mecca and it held a gilt copy of the Koran. The mihrab was topped by a shell-shaped dome. The worn flagstones indicated where pilgrims circled it seven times on their knees. "I think it's now fenced-off to preserve the floor," Leon said.

"Or to save the knees of the faithful..."

He chuckled softly. "Possibly. We are soft in comparison to those of bygone ages."

Then they came upon the cathedral, erected in the center of the mosque. "Some have called it religious vandalism," Leon said. "Emperor Charles V had given unthinking permission for the construction. When he actually saw the result, he was furious with the cathedral builders. 'You have built here what you or anyone might have built anywhere else, but you have destroyed what was unique in the world,' he told them."

Her eyes were moist. "I can see what he meant. And yet, does it not in its way bring together two great religions?"

"Perhaps. But a few extremists might not see it that way..." He paused and peered to the right, down the side of the cathedral. His voice hushed, he pointed. "Look, there he is!"

Geraldo was standing next to a woman dressed in black robes, a shawl over her head. All he could glimpse was her dark features and beaked nose. They appeared to be arguing.

"Move closer," he told Carlota. "Go to the left, I'll take the right..."

"I don't want seventy-two fucking virgins," Geraldo was saying. "Safia, I want *you*!"

"I have already told you, I am spoken for! You should be proud, feel honored! *This* is your great task." She jabbed a finger at the rucksack slung over Geraldo's right shoulder, and then swept a hand toward the cathedral. "To destroy this aberration, this blasphemy!" With her other hand she clutched the hem of the shawl tightly about her head and glanced around, apparently realizing she had spoken too loudly. Sound had a tendency to magnify in this cavernous place.

Boldly, Leon strode forward, arm outstretched, offering his hand. "Geraldo, fancy meeting you here!" he exclaimed, smiling.

Geraldo's mouth gaped. "Leon...?"

Safia hissed unintelligible words between her teeth and snatched at Geraldo's rucksack, pulled it off his shoulder.

Leon grasped Geraldo's arm, led him away.

Safia swerved and darted in the direction of the cathedral's central aisle. But she didn't get far. Despite her limp, Carlota moved fast and leaped at Safia, her arms wrapping around the young woman's legs. They tumbled to the hard tiled floor, the sound echoing. Safia grunted.

Carlota withdrew her automatic, leveled it at Safia's head. "Let go of the bag!"

Safia scowled but complied.

"Now lie very still!" Carlota ordered.

Leon shepherded Geraldo farther away, toward the entrance. Surprisingly, none of the security staff had observed anything untoward yet. A small cluster of tourists stopped and watched but didn't make any move to get involved. Leon approached a stout man in uniform. "There's a female private detective by the cathedral." He pointed. "She's armed and has caught a terrorist with a bomb in a rucksack."

"A bomb?" The man's face paled.

"It isn't active yet. You'll be safe. Go and give her a hand, eh?"

"Is this some kind of hoax? Who are you?"

Leon showed his business card. "I'm happy to answer questions from the police later. I'm staying at the Hesperia hotel."

The security man dashed toward the cathedral, unhooking from his belt a walkie-talkie as he went.

Once outside in the bright sunlight, Leon led Geraldo to one side, a good distance from the milling crowds.

Well away from anyone else now, he turned on the young man and slammed a fist into his stomach.

Geraldo doubled up, wheezing, gasping for air.

"I was tempted to shoot you back there!" Leon snapped. "If it wasn't for your mother, I'd happily have done it!"

Geraldo continued to wheeze. Tears sprang from his eyes.

"The woman—Safia—took you for a fool!" Leon snarled. "All these Islamic bastards—so-called masterminds —do the same. They recruit and brainwash cannon-fodder like you for their cause. But they never knowingly put themselves on the line. They're cowards! For her cause, your precious Safia was willing for you to blow yourself to smithereens!"

"I know... I realized... She used me." More tears streamed down the lad's face.

Leon gritted his teeth. "That bomb probably wouldn't only destroy part of or all of the cathedral. There'd be collateral damage: people—innocent people—maimed and killed!"

"I'm... sorry... She was so... so convincing..."

Moments later, Carlota joined them.

"Is Safia in custody?" Leon asked.

"She is. And the rucksack was handed over to the bomb disposal team. I was impressed. The Antiterrorism Guardia Civil officers arrived promptly."

Leon turned to Geraldo. "Have you ever been in trouble with the law—or had your fingerprints taken?"

Geraldo shook his head, wiped his cheeks with a sleeve.

"Then, I think you need to leave the city pronto—before Safia implicates you. If they can't find you, they can't link any fingerprints to the bomb."

"I only touched it when I was wearing gloves," Geraldo said. "Latex. It will be her word against mine."

"She might have a rap sheet as long as your arm already," Carlota suggested.

"We'll try and discover that when the police interview us at the hotel."

"What happens now?" Geraldo asked.

"You go and apologize to your mother for being such an idiot. Beg her forgiveness. Speaking of which, let's leave here —by the Door of Forgiveness."

———

THE INTERVIEW with the police was a formality. They had apprehended Safia in possession of the explosives and she was refusing to talk, which had to be good news for Geraldo.

Leon and Carlota signed witness statements and were free to go.

Spain's legal wheels turned exceedingly slowly so it could

be many months before they would be summoned to appear in court as witnesses.

They both put it out of their minds, content in each other's company.

Over a coffee in the early evening, Leon concluded, "What is surprising is that, unlike so many other times, the reconquering Christians actually let the original Islamic building stand. After all, they razed many to the ground."

Carlota agreed. "True, this great mosque and the Alhambra palace of Granada suffered privations, but even now they're still standing, captivating emblems of Arabic history and culture..." Then she was interrupted as her cellphone rang. She winked at him. "It's a call patched through from the office." She grinned fetchingly. "You never know, it might be work, eh?"

She tapped the keypad and listened. "Just hold, please." She handed him the phone. "It's from a guy called Hiroki Kuroda. You're old pals, he says." She arched an eyebrow: her look conveyed the thought that "old pals" seemed to get him into trouble. "Calls you 'Santos-san'?"

"Okay." Leon fingered the speaker icon and spoke: "Greetings, old friend."

"Where are you? I dropped by your office, but a note on the door says you've gone away for a few days..."

"I'm in Córdoba."

"Ah, I like it there. Good choice in more ways than one. Listen, Santos-san, I need to meet you tonight."

"Tonight?"

"It is urgent. It will take me about four hours to drive. Do you still frequent the same hammam?"

"Yes."

"Then I will see you there. I will book the 10pm session." Leon recalled the last session was midnight, the first of the day at ten. "I will ensure we will be private."

"I'll bring my assistant Carlota as well."

"You can trust her?" Hiroki queried.

Leon eyed Carlota. "With my life."

She blushed.

"Alright," Hiroki ended.

"See you at ten, then." He closed the call and handed the phone to Carlota.

"You've brought a swimsuit?" he asked her.

CHAPTER 10

WESTERN BARBARIAN

A MOUNTAINOUS LANDSCAPE POPULATED BY dragons strode out of the swathes of hammam's steam and approached Leon Cazador and Carlota.

Leon wasn't surprised when Carlota stifled a gasp.

Hiroki Kuroda was tattooed over his entire torso and down to his wrists and calves. At a glance, he gave the impression that he was wearing long johns; instead, he was a walking exhibition of body art. Ray Bradbury's *Illustrated Man* always sprang to mind when Leon saw him, but this was no fantasy. As a member of the Yakuza—a Japanese criminal organization similar to the Mafia, but much older— Hiroki as a much younger man had endured hundreds of hours of pain from a bamboo sliver simply to show that he could. He waved a greeting with his left hand. The little finger should have been missing at the first knuckle, but a shining substitute appeared grafted in place.

Sitting on the wooden slats of the bench, Leon wore light blue swimming shorts and Carlota, on his left, was skimpily covered by a dark green bikini she'd brought for use in the hotel pool but had yet had the opportunity to christen.

Hiroki adjusted the towel about his waist, acknowledged Carlota, and lowered his huge bulk on Leon's right. "Thank you for coming, Santos-san," he whispered, his voice deceptively smooth, like water trickling over time-worn pebbles.

Even after many years he still addressed Leon by his alias, Carlos Ortiz Santos, rather than his real name: "I first knew you with that name, and I like it," he confessed once.

Leon introduced Carlota then added, "It is good to see you after nineteen years."

"Twenty-one, actually, I think."

Leon bowed briefly, acknowledging his old friend's superior concept of time passed. "I thought the Yakuza had long ago moved out of Spain."

Hiroki chuckled, his dark jet eyes glinting in amusement. "*Hai!* Still direct, I see. Even now, after all these years, I find your *gaijin* ways most difficult."

"There's a time and a place for courtesy and etiquette, Hiroki." Leon's tone implied he should get to the point, but Leon was not so much the barbarian as to tell him so bluntly, despite his "gaijin ways."

Hiroki bowed; his once-raven-black hair, slicked back behind his ears, now contained strands of gray. "Sadly, two new families are operating in Spain, one in Andalusia and one in Catalonia."

"That's two too many," Leon observed. Each Yakuza crime family would comprise dozens of younger brothers and many junior leaders. "They must have kept quiet. As far as I'm aware, the authorities know about the Chinese Tongs, but no Yakuza have shown up on Spain's National Police radar since we closed down the Okudara gang."

"Yes, they are being more circumspect."

"Unusual behavior for Yakuza," Leon said. Unlike other criminal groups in Japan, the Yakuza have never concerned themselves with keeping a low profile. Their social clubs and gang headquarters are blatantly marked with Yakuza signs and logos. "Clearly, their tentacles are moving out," he added, "and they want to continue staying under the radar."

"*Hai*. They spread to other Asian countries, the States, South America. And now they have returned to Spain. They have taken advantage of the chaos caused by the pandemic, I think."

These new Yakuza families must have noted the criminal gains being made by the Russkaya Mafiya and the Balkan syndicates, and decided to carve out a piece of that action. *Just what we need*, Leon thought. "Why are you telling me this?"

"As you know, I left behind my past, Santos-san." He raised his left hand. "I make an honest living now with Nyoko by my side."

"Good." Leon had heard that a good number of ex-Yakuza, having repaid society by doing time in prison, sought gainful employment on release. Unfortunately for them, the evidence of the missing little finger—or more digits in rare cases—signified they had a criminal history and were not considered employable or trustworthy. Hence they had resorted to the use of prosthetic digits or even a graft like Hiroki's.

"The restaurant business thrives?" Leon asked.

"It does."

"And is Nyoko well?" Leon ventured.

"Yes, she is, and she remembers you fondly. She sends her love."

"Thank you, friend."

Carlota gave him a querying look.

"I'll tell you later."

Back in 1988—my God, Leon thought, thirty-four years ago, before Carlota was born!—he had been a member of CESID.

———

1988
Tokyo, Japan

HE'D BEEN STATIONED at the Spanish Embassy in Tokyo, part of an international team working with the Japanese

Criminal Investigation Bureau. His purpose for being there was twofold: tracking Chinese spies and learning about Japanese criminal gangs. Shortly after his arrival he'd been involved in several police raids on the mizu shobai, the so-called "water businesses," the Yakuza's network of bars, restaurants and nightclubs. One particular place of ill repute had been near the Ginza, and there was a lot of confusion as doors had been battered down. Half-dressed people ran in every direction accompanied by screams and shouts.

And inevitably a handful of foolish bad guys didn't want to lose face so they stood and fought with automatic weapons; a couple of them not only lost face but their lives. Two men attempted resistance with jujitsu, they and their opponents crashing through the paper of a shoji screen.

More by chance than design, Leon saved the life of Nyoko, who was in charge of the nightclub's reception desk. He kept her safe under cover from her demented gun-toting colleagues, and afterwards she agreed to testify in court in return for immunity and anonymity.

True to her word, Nyoko gave evidence then went into hiding. She was Hiroki's wife, and he suffered considerable shame at her betrayal of a crime family. He succumbed to the ritual yubitsume and offered his little finger to his boss as an act of regret and appeasement. As he'd been a popular member, that was acceptable—on condition that his wife did not come to their attention again. That wasn't going to happen: Leon later learned she had fled to Spain where she stayed with relatives until Hiroki could follow her.

Leon's last night in Japan had been somber. In his brief stay, he'd grown to like the country and many of the people with whom he'd come into contact, though he still found their culture and ways at times baffling. His final evening was a year after that raid. He was scheduled to fly to China and secretly report on the growing unrest among the populace.

Leon sat on the balcony, watching the bright city lights while savoring a quiet drink of sake and a plate of sushi. His apartment's lights were off, so he could better appreciate the bejeweled nightscape.

Tokyo's lights were mesmerizing, and he reflected on how many cities and countries he'd left for good. Regrets, a few. Memories, plenty. But new challenges always seemed to beckon. Those were the days! He was twenty-five and still craved adventure.

The visitor cracked the lock without a sound, entered his apartment and moved like a shadow.

Even so, Leon had sensed the uninvited presence, perhaps a change in the air as the intruder moved; perhaps it was Leon's training with the monks in the jungle.

Whatever the reason, Leon calmly picked up the remote on the balcony table and pressed the switch: the overhead lights instantly illuminated the entire room.

Hiroki stood there, completely dressed in black, like a ninja but without a mask. His face showed no emotion; it was not threatening. And he wasn't alarmed at being detected and identified.

"Greetings, Santos-san. I am in your debt—a debt that can never be repaid," Hiroki said, and he bowed and left as suddenly as he had arrived. Despite his wife having shamed him, Hiroki knew that Leon had saved her life, and therefore he was in Leon's debt. That debt is known as *giri*, the burden that is the hardest to bear.

Leon heard no more from Hiroki until late 2001, shortly after he quit CESID, which coincided with the organization's name-change to CNI.

———

2001
Southern Spain

HIROKI HAD TURNED up at Leon's Torrevieja office without an appointment. At the time, Leon was struggling to get clients. He was doing everything himself, but he really needed a competent private assistant.

Hiroki lowered himself in the guest chair and it creaked in response to his great weight.

Leon said, "You have renounced your crime family, haven't you?"

"You are as perceptive as ever, Santos-san."

"An educated guess," Leon said. "They allowed you to quit?"

"Yes. The family is honorable..." Unlike most Yakuza, Leon mused.

"But...why are you here now?"

He smiled, not a wholesome sight, and his dark jet eyes shifted from Leon's. "The Okudara-kai has always blamed me for one of their number being killed in that raid. But my family rejected their claims and warned them to stay away or gang warfare might result."

"Something tells me the Okudaras are still disinclined to comply?"

"Indeed. It made sense for us both to move here. We remembered you telling us about it—the opportunities. We did not wish to contact you, however. I was already in your debt. And we prospered—in a legitimate restaurant business in Alicante."

"And yet now you have come to me."

Hiroki didn't respond, but seemed evasive, and went on, "The Okudara-kai has been quietly moving in on the Romanian and Bulgarian gangs in Spain and France, taking over their 'comfort workers'. Sex tours are getting more popular in East Asia, as you know. The Yakuza have their hands in that trade as well. Organizing holiday tours to cities in Bangkok, Manila and Taipei, where special hotels offer every kind of fantasy."

The Yakuza perfected the art of people smuggling way back. They took girls from impoverished villages of the Philippines and bought unwanted girl-children from Chinese parents. But with the Westernization of China, that source was not so plentiful. Besides, many of their clients desired young Europeans rather than Asians, and they found that these could be sourced from the mess that was the new expanded European Union, which was now awash with thousands of illegal immigrants who wouldn't be missed.

The cost in human misery, disease and death was horrendous. Once, bringing the ungodly to justice was Leon's duty; now it was a calling. However, this well-organized trade in human beings was too big for him. Out of his league. There was something else Hiroki hadn't told him.

"I ask again, my friend: why are you here?"

"Nyoko vanished yesterday. While she was shopping in the Habaneras mall. They took her in the underground car lot. Last night I had a message waiting for me when I got home from the restaurant. From Kaito Okudara. He had followed us. Now he gloated, said he had arranged the abduction of Nyoko. He wants me to sweat, and eventually he will demand his pound of flesh from me..." He shifted in the chair and it creaked in protest. "My friend, I fear for her life."

This was personal now. "I'm interested," Leon said. "Go on."

"I am frustrated. I do not know where Okudara is. I have made enquiries, but they have been limited as I am no longer in the business. It is clear he keeps a low profile."

"He clearly hasn't reformed, he's still involved in crime. So we can start from that premise," Leon suggested. "I'll call in a few favors of people I know in the business. We should unearth something."

As Leon predicted, useful information materialized.

On the outskirts of Alicante, near one of those immense polígonos, stood a warehouse, one of hundreds. Cars rather than trucks visited this particular warehouse on a regular basis.

Inside, it gave the appearance of a furniture outlet, with open-plan sections divided into several salons occupied by scantily clad masseurs and their clients. A staircase ran up to a landing and ten closed doors.

Two Japanese men in dark pinstripe suits occupied the salon opposite. Wearing short black cocktail dresses, a couple of Eurasian comfort women were fawning over the men in a studied, insincere fashion.

From the adjacent salon, Leon heard the whir and clang of pachinko slot machines. Two spotty youths squatted on a futon, waiting their turn with the hostesses. These people were exhibitionists. Those who required privacy went upstairs. Others lounged, smoking, drinking and popping pills. The place was pervaded by a sickly-sweet smell of cheap perfume, sweat, cannabis, and general corruption.

Pretending to be a client, Leon sat with his back to the bar and sipped a very expensive tasteless drink.

Moments before he'd watched a number of prime suspects enter the rooms upstairs.

Leon spoke into the small lapel microphone and, within minutes, all hell broke loose.

The raid was well coordinated between the *policía national, the policía local* and the *Guardia Civil*. They netted thirty-two illegal immigrant women, twelve very embarrassed clients, four Yakuza regional bosses and two Spanish strong-arm men. Also in the haul was ten kilos of meth-amphetamine, six pistols and a sub-machine-gun, and two stolen BMWs. Before the lawmen could impound the only computer in evidence, Leon hacked it and found an inter-esting database. He downloaded several files to a memory-stick.

"The information was good," Guardia Diego Estrada said as they carted away the criminals. "We owe you, Leon."

The world seems to run on favors and debts. Though not perhaps as formalized as the Japanese variety. "Glad to be of help, Diego," Leon said, shaking his hand.

As Leon drove away, Hiroki moved in the well at the back and then, when they were clear of official observation, he struggled to get up to sit on the seat. "They should be able to close down the Okudara Yakuza," he said, "now they have that database."

Leon tapped the memory stick in his breast pocket. "Let's hope so, Hiroki."

In his Torrevieja apartment Leon slotted the memory stick into his laptop and Hiroki scanned the files. A smile transformed his features. "I have the address."

"Good. We don't have long. The Guardia will be looking at that database pronto, I reckon. Word will soon get to the Okudara-kai."

"You do not need to come with me," Hiroki said. "My debt is large already."

Leon drew from his shoulder holster the Astra A-100; it had its full quota of 9mm cartridges. "I'll watch your back, Hiroki. Let's go."

"Stubborn arrogant Western barbarian!"

"That's me," Leon said, and they left.

It was only a short drive. Leon parked the car on an area of waste ground—there's a lot of waste ground in Spain. They got out. Hiroki was ten years older than Leon yet moved like a panther, sleek and silent. Leon was behind him, but it was hard work to keep up and he was only thirty-seven.

Within secluded walled grounds the two-story six-bedroom villa was floodlit. They hadn't bothered with electronic surveillance because they employed cheap Bulgarian guards. Leon knew they were cheap because none of them saw Hiroki until it was too late.

The door was unlocked and the lobby wasn't covered by any CCTV cameras that Leon could detect. Arrogance or carelessness? Nobody seemed to be living here, which was odd. The upstairs and downstairs rooms, appointed with modern expensive furniture, were empty.

Leon gestured at the door leading to the basement. Hiroki nodded and it offered little resistance to his lock-picks.

Stealthily, they descended the stairs and at the bottom

walked along a short passage. Leon had drawn his automatic, safety off.

Immediately in front of them was a door. Leon slid it open and the strong scent of orange blossom floated to meet them.

Dressed in a gold-trimmed kimono, Nyoko was on her knees in the center of the ornate room, sideways on to the door. Her hands were tethered behind her back with red silk. She turned her head as they entered and her gorgeous eyes lightened as she saw her husband.

A stout Japanese man dressed entirely in black stood behind her with a samurai sword raised. His features were flabby due to too much good food and alcohol. His black hair was severely swept from his forehead. He eyed Hiroki and let out a low guttural laugh.

Hiroki said, "Kaito Okudara, you have brought your family low."

Okudara cursed Hiroki's ancestors and then said, "I have been waiting for you. So has your late wife."

The terrible meaning of his words registered as Leon watched the sword descend.

Before the blade could do its grisly work, however, two *shuriken*, or throwing stars, smashed into Okudara's right wrist and the sword clattered to the floor. In that same instant, Nyoko rolled out of the way and Hiroki withdrew a knife and dashed toward his wife's captor.

Bloody wrist by his side, Okudara adopted a karate stance, ready.

Before their bodies met in combat, Leon fired his automatic once and Okudara tumbled backwards, a hand grasping his wounded shoulder.

"Leave him for the law, Hiroki!" Leon urged. "Being charged for his murder won't help you or your wife."

"He deserves to die! His life is mine to take!"

"No, Hiroki, now I declare his life is mine. Your debt is cleared, your duty done."

Hiroki stopped in his tracks and looked down upon the once-fearful crime-lord.

Okudara's dark eyes glared defiance, and his lips curled in disdain.

The knuckles on Hiroki's knife-hand whitened.

Nyoko was still sprawled on the floor, her face ashen, eyes pleading with her husband. But, ever dutiful, she would not presume to tell him what he must do.

Those seconds seemed to stretch into a long time.

Finally, Hiroki turned to Leon and bowed. "Very well, Santos-san. I am duty-bound to accept."

Debt repaid.

Okudara was sentenced to serve twenty years in prison and Hiroki moved to Granada with his wife and opened a new restaurant there.

———

August 2022
Córdoba, Spain

THAT WAS IN 2001. And Hiroki and he had not been in touch since.

Until Hiroki telephoned the Torrevieja office number, and his call was automatically transferred to Carlota's phone here in Córdoba.

So, twenty-one years later, Hiroki was back in his life. But why?

"I need your help," Hiroki explained as the steam increased. "What I ask of you, it is dangerous."

"Old pals again, eh?" Carlota whispered in Leon's ear.

Leon grinned but didn't comment. He let the sweat ooze from his pores. Sure, he was fifty-eight and had had a good life, but he was still fit—though not in the Tom Cruise league—and didn't want to die any time soon. "How dangerous?"

"Very," Hiroki replied. "Big money is involved. It is the illegal organ traffickers who are operating hereabouts."

"In Córdoba?" Leon's mind flashed fleetingly to his attachment to the FBI in South Carolina. That was the last time he'd been involved in tackling lowlifes who dealt in that filthy trade. He briefly wondered how Sister Cristina was coping. Last he'd heard from her newsy annual letter she was, after a brief stint in Belize, again running the homeless hostel in Charleston—when not combating the odd crime or solving a mystery or two.

"Yes, I believe so," Hiroki replied, fracturing the memories. "And other places..."

Leon was only marginally surprised. True, organ-trafficking had only been considered a crime in Spain since 2010, when it was first highlighted here. He recalled only a few weeks ago a man bribed a homeless man into agreeing to donate a kidney for his wife, falsely declaring he was related. After tests, it was announced that they were compatible. Unfortunately, while at the notary's where he was to sign the consent form, the potential donor went queasy on the deal, refused to sign and exposed the bribery. "I'm aware of a little trafficking here, but I haven't encountered any traffickers myself. What is your involvement, Hiroki?"

"Our daughter Akemi—she's twenty now—"

"Congratulations. I never even knew you had a daughter."

"When Nyoko came so close to death, we decided every day was precious." He made that unsettling smile face. "Once we had settled in Granada we celebrated and we were blessed with Akemi..."

"But...?"

"She is a junior investigator with the World Health Organization, a unit who are looking into rumors of illegal trafficking of human body organs..." He hesitated and then went on, "She and her team—there are three of them—have gone missing."

"When was this?"

"Yesterday, Wednesday."

"Isn't the WHO being alarmist?"

"You'd think so. Geneva HQ didn't receive the regular evening report last night. So they did a bit of checking. Their suspicions were aroused when they realized they were unable to track any of their agents' cellphones; one, maybe a glitch, two's pushing coincidence; but three, something's wrong."

"Good logic," Carlota said.

"Agreed," Leon said. "Is WHO sending someone?"

"Yes, the head investigator—a Frenchman, Gabriel Laurent—flew in here in a private jet from Geneva this morning. But," he sighed, "the police are involved, and as you know, politics and diplomacy make uncomfortable bedfellows, so everybody is being very careful, walking on eggshells... And that makes for slow response-times. Laurent was good enough to speak to me as her next-of-kin. Alas, I fear he is out of his depth. He says, 'Nothing like this has happened before,' so it's as if he is in complete denial. He's staying at the same three-star hotel their team is booked into, the Córdoba Califa."

"Head Investigator not opting for a five-star?" Carlota huffed. "He must think he's slumming it."

She had a point but Leon didn't comment. "Can't you call on the families to help?"

Hiroki shook his head. "That is not possible. For Nyoko's sake I cannot get sucked in with them again. That is why I have turned to you. It's fortunate you were in the city."

"Coincidences, don't you just love them?" Carlota commented.

CHAPTER 11

ORGAN SYMPHONY

Wednesday—almost two days earlier

ETHAN WARD WAS THIRTY-NINE AND SOON TO reach that threshold age where life supposedly begins. He'd been working as an agent on the World Health Investigation Team for eight years and had only now been promoted as senior agent, a position he'd hungered after for ages. But now he found the responsibility daunting. His two colleagues— Reed Carter and Akemi Kuroda—looked to him for guidance and decisions. Yet he felt like a fish out of water. Córdoba was so far removed from his home patch of Charleston, South Carolina. The heat might be similar, which he was comfortable with, but everything else seemed alien. His one big drawback was that he didn't speak Spanish fluently and relied on Akemi and Reed when putting questions to the locals. Sure, his tall height made him dominate most Spaniards. He was also conscious that he was overweight but couldn't see how he could correct that any time soon: the food here was too darned tasty! He marveled at Akemi; she was so slight of frame yet had a voracious appetite. Maybe it was to do with her being twenty. Food didn't yet deposit fat on her bones. Thinking of bones, he'd really like to jump hers. Hey, he told himself, act professional. She was alluring, though, with those big eyes enhanced by her mauve eye-shadow.

The lead that Reed had picked up had been slight, but as it was their only break to date, Ethan had authorized round-the-clock surveillance. "We'll change watch at 10pm each night," Ethan declared.

Late last night Ethan reported to Geneva HQ that they were tracking a suspect who went by the moniker of Daigashi. Akemi pointed out that it probably wasn't his real name, since one meaning pointed to it being a deputy-boss in the Japanese underworld.

"How do you know that?" Reed had asked her in a disparaging tone.

"I studied criminology." Her voice was gentle yet Ethan detected firmness beneath the surface which he noted Reed was loath to engage. Reed hadn't commented further.

Today it was Reed's turn; he'd been on watch since relieving Ethan last night. Now, Ethan and Akemi waited in their three-star hotel, the Córdoba Califa.

"It is so tedious, all this waiting," Akemi had remarked to Ethan on her cellphone. "I had hoped this job would be more exciting!"

"It will have its moments, I assure you," he replied. Then, added, "Wait!" His adrenaline started flowing when he received the phone call from Reed. "Akemi, switch to conference call mode.

"Go ahead, Reed," Ethan said.

"Daigashi's on the move, people, and the intel is good. He's carrying a box."

"What kind of box?" Akemi asked.

"The kind you transport human organs in," Reed replied.

A mite flippant, but Ethan let it go.

"Ethan, what's our move?" Akemi asked.

"Keep him in sight, Reed," Ethan said. "Follow and keep us apprised of your direction. We'll join you shortly," Ethan promised.

———

AKEMI WAS EXCITED. At last, the chase was on! True, they could have apprehended Daigashi at any time, but they not only wanted him caught with the goods on him but also needed to identify the next link in the trafficking chain.

Dressed in her turquoise blouse, tailored cream linen jacket and pants, she exited the elevator and crossed the cool air-conditioned foyer, her white fedora clutched in her hand. Her billfold was snug in her back pants pocket. She didn't want to bother carrying a purse. Besides, she wanted her important stuff with her. As she approached she could see through the glass entrance doors that Ethan was already outside on the porch, waiting for her. She made brief eye-contact with the receptionist and he smiled at her and waved. She returned the smile and wave. The clock behind him read 1pm. Putting on her hat with one hand, she opened the door with the other.

The heat hit her immediately. By now she should be used to it, but she wasn't.

"Glad you could make it," Ethan said sarcastically. She immediately felt overdressed. He was wearing a Green Lantern T-shirt, khaki shorts and scuffed sandals. Draped round his neck was an old camera actually fitted with a viewfinder. He presented the typical tourist image.

According to personnel, he was about twenty-one years her senior, so she was tempted to let his comment ride. *Like hell.* "Call of nature," she offered, though her tone implied: *Truly, you piss me off!*

"Yeah, well..." Ethan held his cellphone horizontal in front of his chin and spoke into it: "Reed, we're leaving the hotel together now." He gestured at Akemi.

She unfolded a street map she'd taken out of her pocket.

"He's passing the Almodóvar Gate, going in a southerly direction," Reed said. "Taking his time. Can't be far to their OR, I reckon."

"Don't speculate," Ethan admonished. He turned to Akemi, raising an eyebrow.

She pointed on the map. "I've found it. Here—at the end of Calle Tejón y Marín..."

Ethan keyed his phone, brought up on the screen the local map and his position. Akemi did the same.

"We need to go separate ways," Ethan said. "Converge later when we're closer. We'll look less conspicuous then."

Conspicuous, right! "I should've worn something different!" she moaned, brushing a hand down her suit.

He studied her, head to toe. "Don't worry. You look great."

His comment mollified her a little. "Thanks." A least she was wearing sensible shoes—lace-up tan leather.

"We'll take parallel streets. I'll go down Cally Tedjion why Marine." She reckoned he meant Calle Tejón y Marín. Plainly he didn't have an ear for foreign names and words. "You stick with this one."

Plaza de la Trinidad. "Okay." He's the boss.

He went down the steps and hastened across the road, dodging traffic, and entered the street to the right of the hotel entrance.

Holding her cellphone in front of her, she descended the steps with care and moved to the left of the hotel, crossed the same road and hastened along Lope de Hoces until she reached the right-hand turn into Plaza de la Trinidad.

By now she was familiar with the Spanish house electrical wiring—it was on the outside of the buildings, snaking along the streets. Windows and doors were fitted with black metal grilles. Spaced at regular intervals metal lanterns on wall brackets would offer illumination when night fell, though she didn't particularly fancy walking along here then. Despite those misgivings, she felt an adrenaline rush. The chase was on, indeed. Trouble was: the Spanish didn't always bother putting name-plates at each end of a street.

She entered Sánchez de Fería.

Thankfully, Reed's resonant voice kept a running

commentary going, narrow street after narrow street, a seemingly tortuous trail. It gave her the impression she was negotiating a maze, reinforced by the fact that most thoroughfares were not wide enough or suitable for modern cars.

Consulting her phone map, Akemi kept track and was grateful for the narrow confines: shadow was cast by the white cliff-like walls and the heat of the sun did not penetrate. She was already quite clammy anyway.

She veered right, attempting to converge on Ethan, entering Calle Fernández Ruano.

Here, she saw a well-dressed white-bearded man emerge from a house doorway. He wore a beret and carried a bulky briefcase. And, an instant later, surprising her, another man appeared from an adjoining building. This second man looked completely out of place; he wore a black frock coat, a red cloak and a black top hat—as if he was auditioning for the theater.

A moment later, the bearded man turned right into Calle Tejón y Marín, glanced over his shoulder and shouted at Top Hat, "Go away! I owe nothing!" He quickened his pace. "Stop tormenting innocent businessmen!"

Top Hat ignored him and continued to follow.

And then the two of them moved out of sight as the street gently curved to the right.

She stopped at the corner, hoping to catch a glimpse of Ethan coming down Calle Tejón y Marín, but he didn't appear. Must be ahead.

"He has just passed the synagogue," Reed declared on her phone.

She could see the synagogue on her phone map, not far ahead.

She went left into Calle Judíos. She continued on and soon came to the synagogue.

But she didn't glimpse Reed—or Ethan for that matter.

There were no more instructions.

A man with a many-lined face and wearing a yarmulke

stepped out, lips murmuring a brief prayer. He noticed her and bowed his head respectfully.

She nodded in response.

Calle Judíos seemed quite long. She assumed she should go on. The conference call was still open, so she said, "Ethan, have you heard—"

"No, I'm going on ahead," Ethan said.

"Where are you?"

"I'm at a statue of a guy called Maymonidess."

"Maimonides," she corrected. "Right, I've found it on the map. But, Ethan, why hasn't Reed reported again? You sure you didn't pass him?"

"No, I know what he was wearing. To be honest, I don't know what's going on now. But there has to be a reaso—"

State the obvious, she thought, and then realized he hadn't finished speaking. The sudden quiet on the line made her jittery. "Ethan?"

No response.

The shadowy street she was in suddenly felt cold. She longed to be away from here, in the open, in the sun, basking in the warmth.

She walked hurriedly. Sweat collected at the small of her back and in her armpits.

She went on for about five minutes.

Nobody about; probably because it was too hot. Nothing unusual. But no Reed and now no Ethan.

Her heart was hammering away.

She felt alone. A rookie investigator.

At least she could rely on her Spanish. Ask a policeman? Ha!

Then, roughly three paces ahead of her a man strode out from a doorway. He was dressed in loose-fitting black pants and an open-necked shirt.

She stopped at once, sensing a threat.

Her mouth was dry.

It wasn't Daigashi.

The man swaggered toward her.

Shoes scuffed the cobbled ground behind her and sent her heart fluttering wildly.

She peered over her shoulder, ready to run. Another man stood about ten paces away. He had a big round flat face, a double chin and wore similar clothing.

"Sasakawa," barked the first man in Japanese, "don't let her pass!"

Sasakawa grunted and crouched, ready, broad of frame, feet firmly planted, much like an immovable object, blocking her way.

Both of them were obviously Japanese.

The man in front of her spoke in English, "You shouldn't be interfering with our work, young lady," he said. He had wide-apart eyes and eyebrows, thick dark brown hair, a flat nose, wide nostrils, a thick lower lip, a high forehead and a rounded chin with dark stubble. She'd remember him again, if necessary. He held out a hand, wiggled his fingers playfully. "Come, join your colleagues."

They know about Reed and Ethan? She swallowed and her throat felt raw.

Was this some kind of elaborate trap?

Forcing herself not to panic, she murmured "Yes" to put Flat Nose off guard, and moved forward, as if complying. Then, without hesitation she leaped toward him, landing her right foot exceedingly hard on the man's kneecap, using it as purchase to spring to the left, then kicked off the building's wall—disturbing cement dust as she did so—and landed on the cobbles behind the man.

She didn't wait to see what damage she'd done to the man's knee. She ran.

Ran full tilt into another Japanese man who had stepped in front of her. *Where the hell had he come from?* His appearance was so unexpected that she was caught unawares, his chest impervious to her unwitting onrush. She gleaned the imagery of slate colored almond-shaped eyes, a black ducktail beard and a bent nose before stumbling backwards. Her ass landed painfully on the cobbles. She flipped onto her feet in a second; crouched and ready, hands rigid to confront this third man—who she recognized as Daigashi. She should know...she'd tailed him two days earlier, and he still wore the same lightweight gray suit and blue open-neck silk shirt. His oval face and short greasy black hair were unmistakable. Of medium height, he possessed a wiry body, judging by his tight-fitting shirt and pants. His olive complexion leaned toward being sallow, and he had leathery pitted cheeks. A scar snaked down the left side of his face. She noticed he only had a gold stud earring in his left earlobe; possibly because he had no right lobe.

He didn't adopt any kind of defensive stance, simply holding the box in his left hand. "It's rude to refuse a polite invitation," he said, his voice sharp and shrill.

"He didn't say 'please'," she replied.

Daigashi absently rubbed the scar on his face and said to his confederate, Flat Nose, "Come, Ishii, say 'please' for the lady!"

"Pretty please," said Ishii, grinning, arms akimbo.

Akemi shook her head. "Sorry, on second thoughts, I'll take a rain check."

"Abject apologies, young woman." Daigashi smiled, revealing buck teeth, and gave a mock bow. "No rain, no check!"

The three of them closed in. She might be able to handle one at a pinch, but not all of them. She was consoled by the fact that they didn't produce any weapons. That implied that they wanted her alive. She swallowed. That wasn't necessarily a good thing, she knew. But, as her father had instilled into her, while there was life, there was hope. She'd undergo a beating at best, she supposed; worst, possibly gang rape.

That thought chilled her to the bone and she felt vomit rise; she swallowed again, this time with distaste.

Then, resignedly, she bobbed her head briefly. "Since you asked nicely, I will be pleased to join my colleagues."

The one named Ishii groaned, rubbing his knee. "Shame. I was looking forward to fighting you. Returning the favor."

"Another time, perhaps?" she said. "Rain check, eh?"

Daigashi laughed. "You have spirit, woman." He signed to the two men. "Bring her." He turned and began walking ahead. His right leg had a pronounced limp.

Strong hands gripped her upper arms and she was frog-marched between them. Both men stank of marijuana.

They moved further down the street, which in places was so narrow the shoulders of the men on either side of her occasionally grazed against the walls of the buildings.

Presently, Daigashi stopped at an old wooden door, its green paint faded. He produced a key and unlocked the door and opened it and went inside.

They followed him, shutting and locking the door after them, and entered a large patio, its walls decorated with Moorish azulejos and metal lanterns. They passed a central tiled fountain; on the water's surface floated hibiscus petals. The heady fragrance of jasmine accosted her but didn't quell her nerves.

At the far end was an arcade with arches. Here, they turned left and moved along the arcade and a door at the far end opened.

A very tall woman dressed in the white uniform of a nurse came out and strode up to them; her name-badge over her prominent bosom read *Ma. Inés Jara*. She raised a gun and pointed it at Akemi.

And Akemi sensed the blood drain from her face and her heart fluttered and her stomach lurched.

The weapon made a *phutt* sound and Akemi winced as she saw and felt the tiny dart hit her neck.

She lost consciousness almost immediately.

———

Thursday

RENZO RAGAZZO WAS a sixty-year-old Italian politician who had things to do and yet had so little time left in which to do them. Official channels were no longer open for him to undergo heart transplant surgery due to his age. Instead, he had let it be known he was willing to pay handsomely if a new heart could be obtained for him from other sources.

Over the years he had sequestered countless Euros during his nation's various and seemingly never-ending financial crises. He was a good orator, a populist, and adored by women. He had much to give.

It was an anxious time. Earlier the plain-looking female nurse had entered his private ward. She had fastened a tourniquet around his wrist and pulled it tight. "I'm drawing blood for one final check, sir. A blood cross-match to ensure your new heart will not be rejected."

He nodded docilely. He hated needles. He was tempted to look away as she tore open the packets containing the needle and the alcohol sponge, but he realized that he was paradoxically fascinated in the entire procedure. Life-giving procedure, in fact. The nurse then softly tightened the tourniquet a little more. Now the veins on the back of his hand stood out. She wiped the skin with the sponge and inserted a needle and expertly connected it to a syringe and drew off blood. She unscrewed the self-sealing syringe and connected a new one to the needle and repeated the procedure, and finally labeled them both "Recipient". As an anticlimax she had stuck a sterile patch over the pinprick. "There, that didn't hurt, did it?"

"No. But surely you know the heart is suitable if the operation is imminent?"

"We try to leave nothing to chance, sir. All the tests so far have been very positive."

He had lain against the pillow and released a sigh of relief.

And now, at last, the time had come.

He lay fully prepped on the operating table, listening to the surgeons' piped music. He'd been told it was played supposedly to calm him, the assumption being that patients listened even while unconscious. He had to admit, though, the choice didn't seem appropriate: Saint-Saëns's Symphony No.3. Then again, when he remembered its popular name was the *Organ Symphony*, he could appreciate the irony. Not that it was settling in the least.

Quite bizarrely, the French surgeons scheduled for the transplant operations were twins, Doctors Roland and Yves Dubois. Although they were not identical, their resemblance to each other was striking. Both were in their mid-thirties, he guessed, and had hooked noses, steel gray eyes, and broad shoulders. Their long fingers seemed well suited to surgery or perhaps even the piano, he thought. Roland had bushy black eyebrows and curling black hair almost down to his shoulders, while Yves had thin black eyebrows and straight black hair. Dr. Roland was the Saint-Saëns aficionado.

On the nearby table lay a naked man considerably younger than Renzo. A fine specimen: tall yet slightly overweight. But then again, Renzo admitted he was no longer as slim as he used to be. The man had a bronze complexion, a square jaw, a straight rather than a Roman nose, and crewcut blond hair.

He wondered how the man had died. The surgeons had emphasized that the donor had to be brain-dead before they would attempt to excise any organ.

Renzo's troubled heart missed a beat.

I must be mistaken, he thought.

The donor's eyelids flickered for a fraction of a second, as if he were merely in REM sleep.

Renzo stared, fascinated, and saw the chest cavity rise and fall, ever so slightly.

The man, his donor, wasn't dead.

The two transplant surgeons entered: Dr. Roland Dubois first, followed by Dr. Yves Dubois.

Dr. Roland hummed the *Adagio* from Saint-Saëns, and walked up to the side of Renzo's table. His mask was lowered, resting at his Adam's apple.

Silently, Dr. Yves approached the side of the donor, his steely gray eyes serious above his surgical mask.

"How are we feeling?" Dr. Roland looked down his hooked nose at Renzo, his voice quite throaty.

"Well, Doc, 'we' are really concerned." Renzo jutted his chin at the man on the other table. "If he's my donor, then you should be aware that he isn't dead."

Dr. Yves lifted the donor's eyelids and then made a nasal chortling sound. "Oh, that's not a problem, I assure you." His voice, in contrast to his brother's, was reedy. "Your donor is terminally ill—nothing wrong with his heart, fortunately for you; no, it's his brain. Our tests signify he has less than an hour to live."

"You can be that accurate?" Renzo queried.

"Oh, yes," Dr. Yves replied firmly.

"I see. A pity, he looks in pretty good shape, too."

Clucking his tongue, Dr. Roland interjected, "That's the trouble with so many of our patients. They look after their outer body but neglect the innards."

"Too cavalier in their life-style," agreed Dr. Yves. "Sadly."

A nurse entered wearing her face-mask and carried a kidney-shaped metal tray. "Everything checks out, doctors," she said. "Our immunologist has given the all-clear to proceed." The final blood cross-match was good, so they were as certain as they could be the donor heart would not be rejected.

"Then, let us get under way," Dr. Roland said.

Dr. Yves nodded.

"Time for your shot, sir," the nurse said and swabbed Renzo's hand with cool alcohol and inserted a cannula with two fine tubes attached and taped it to his hand.

Dr. Roland said, "This is the turning point of the symphony," he enthused. "The organ is about to enter in all its glory!"

Dr. Yves raised his mask to cover his nose and mouth and picked up a metal rod-shaped item from the stainless steel tray at his side.

His brother Dr. Roland said, "Hah, here's the major key

version of the *Dies Irae* theme! A pity you're going to miss it, Monsieur Renzo. Are you ready?"

"Yes," Renzo croaked.

"When you wake, you will have a new heart." Dr. Roland promised. "Death redeemed, indeed, a kind of resurrection!"

The anesthetist placed what appeared to be an oxygen mask over Renzo's mouth and nose. "Take five deep breaths," she instructed.

Obediently, Renzo began: "One, two, three..." He got no further; Renzo was anesthetized.

Dr. Yves addressed the nurse and patted the head of the naked man next to Renzo. "Are we ready to harvest his kidneys as well for our other lucky clients?"

"Yes, Dr. Yves. The preservation tanks are on the counter, in readiness. As usual."

"Ah, so they are." He now took up the music's theme in unison with his brother Roland, waving his arms as if conducting the orchestra, and then called to his brother, "Time for him to die."

He lifted the metal rod and leaned over the unconscious man and pressed the tip against the donor's temple. He pressed a button and a dull thud sounded. The contraption was his own invention, inspired by a trepanning tool: it sent a tiny electrical node into the patient's brain and then it detonated, transmitting a disruptive electrical charge that entirely stilled the brain function.

He removed the rod and a small hole seeped a tiny amount of blood. "I consider he's now terminated. Nurse, you can bring in the team and we can start."

"Yes, Dr. Yves," she said, making for the door.

Dr. Yves lowered the rod to the tray at his side. "Oh, nurse, for the record, what's the donor's name again?"

She turned. "Ethan Ward."

CHAPTER 12

LITTLE FINGER

AKEMI WOKE WITH A SPLITTING HEADACHE AND A terribly dry mouth. She opened her eyes and then sat up with a jolt. This wasn't her hotel room.

And then it all came flooding back: the three Japanese men, forcing her to go with them, the deceptively blissful courtyard, the arcade and the nurse with the anesthetic gun.

She was lying on a single bed pushed against the wall. She swung her legs round and sat up. The room she occupied was small and had seen better days. Parts of the walls were decorated with colorful tiles, but sections had fallen away and lay broken on the floor, leaving bare plaster. There was one door, at the other side of the room. In the room's center were two straight-backed chairs and a cheap wooden table. A single light bulb provided illumination; there were no wall windows, but there was a skylight window, its panes spotted with bird-droppings so only a small unblemished patch admitted light from the sun.

Where were Reed and Ethan? Had they met a similar fate?

She licked dry lips. Her tongue felt thick, almost bloated.

How long had she been unconscious? Looking at the skylight, it was daylight.

She checked her Fitbit Versa on her wrist: it was midday, so it had to be at least a day later. So she'd been out of it a long time.

Standing up, she walked to the table a little shakily, and then sat on a chair.

Absently, she tapped her back pocket. Her billfold was still there. So they hadn't robbed her. Her clothes were rumpled, not surprising since she'd been lying in them for roughly twenty-two hours. Her stomach made gurgling noises and she felt weak. Being all too familiar with dieting, she knew the weakness and hunger pangs would go if she ignored them.

She got up again and believed that her legs were stronger now. She went over to the door, tried the handle. It was locked. No surprises there, she supposed. She moved again, until she stood directly under the skylight, bathed in a narrow shaft of sunlight that percolated through the shit. She could understand how prisoners in solitary confinement could go stir crazy if they saw no sunshine from one day to the next.

And now she experienced uncomfortable pressure on her bladder, despite feeling dehydrated.

She looked around. There was only the one door, so there was no toilet cubicle. Only a bucket at the foot of the bed, its purpose obvious now. She only hoped nobody entered the room while she squatted over it and relieved herself.

———

AN HOUR PASSED. Akemi sat on the edge of the bed, hands on her head, elbows on her thighs. Thoroughly dispirited. Careful what you wish for, she told herself. Not so long ago she'd been craving excitement. But then she hadn't really appreciated it could be life-threatening.

Her heart skipped a beat as the door to the room opened.

Three men strolled in and shut the door after them. She

recalled their names. Daigashi's thin lips curved but it wasn't a genuine smile. "It is good to see you are awake at last, young woman," he said. He carried a box which appeared familiar and put it on the table. She could clearly see the writing on it now: *Cardiac Preservation Transport System*.

She didn't answer him. The other two—Sasakawa and Ishii flanked him; both smirked.

Then Daigashi said, "Stand up, woman so Ishii can search you!" Not so polite now, was he?

It crossed her mind to wonder why he—or somebody else—hadn't already searched her.

Nothing was to be gained by being bloody-minded or obstinate. She got to her feet and stood quite still, though her knees tended to quake.

Sasakawa walked behind her and gripped her upper arms while Ishii strode up to her, his face close to hers, his foul breath making her want to retch—if only her stomach hadn't been empty she could have directed projectile vomit into his eyes.

She braced herself, nostrils flared and her breathing accentuated, which was annoying as it meant she smelled the breath from the pair of them so much she was liable to get high.

Ishii first shoved his hands in her jacket's side pockets and extracted her cellphone. It was still on and in conference mode. He handed it to Daigashi, who turned it off and put it in his jacket pocket.

Then Ishii opened her jacket and his hands slowly made a rough and personally uncomfortable search, pointedly lingering over her breasts. "Pert," he said. "I like them pert." He continued, sliding his hands down her legs and quickly found her billfold in the back pocket. He handed this to Daigashi, too.

She cleared her throat. "Where are the others?" she asked, attempting to control her traitorous trembling body. "My colleagues."

Opening her billfold, Daigashi said, "If there are to be

any questions, lady, *I* will ask them." He glared at her. "Understood?"

"Yes, I understand," she said.

"Good."

———

DAIGASHI GRINNED as he withdrew from the billfold bank notes in Euros, Dollars and British Pounds, which he shoved into his jacket pocket. He glanced at her American Express credit card and threw it on the floor. Then he removed her World Health Investigation Team ID card in the name of Akemi Kuroda.

Reading that name sent a shiver down his frame and he took a step back, a crooked smile on his narrow mouth.

Oh, the gods are good! He rubbed the scar on his face—gained from a fight in prison. Hiroki Kuroda had been responsible for him being sent to prison. While it was a long sentence, he should have been released earlier for good behavior. Unfortunately, his fellow inmates didn't take to him much. One of them broke his nose on two occasions and now it was permanently bent.

He circled Akemi, leering at her, rubbing his right ear; the earlobe had been bitten off in a fight in the prison laundry. Finally he'd lost patience with the constant bullying and fought back; but to no avail. There were too many of them: his right leg was seriously damaged when he didn't show enough respect to the prison kingpin. "Next time, both your legs will be broken," he was told. By then, of course, the authorities put him down as a trouble-maker and he was never going to get released before serving his time, the full twenty years.

"Oh, this is going to be so sweet," he whispered with a nasal twang. He put her ID into her billfold and left it on the table. "Alright, you two," he ordered, "put her in that chair —and hold her down!"

They did as bid and she sat on the straight-backed wooden chair, the table in front of her. She wondered how long the heart in that box would be viable. She'd been told the norm was six hours. Time was running out for a lucky and doubtless wealthy transplant recipient. She feared that time might be running out for her, too.

"Place her right hand on the table," Daigashi ordered.

While Ishii clamped hands on her shoulders, the huge hulk named Sasakawa grabbed her arm and slammed her hand on the table.

She gasped, sure that the heel of her hand would be bruised, but made no other sound.

Daigashi removed his suit jacket and carefully draped it over the second chair. Slowly, methodically, he rolled up the sleeves of his shirt. He walked round the table and held his right wrist in front of her face. "See this?"

His sudden movement made her flinch.

The flesh was badly scarred; the wrist was markedly thinner than the other one. "Your fucking father did this to me," Daigashi snarled. "He not only took twenty years off my life but made this wrist as weak as a child's!"

Uncomfortable, she moved slightly in the seat, and Ishii pressed down hard on her shoulders, forcing her to sit still. "My—my father?"

"Yes—Hiroki Kuroda!"

She hid the shock well. "But there must be many men with the name Kuroda," she argued.

Daigashi shrugged. "Well, if I'm wrong, it will be a pity —for you."

"Wh-why?"

"I want to find him, repay him. You could tell me where he scuttled off to."

"Scuttle off? My father does not scuttle anywhere. He is a brave man!"

He gave her a slap with his left hand, but she didn't cry out. "Daughter like father, I see only too well!"

"Even if he were my father, I would not tell you!"

Abruptly he held her chin in his hand, shoved her head back against the belly of Ishii. "I think I could make you!" He let go, stepped back. "But I could also use you as bait. Bring him to me."

"What if he isn't my father?"

"Then you will be a donor. We will keep you on ice until your organs are needed."

"On ice?"

"Oh, don't worry, we'll keep you very much alive. Cryogenics isn't so advanced yet..." He gestured at the room. "We will keep you here."

She struggled, trying to extract her arm from Sasakawa's grip.

Daigashi went over to his jacket, fished in the inside pocket and produced a narrow metal object. He flicked it and a blade appeared. It shone in the light. "Hold her steady," he ordered.

Her heart was pounding now. She was weak with hunger, defenseless. At the mercy of these thugs. "Why are you doing this?"

He laughed. "Still with the questions, eh?" He stepped closer, threatening. "Perhaps you deserve some answers. My name is Kaito Okudara. Your father—with the help of a private investigator—conspired against me and handed me over to the police. I was jailed." He waved the knife-blade. "Now do you see? It is my good fortune that you have fallen into my hands." He chuckled. "Speaking of hands..." Slowly, he spread her fingers on the table and deliberately sliced off her little finger at the first knuckle.

She clenched her teeth and made a seething sound while fighting the obvious pain; tears ran from the corners of her eyes. But she didn't scream or faint.

He produced a clean linen handkerchief from his pants pocket, draped it over the bleeding hand. "You would be a credit to any Yakuza family," he told her. "Let her go."

As his men released their hold on her she pulled her hand to her and wrapped the handkerchief round it and clutched it to her chest. Drops of blood stained her jacket but she felt sure that was the least of her worries.

Okudara held up the severed digit which dribbled a little blood onto the table top. "This will be a souvenir—unless of course I discover where your father is." He licked blood from the small stump. "And if that is the case, then I will send it to him as a keepsake—with an invitation..."

———

THE TWIN DOCTORS were surrounded by medical staff now, many of them monitoring via the life-support equipment the vital signs of Renzo the politician.

The Organ Symphony was on a loop; no sooner did it end than it began all over again. Presently, it was the symphony's most famous melody, which Saint-Saëns described as a "totally transformed" major key version of the *Dies Irae* theme, with piano in place of a heavenly harp followed by the organ punctuated by trumpet fanfares: death has been transfigured.

"This is so apt!" Dr. Roland said, gloved hands poised, "Ready, brother?"

Dr. Yves replied, "Ready."

"Then let us begin. Keep in step with me."

"I always do, brother. Those six minutes will always make me your junior."

The nurse rolled her eyes to the OR ceiling.

"Scalpel," said Dr. Roland. A nurse at his side slapped the tool into his waiting gloved palm.

"Scalpel," echoed Dr. Yves, receiving the knife from his nurse at her station by his elbow.

"Incision started," said Dr. Roland.

"Incision started," echoed his brother.

They worked as a precision team, their every move

seeming to beat time to the piped music. Until finally the donor's heart had been transferred to the recipient, Renzo, and donor's two kidneys were ensconced in separate preservative containers.

———

AKEMI'S HAND THROBBED DULLY. The extreme pain had diminished. She didn't dare to peel the handkerchief back and look at the damage, the cruel amputation.

"Sasakawa, bring the box. We have a heart to deliver!" Daigashi—no, she must think of him as Okudara now— strode to the door.

Obediently, without a word, Sasakawa grabbed the box.

Opening the door, Okudara turned and eyed her up and down, a slight curve on his lips. "Ishii will guard you while we're gone."

The two men went out and the door was shut and locked.

Ishii crossed the floor and retrieved her American Express card. "Sometimes, I wonder about our leader. So wrapped up about the big picture and getting even with your dad, he doesn't bother with the little financial picture. This is a perfectly good card—if you know the PIN number." He waved the card at her. "You can tell me that, can't you?"

"I could—if you let me go," she suggested, still clinging to her wounded hand. Clutching at a straw.

He made a grating sound that approximated a laugh. He put the card in his shirt breast-pocket. "No, I can't do that. I can make you tell me, of course."

Rhetorical. She didn't doubt he could. She said nothing.

He sighed, sat opposite and stared at her, absently fingering her billfold, and then glanced meaningfully at the bed across the room. He grinned and his tongue slid over his lips.

Creep! She lowered her eyes.

"That's a shame," he said.

She would not answer him. Keep your gaze averted, she told herself. She had the feeling that any kind of eye-contact would only antagonize him or further inflame his obvious lewd thoughts.

"I meant," he said, "it's a pity your jacket's got blood on it."

Oh, really? She said nothing.

"Take it off!" he ordered and banged a fist on the table, making her jump. He laughed at her response. "Do it, take off your jacket!"

Holding her breath, she awkwardly eased the chair away and stood up, still careful not to look directly at his face. Although it was difficult to maneuver with only one fully functioning hand, she managed to shrug out of the jacket and hung it on the back of the chair.

"Nice blouse," he said.

I'm not taking it off, damn you! She bit her lip and now, furiously angry, she glared at him.

He leered and pushed his chair back, got to his feet. "You're not seriously going to fight me, are you?" He limped toward her. "My knee still hurts. I owe you for that."

"You owe me nothing."

He licked his thick lower lip. "I won't hurt you like you hurt me—*if* you take off your blouse."

She shook her head.

He came closer. "Then I'll have to take it off for you—and hurt you as well." Closer still he came, his eyes on her heaving chest, she noted.

Breathing heavily, he stopped and reached out to grab the collar of her blouse.

She kicked him between the legs. It was *so* gratifying as he emitted a high-pitched groan and bent forward in response.

Training set in. Almost instinctively she slammed the ridge of her left hand against his neck, twice in rapid succession, briefly blocking the blood flow to his brain. He expelled a loud gasp and flopped sideways, hitting his head on the corner of the table, which proved a bonus from her point of view.

He lay there on the dusty floor, blood on his temple. Out cold, she guessed. Better check, though.

Steadying her breathing, she knelt down and checked his pulse. His flesh was clammy. He'd live.

Her thoughts were in turmoil. She was pleased he was incapacitated, but surprised at how she'd reveled at inflicting those blows. What was she thinking? These people were quite comfortable killing innocents to harvest their organs and yet she had qualms about slaying her captor? But she'd never killed before. Sure, she'd hurt a number of opponents in martial arts sessions and sustained more than a few bruises herself, but she'd never broken anyone's bones. Maybe she needed to start learning now. She shuddered. That required cold calculated willpower.

Self-justification: she'd reacted before Ishii attempted to violate her. A pre-emptive strike. But when Okudara and Sasakawa came back, they were unlikely to be sympathetic. She rolled her eyes in disgust at herself. She'd only delayed the inevitable pain they'd inflict.

She saw the skylight and smiled. It was an idea; it might work.

First, she put her jacket on. Then she retrieved her American Express card from Ishii's shirt and shoved it in her billfold. She decided she might as well search Ishii's pants; he might have something useful. In his back pocket she found a small collection of pornographic photographs and also a wad of Euros. She had no qualms about taking the money, which also went into her billfold. In another pocket she found a Spanish driving license, so the villain wasn't merely a tourist. He plied his trade regularly. No key for this room's door, sadly. And no cellphone. Nothing else. She shoved the billfold into her pants back pocket.

Before she put her plan into effect, she dragged Ishii by his collar along the floor and dumped him in front of the door. If anybody attempted to open it, she hoped his inert form would provide an obstruction.

Next, she moved the table until it was directly under the skylight, and then lifted the chair she'd used and put it on the table. Gauging the height, she reckoned it might suffice. The bed under the table would guarantee about another foot in height, but she feared the stability would be highly suspect. She must hope her guesswork proved okay.

Crossing the floor to the other chair, she tipped it on its side, stood on one of its legs and with her left hand applied pressure to the rest of it until the leg snapped off. Since Ishii hadn't carried a weapon, this was all she had for the time being. It wasn't quite a nunchaku or even a cop's nightstick, but it would have to serve.

With the utmost care she clambered onto the table top, the chair leg gripped in her left hand. She lifted her knees onto the seat of the chair and, holding onto its back, straightened up and stood on the seat. It was just as well she wasn't queasy about heights. There was a slight wobble, but that was her knees, not the structure she'd built. Only nerves.

It was enough. She could stretch and touch the skylight catch!

———

OKUDARA WALKED a couple of paces ahead of Sasakawa across the courtyard and entered another door.

Inside was a complete contrast. No expense had been spared; the place was completely modernized. The corridor's tiled floors echoed their footfalls. Although there were strip-lights along the edges of the ceilings, there was also an array of skylights offering natural light which made the place gleam and appear less clinical, despite the pungent smell of chemicals drifting through the air-ducts.

"Keep up, we have a delivery to make!" he barked.

Sasakawa shuffled behind him a little faster. "I don't want to drop it," he said.

"No you don't—or there'll be hell to pay!"

They entered another door which was at the end of a long corridor.

About halfway down this corridor, Okudara barged through a door labeled *Receiving Room*. He held it open for Sasakawa.

This was familiar, an anteroom he'd been in a number of times. The usual nurse with a long face and soulless black eyes sat behind a reception desk. A pile of manila folders were stacked on the desk surface, alongside a telephone. The only other furniture was a wooden four-drawer filing cabinet and a single matching wooden chair. Two walls were adorned with framed illustrations of male and female anatomy, showing muscles, tendons, bone structure and organs. A door to the left was labeled *No entry except to OR staff*. Again, a skylight allowed sunlight and a shaft of light shone through a slightly open window, highlighting the swept-back jet-black hair of the nurse.

"Your delivery is an hour late," she said sternly.

"It's still well within the margin," Okudara replied coldly. He signed to Sasakawa, who nodded and lowered the transportation container on her desk.

She checked the readout and seemed satisfied—if anybody could satisfy this witch, Okudara thought. He certainly didn't want to even consider trying.

"Payment?" he said, extending his hand, palm up. Not so much begging as demanding.

She opened a drawer in the desk and lifted from it a thick brown envelope which she handed to him.

"Thanks. When do you want the next delivery?"

"Tomorrow, Friday. You shouldn't need to ask. It's on your schedule. A busy week for you, isn't it?"

"You're right, it is." He was about to turn away and leave but hesitated. "The live donors we've delivered."

"What about them?"

"We reckon the payment should be greater than for

merely delivering this box of an organ. A live donor has lots of organs, after all."

Her thin lips approximated a smile. "I like your chutzpah. But I do not make the financial arrangements."

"Then will you get somebody who can? Another plus is, the organs in a live donor are really fresh, aren't they?"

"He can go," she said, pointing to Sasakawa, "but you wait here."

CHAPTER 13

LIVE DONORS

AKEMI MANAGED TO UNLATCH THE SKYLIGHT window-catch and then used the chair leg to raise the window; it fell back with a crash and she winced, hoping the sound didn't alert anyone. She waited anxious seconds but nobody came. Then she firmly wedged the wooden leg across the corner of the window and tested that it would take her weight. She was relieved to find that it would.

Gripping the chair-leg, she pulled herself up and at the same time felt the chair wobble under her feet. A second later, it clattered to the floor. She rested her forearms on the window edge, her legs dangling, and then heaved herself through, and breathing heavily crouched by the edge of the skylight.

Did anybody hear the chair falling?

The door to the room remained shut.

Looking around, she saw the tiled rooftops were a jumble of various shades of red and brown. Further along the roofs appeared more modern, smooth cement surfaces and modern skylights.

Tentatively she walked along the roof; the slope wasn't too severe. When she reached the next skylight she peered down.

It was a modern corridor interspersed with doors.

She moved to the next one and found the skylight was slightly open, just a notch.

Voices carried up to her.

She crawled to the edge of the window and peeked through the gap.

"My God," she breathed softly, and raised her good hand to stifle a gasp.

It was Reed and he was talking to Okudara and a stern-faced female nurse. They were speaking English.

"Our disappearance will give the WHO pause for thought," Reed was saying. "Working on the inside, I found they were getting too close to the true purpose of the Black Foundation clinics—so our little decoy ploy proved necessary."

"What do we do with the pair of them?" Okudara asked.

"Ward is already undergoing surgery as we speak," the nurse said. "Kuroda's op is scheduled for tomorrow."

"A waste," Okudara said. "I don't know why we couldn't have had a little fun with her before she's on the butcher's slab."

"Live donors must be unsullied," Reed said, chuckling. "There's no telling how much bacteria you and your pals might pass on to her!"

"I am not amused!" Okudara snapped. "Now, what's my —our cut?"

"Dr. Godsafe agreed you get ten percent more than the usual." Reed turned to the nurse. "Make the arrangements, will you?"

"Yes, sir," she said.

Reed rubbed his hands together. "Now, since I have to all intents and purposes disappeared, I must return to Venice and report in person to Dr. Godsafe."

"On a different passport, I suppose?" Okudara said.

"Oh, of course. Have fun." He exited the room.

Akemi sank back on her haunches, her whole body trembling.

Then she thought of Ethan. And smothered a sob.

She rose to stand and skirted the skylight and hesitantly walked across the roof-tiles to the next skylight. This one was shut. Below was what looked like a private hospital ward, with a man lying on a bed, surrounded by monitoring machines and hooked up to an IV stand.

Further along, she came to a third skylight.

Below was a brightly lit white-tiled room.

The grisly scene made her dizzy and weak. She sank slowly to her knees. But she couldn't move her gaze from what was happening.

His face serene in death, Ethan Ward lay on the operating table, his chest cavity opened as if an alien had burst forth from it. To the side stood a standard surgical trolley containing an assortment of pathologist's scalpels and bone-cutters, plus an electric saw; all of them blood-stained.

On the adjacent operating table was an elderly man whose chest was being sewn up presumably by a doctor in scrubs. Two nurses and two other staff attended, monitoring the machines.

Over on the counter she glimpsed two boxes, the same kind that Okudara had been carrying.

Tears streamed down her cheeks.

She backed away from the skylight.

Must find a way down, to get away, to alert the police.

Again, she skirted the skylight and moved to yet another.

She steeled herself for more grisly medical transplantations.

But this wasn't an operating room. It was another private ward. A middle-aged man in civilian clothing paced the room while an elderly gray-haired woman sat on the edge of the bed. She was wearing a surgical gown and yet still managed to appear elegant.

PACING THE WARD, Remy Leroy, a fifty-year-old French concert orchestra conductor, huffed and puffed. "You're being unreasonable, Delphine!"

"I do not think so, my dear." She slid off the bed and padded toward him. "Now stop striding up and down and give me a hug!" Standing in her hospital shift, she opened her arms to accept him. Her lined face creased in amusement and her rheumy blue-gray eyes still held the allure of old times.

He expelled an exasperated sigh and stopped in mid-stride. He walked to her and obediently hugged her, though gently, with little pressure. "Not too tight," he whispered, "I don't want to hurt you, ma chère."

She trembled in his grasp and he remembered those heady days when they had been young, carefree, and deeply in love. In love with each other and with classical music. In truth, he was still in love—with both.

Chuckling softly, she brushed a hand against his salt-and-pepper hair, which moved as if of its own accord. "Oh, Remy, dear, you've been hurting me for the last ten years."

His face paled and he abruptly pushed away from her. He wiped a hand across his brow to adjust his skew-whiff toupee. "What do you mean?"

"Your dalliances with sopranos. It's always sopranos, isn't it?"

"You—you knew?"

"Yes, of course."

His eyes avoided hers. "That's all they were, you know, dalliances."

"I know."

"But—but I do honestly love you, you know that. I don't want to lose you... that's why you're here!"

She raised a hand, gently brushed her knuckles against his cheek. "I know, I know. Despite your infidelities, you have always been considerate—and loving. The fifteen year age difference never seemed to matter, I thought."

"It didn't." He sat on the chair next to the bed. "But... I'm weak."

"You are." She patted him on the shoulder. "Now what are you going to do about the deposit for this operation I don't want?"

"But—but you'll die without it!"

Tears shone in her eyes. "I've had a good life, Remy. You've given me many lovely years. While you are still young enough, you should find someone else. As for the heart allocated to me, arrange for it to go to somebody younger, more deserving."

He stood up and embraced her none-too-gently this time. "More deserving?" His voice cracked. "I don't deserve you, Delphine. Really, I don't!"

————

THE TALL NURSE, *Ma. Inés Jara*, held the anesthetic gun in one hand as she unlocked the door. It was best to keep the Japanese woman unconscious—less trouble, she'd learned; some live donors could be very refractory. With her free hand she pushed the door but couldn't budge it more than an inch. Something was obstructing it. She clicked on her lapel microphone and said, "I need security. Quickly!"

Within five minutes, two burly men appeared at her side. She told them to force the door. Between them, they managed to open the door enough so that she could squeeze through the gap they made.

She swore. "It's one of our harvesters!" she cried. "The donor's gone!"

Bending down, she clamped her hands under Ishii's arms and heaved him to one side. He was still breathing.

The two security men entered. "She's gone out the skylight!" one of them exclaimed.

Stating the obvious, the simpleton!

"Well go after her!" Nurse Jara barked. "Here, take this!" She handed Simpleton her anesthetic gun. He tucked it inside his zipped-up jerkin.

One man picked up the fallen chair and put it on the

table top and held it steady while the second, Simpleton, clambered up. He was tall so had no difficulty in reaching the edge of the skylight window and heaving himself through. "I'm up!" he called.

Well, fancy, I wouldn't have noticed! Nurse Jara said, "Can you see her?"

"Yes! She's moved well along the roof—I reckon she has even gone past the OR..."

Nurse Jara said, "Well, go after her!" And then she turned and left the room.

She raced to her nurse's station and extracted another anesthetic gun from the cupboard. She hurried down the corridor, passing the OR where the operation-in-progress lamp still glowed red.

She passed the ward where Madam Leroy was soon to be prepped, and entered the adjoining ward, which was vacant. She wheeled the nightstand under the skylight and clambered on top of it.

Being tall, she could easily reach and opened the latch. Stretching, she raised the window.

The Japanese girl was walking toward her. Then the girl spotted her peering from the skylight window and twirled round and hurried back the way she'd come. Yet she must have realized her escape was stymied by the security man; Simpleton, was on the roof and closing in on her.

Nurse Jara aimed the anesthetic gun and fired.

Good shot! The dart hit the girl's thigh. The result was remarkably fast and catastrophic.

The girl fell sideways, onto the skylight to her right. The frame didn't survive the force of her falling weight but shattered: glass, wood and the girl fell through into the private ward. The sound of her landing was loud, coming from next door.

Nurse Jara jumped down from the nightstand, rushed to the door and ran along the corridor to the Leroy private ward. She flung open the door.

The Japanese girl lay unconscious on top of the bed,

pieces of glass and wood littering the room. Amazingly, there was no blood. Monsieur and Madam Leroy stood in the far corner, hugging each other and were clearly in shock.

Not too much shock, however. "I require my deposit returned immediately!" Monsieur Leroy stated firmly.

"I'm terribly sorry, Sir, Madam," Nurse Jara said in the most sincere voice she could muster. "This is awful. You could have been seriously hurt!"

"I could have been killed before my time, which is limited as it is!" rejoined Delphine Leroy.

"Quite so. I will arrange for the return of your deposit, Monsieur Leroy."

Nurse Jara was pleased to see that Akemi was only bruised and none of her bones were broken. She wanted the young woman intact, otherwise it reflected badly on her. She would ensure that Akemi was kept sedated until she was needed for the next operation, which was scheduled for tomorrow.

———

HIROKI, Leon and Carlota agreed it was too late to attempt anything tonight, certainly there was no need to curtail the hammam session. The booking for the hammam was for ninety minutes' duration; they each wore a color-coded wrist-band to denote when they were due to leave; their changing room locker keys were on the same band. All three of them exited the sauna. Hiroki removed the towel; thankfully he was wearing briefs, though they left little to the imagination.

They showered then plunged into the thermal bath, a large swimming pool surrounded by Arabic arches. Hiroki made an enormous bow-wave at his immersion.

Every time he frequented the hammam, Leon found it invigorating.

After about ten minutes a male masseur dressed in white

pants and short-sleeved jacket approached and advised all three of them it was time for their massage.

The two men stepped out of the pool and were led along the ornately tiled side and behind a curtained area. A second masseur awaited them. A half-dozen couches covered with towels lined the room. Leon saw Carlota being led through the same opening in the curtain and then she went behind yet another opaque curtain. The two masseurs gestured for the men to lie face-down on the couches.

Leon's masseur applied scented oil to his back and firmly rubbed it into his muscles. The masseur was the height of discretion and made no mention of the number of scars on his body.

Later, as they repaired to the changing room, Leon promised, "We'll go round to the Califa first thing in the morning. Where are you staying?"

"At the Maestre," Hiroki said. "It's central and economical."

"I know it, near the Mezquita. I've got your cellphone number."

———

Friday

THE FRENCHMAN, Gabriel Laurent was waiting for them in the foyer of the NH hotel Córdoba Califa.

Leon estimated he was in his early forties. He was short, with a pale complexion, swept back curly black hair, a typically Gallic hooked nose, and a small mouth. He wore a tight-fitting light gray suit, an open-necked shirt that displayed black curly hair on his chest, the look no doubt inspired by his president.

"Mr. Kuroda phoned me to expect you, Señor Cazador," he said, extending his hand. His English was slightly accented, and possibly attractive to certain ears.

It was a firm shake, quickly disengaged.

Leon introduced Carlota.

Laurent bowed slightly, took her hand lightly, and his hazel eyes sparkled. "Charmed, Mademoiselle. Perhaps we could continue in my room?" This last was not provocatively aimed at Carlota but both of them.

"Yes, that would be fine," Leon agreed.

Today Leon wore a black short-sleeved shirt with an open neck, the same slim blue jeans and suede jacket. Carlota had chosen a black blouse and the same light purple jacket and pants she wore yesterday.

As Laurent shepherded them to the elevator, Leon noted that there was a CCTV camera aimed at the foyer entrance.

In the elevator, Laurent said, "I have been puzzling what the 'NH' stands for, precisely."

Carlota smiled. "It's the Navarra Hoteles Group—it began in the province of Navarra and has expanded."

"Oh, I see. A bit like our Ibis hotels."

She shrugged. "Maybe, though I think NH do not consider their hotels are in the economy class."

Laurent said nothing in reply.

When they reached his room he poured three glasses of still water. The curtains were open to reveal a balcony that overlooked the city. Not exactly slumming it, Leon thought.

After settling in their chairs, Leon asked, "What have you found out so far?"

Laurent cleared his throat. "Sadly, my Spanish is of the 'get-by' type. I can speak perfect English."

"We'll stick to English, then," Leon said.

"The staff speak French, I presume?" Carlota asked.

"Some do, some do not. However, I have ascertained that the CCTV camera was functioning and I have viewed the images for the day in question. Both Ward and Kuroda left the hotel at 1pm precisely."

"What about Carter?" Leon asked.

"I must admit I didn't think. I was pleased to note those two and the time..."

"That was the last time those two were seen here?" Carlota pressed.

"Precisely."

"We'll search the CCTV footage for Carter later," Leon said.

"Yes," Laurent said, "I should have thought of that."

"Never mind," Leon said. "Can you give us any details about Ethan's last report you received?"

"He said they were tracking a possible suspect." Laurent pulled out a notebook, flicked through its pages, then stopped. "The suspect's name was Daigashi. That was the last we heard of note."

"There's something about that name that sounds familiar," Leon said. "I've come across it before—a long while back."

"Before my time, I imagine," Carlota said.

"Oh, definitely," he said with a grin.

"Well, Monsieur Laurent," Carlota said, "nothing else to add?"

"No, not really. Even though the languages are not dissimilar, as I have inferred already my Spanish is not too hot. They pronounce all the letters, which is confusing as we do not... The local police have, I understand, 'looked around' but have no information to impart."

Leon eyed his watch. "I think we should begin our house-to-house inquiries at 1pm—maybe we will encounter some people who are out and about regularly around that time, and we can question them."

"Yes," said Laurent. "I perceive the sense in that."

"In the meantime," Carlota said, "we'd like to examine their rooms."

"Yes. That can be arranged with the manager. What precisely do you think you will find?"

Carlota smiled sweetly at him. "When we find it, we'll let you know."

After the manager had given them duplicate key-cards, they left Laurent in his room and began their search.

First, they entered Akemi Kuroda's room. The bed had been turned down by staff. Everywhere was very neat, and Leon suspected it was not due to the cleaners. Hanging in the closet Carlota found two summer dresses, a lightweight waterproof, two pairs of high-heeled shoes, and in the drawers neatly folded were white lace briefs and bras, and an unopened box of tampons. Her suitcase was quite small and empty. The dressing table was lined up with a hand-lotion bottle, make-up, a single deep red lipstick, a black eye-liner pencil, mauve eye-shadow, and a small pack of tissues, all in a neat row. The bathroom was the same: toothpaste tube, toothbrush and female razor all neatly in their place. A black silk kimono hung on the bathroom door. On the nightstand lay a guidebook of Córdoba, a well-thumbed thick paperback *The Tale of Genji*, with a bookmark two-thirds in, a novel entitled *The Lute and the Pen* about tenth century Spain and Córdoba, and a framed color photo of an elderly couple with Akemi standing beaming between them. The room wasn't quite the Mary Celeste.

Next, they tried Ethan Ward's room. In contrast, his clothes were bundled in the suitcase, which was on the floor to the side of the closet. His shoes were scuffed and his toiletries lay haphazard on the shelf by the washbasin. There were two color photographs, unframed, tucked behind an electric razor on the dressing table: a young blonde woman and an elderly couple. A copy of the latest issue of *Time Magazine* lay on the nightstand, alongside an analogue alarm clock. Perhaps Akemi relied on a smart wristwatch to wake up.

Lastly, they walked into Reed Carter's room. Three shirts and two jackets were hanging in the closet and on its floor were a pair of black leather shoes and a pair of sandals; his underwear was in one drawer, socks in another. On the nightstand was a paperback, a Lee Child thriller *Worth Dying For*, the corner of a page folded back halfway through. Crumpled clothing was bundled in the suitcase, probably dirty washing.

"That's odd," Carlota called from the bathroom.

"What is?" Leon asked.

She came out, stood hipshot in the doorway. "Neither in this room nor the bathroom can I find any razor or toothbrush or toothpaste."

"Deodorant?" he said.

"Yes. That's here; the spray kind."

"Which suggests when he left he hadn't planned on returning, he was spending the next night elsewhere."

She bit her lip in thought. "But he left all his other stuff —even his change of clothes. To lay a false trail?"

"Quite possible... This is not good. We'd better talk to Laurent."

They went to Laurent's room. They stood in the center of the bedroom and explained their theory.

Laurent sank onto his bed, head in his hands. "I can't believe it!"

CHAPTER 14

EL COBRADOR

SITTING ON LAURENT'S BED, CARLOTA CHECKED her watch. "We've got time to look at the CCTV before we start our search."

"Should I come with you?" Laurent asked. His tone implied he wasn't keen.

"No," Leon replied. He keyed Laurent's number into his cellphone. "We'll keep in touch."

Leaving Laurent in his room, they rode the elevator down.

Before going into the back room, they interviewed the receptionist, who was on duty Wednesday. "Yes, I remember her. I said to myself it was odd, a Japanese tourist without a camera!" He described her wearing a cream jacket and pants, a blue shirt, and a white fedora. Distinctive enough, Leon thought.

They scanned the CCTV video that covered the departure of Ethan and Akemi, and the receptionist's observations were accurate. It was noteworthy that Reed had exited the hotel the previous night at 9:30pm and had not been seen since.

Leon said, "If they're tracking the mysterious Daigashi, then they could have been taking turns monitoring the guy. And it was Reed's turn the night before the disappearances."

"That's a likely scenario," Carlota agreed.

"If we persist with our theory, Reed might have set them up to be snatched."

"Bastard," she murmured.

They exited the hotel at 1pm and stood on the entrance steps.

"The pair could have gone left or right along Lope de Hoces," he said. This was the main road passing the hotel.

"Or they could have split up?"

"And gone where?"

She shrugged. "Your guess is as good as mine. Four options. Left, right, over there, down Tejón y Marín, or along there, Sánchez de Fería."

"Let's strike this street from the equation. We suspect they've been abducted or murdered and I reckon this thoroughfare is too busy, too public." He pointed to his map. "Our two other options are narrow streets in built-up areas —ideal for disappearing in. When questioning, use Akemi's description, it's more distinctive."

"Okay. I'll take Calle Tejón y Marín," Carlota said.

Leon smiled, kissed her and said, "Take care, my dear." Then he headed along the street and crossed the road to enter Sánchez de Fería. He knocked on several doors, but the majority didn't answer. Of those that did, the occupant did not recognize the description he gave of Akemi.

He veered right into Calle Fernández Ruano.

No sooner had he entered than he saw a well-dressed white-bearded man emerge from a house doorway. He wore a beret and carried a bulky briefcase. Leon hurried to accost the man and asked him if he'd seen Akemi on Wednesday. The man stopped, gave it some thought, and then beamed. "Yes, she was walking down here, talking into her smart phone. A pretty young Japanese woman." He paused, glanced over his shoulder and scowled.

A man came out of an adjoining building; he was dressed in a black frock coat, a red cloak and a black top hat.

Leon said, "You're being plagued by a cobrador, I take it?

And that's him?"

"Yes, damn the man. He is a complete nuisance, an embarrassment!"

"But isn't that the point?" Leon asked reasonably.

"There should be a law against it—it's harassment, that's what it is! We all have money troubles these days!"

The man in a top hat stopped walking while Leon talked to the cobrador's victim. Chasing money in Spain had always been an expensive and slow process, Leon knew. So for decades Spaniards had tried this other way: humiliating debtors with attention-grabbing stunts. If somebody is being pursued by a man in outlandish costume, then most Spaniards assume that person hasn't paid their bills. In these straitened times, many firms and individuals were owed money, usually late or delayed payment, which could seriously disrupt cash-flow or even ruin a business. Such costumed nuisance-makers reputedly earned anything from twenty to sixty percent of the money collected; so this form of debt-collection has become a worthwhile occupation. More cavalier and less harmful than sending in the heavies, he supposed.

"I must go and try to shake off that pest," the man said, and scurried right into Calle Tejón y Marín.

The debt-collector in the top hat continued to follow, and then the two of them were out of sight as the street curved.

Leon phoned Carlota. "I've had a sighting. Akemi went this way," he told her. "Meet me at the synagogue."

"Right. Got it," she replied.

Leon turned left into Calle Judíos and continued on and soon came to the synagogue. He stood outside, waiting, and a minute or two later, Carlota appeared.

A short elderly man wearing a yarmulke opened the door of the synagogue and murmured a brief prayer as he came out and then shut the door after him.

"Excuse me, sir," Leon said, accosting the man.

"Yes?" His rheumy eyes squinted up at Leon.

"Do you leave the synagogue at the same time most days?"

"Yes, I do." He looked askance at Leon. "Was there something you wanted to ask me?"

Was he prescient? "On Wednesday, did you see a woman dressed in a cream suit and white hat who—"

"I certainly did. I bowed to her and she responded politely."

"Did you see where she went?" Carlota asked earnestly.

"She went further along Calle Judíos. I went in the other direction."

"Many thanks."

The pair of them continued along the street and tried door-to-door, but whenever somebody did answer, no more sightings of Akemi were confirmed.

Leon noticed a partial footprint indentation about waist high on soft cement on a wall, but it could be anybody's and even made much earlier than Wednesday.

"We've hit a dead end," he said and then gently eased Carlota's shoulders against the wall of a building.

"This isn't the time or the place, dearest," she whispered with amusement.

"Those two men coming toward us. Watch them." He turned his back on them and took her in a clinch, allowing her to view them around his shoulder.

One was squat and broad of frame; the other was medium height with buck teeth, a black ducktail beard and walked with a limp that affected his right leg. The squat one was carrying a gray container. They were very probably Japanese.

When they had passed, Leon kissed her cheek.

"Was that box what I think it was?" she asked.

"Yes. Organ transportation. A mite bold, walking about like that with it."

"Where did he come from, though?"

He winked. "Let's ask him, shall we?"

At a discreet distance, hand-in-hand, they followed the

two men.

"The bearded one looks vaguely familiar," Leon whispered and then sucked in his breath as the thought struck him.

"What is it?"

"Daigashi—it's Japanese for deputy leader."

"So? We can see they're Japanese. Are you saying they're Yakuza?"

"Might be. Remember, Hiroki said they're operating around here."

"I have a nasty feeling about this," she said.

"You know the incident I told you about—with Nyoko's abductor?"

"Yes."

"Well, the bearded guy looks like Okudara—only twenty years older."

"So he might recognize you? That's why you turned all romantic, is it?"

"I could turn romantic anytime with you, dear. But yes, I'm sure he has my features etched on his memory."

"That was twenty years ago," she observed. "You've aged, as has he."

"You say the most flattering things, Carlota."

"Just saying that time doesn't stand still." She cocked her head to one side. "You're not bad for your age, anyway."

"Oh, thanks." Then he paused, gestured. "Look."

The two Japanese men stopped outside a door, its green paint quite faded. Okudara fished out a key and unlocked the door. He pushed open the door and as Leon and Carlota passed them in the street they glimpsed an attractive courtyard inside, and an arcade beyond. Then the two men went in and shut the door after them.

The exterior walls of the place were old; this entire block appeared to be one building, with only one door.

Leon glanced up.

Three upstairs French doors had small balconies; windows placed between the balconies were barred with elaborate black-painted iron grilles. Further along was a wooden telegraph pole tightly pressed against the wall; wires and cables proliferated; it passed close to the third balcony.

An old man rode a bicycle past them, and two young tourists sauntered by. Otherwise, the street was deserted.

Leon climbed the telegraph pole first, while Carlota stood as lookout. When he was level with the nearest iron balcony balustrade, he made the short jump and clamped his hands on the top rail. It was rusty but otherwise firm. He cocked one leg over, and then the other, and then beckoned to Carlota, who made short work of the climb.

The balcony was hardly that. It was narrow and barely provided room for two people.

Leon crouched and used his lock-pick to gain entry through the French doors.

He swept the lace curtain aside. This was the end of a corridor. Four anonymous doors were placed on either side of the corridor.

He waved "all clear" to Carlota and she ducked through the curtain and shut the French doors with nary a sound.

Okudara and his huge pal had entered the building downstairs. He needed to find a staircase and go down and confront the ex-con. Leon screwed on the silencer to his automatic and Carlota did likewise.

Then they stalked along the corridor. He tried one door and it opened.

A man lay asleep on the bed, hooked up to IV drips and monitors by the far bedside. Gas and suction lines snaked to his body too, signifying he was alive. He was naked save for a dressing that presumably covered his surgical wound, the area appropriate for a liver operation.

Leon checked the chart at the foot of the bed: Domingo Rivera; his birthdate gave his age as fifty-nine.

They left and he closed the door soundlessly, though he doubted if Señor Rivera would hear him.

This floor was clearly for patients in recovery after an operation.

His heart sank at that thought. "We might be too late already," he whispered.

Carlota nodded. "But let's not go there just yet."

Finally they came to an open landing. At the end was a side-wall window which looked onto rooftops of single-story wing extensions of this building, and several of them had skylights. To the left was the staircase.

"Cover me," he whispered and descended slowly, gun ready.

Carlota followed about five steps behind.

They reached the bottom of the stairs without seeing anyone.

Another corridor, the doors labeled with names. Clients, maybe. He didn't expect to see Akemi's name on any of them.

Tentatively, he tried a couple of unmarked doors. One was a broom cupboard, and another was a store room with shelves of bandages, boxes of tape and plasters, and racks of hypodermic needles sealed in polythene packs.

A door marked *Receiving Room* was opening as they approached it.

They had nowhere to hide. "Get ready," he whispered and raised his gun.

Carlota was already aiming hers.

The two men they'd seen earlier emerged and closed the door behind them. Okudara and his pal noticed the armed presence of Leon and Carlota as the door clicked shut and immediately raised their hands in surrender.

"Don't make a move for that door-handle," Leon ordered in a harsh whisper.

Okudara's eyes widened and he hissed, "Shit, it's you!"

Leon ignored the comment and gestured at the reception room door with his gun. "Who is in there?"

"Just a nurse."

"Okay," Leon backed along the way they'd come. "This way, the pair of you."

Okudara limped past them and the other guy sullenly

followed.

When they reached the door to the store room, Leon opened it.

"Go on, inside!" Leon said.

It was quite cramped in here, he thought. Leon eyed Okudara. "So you do recognize me, eh?"

Okudara bit his lip then cursed.

The big guy pushed past Okudara, his fists clenched, muscles bulging, his Neanderthal brow creased.

"Don't move any closer!" Carlota warned him, raising her gun.

"Don't be foolish, Sasakawa," Okudara said

Sasakawa stopped, his eyes blinking, as if gauging the distance: could he beat a bullet? His entire bulk slumped: he couldn't, and he knew it.

Leon jabbed the snout of the silencer into Okudara's groin. He was unlikely to attempt anything with the weapon pointing there. "Tell me, where are Akemi Kuroda, Reed Carter, and Ethan Ward."

"Never heard of them," Okudara said with a smirk. "Pals of yours are they?"

In the blink of an eye Leon raised the pistol and harshly whipped Okudara's face with the silenced barrel.

The man backed against the shelving and rubbed his chin.

"Carlota," Leon called over his shoulder, "shoot the other guy's knees from under him if he so much as blinks!"

Leon aimed his automatic at Okudara's left knee. "I can even things up," he said. "You can limp with both legs."

Okudara let out a resigned sigh. "They're getting her ready for her op—operation..."

"Tell me where!"

"There are five preparation rooms. I don't know which one she'll be in." He pointed at the shut door. "Further down from where you found us. Go to the end, turn left."

"If you're lying, I'll definitely shoot you in the knee," Leon warned.

"I've got no reason to lie." Okudara shrugged. "You're probably too late anyway."

"Cover them," he told Carlota. He ransacked two shelves and came away with rolls of bandages and surgical tape. "This will do."

He told the two men to sit down on the floor back-to-back.

When they were sitting, Leon draped the bandage round Okudara's neck and then his pal's so that if either one moved too suddenly the other would choke. He continued to tie them up with bandages, using four rolls. There was some stretch in the material, but he'd used so much they wouldn't be able to break free. Then he wound strips of surgical tape round their mouths, keeping their nasal passages clear.

Okudara's slate-colored eyes lanced hate at Leon.

"That should keep them on ice while we go find the others," Leon said.

They both left the store room and shut the door and made their way down the corridor, quietly passing the reception room.

Eventually they came to the end of this corridor, which then turned left and right.

They went left, as instructed.

Their luck held and they didn't encounter anyone.

Finally, they came to several doors with light-boxes above them labeled *Unauthorized entry forbidden*. Between them was a door without a light-box labeled *Prep Room*. All the labels were in English; he guessed that because they had a variety of nationals working here, there was an expectation that they all spoke English.

Gripping his automatic in readiness, he tried the door-handle, and it worked, and the door opened.

It was a large room, lined with tall metal lockers on two sides. Eight people were dressed in white scrubs, sitting on wooden benches or lounging against lockers. None of them were wearing their surgical masks: four men and four women. At the other end of the room was a door with a round glass window in it. Above the door were two lights, one would show red and the other green. At present it shone red.

His heart skipped and his mouth felt very dry: an operation was in progress.

A couple of them had looked toward the door as he and Carlota entered. Their eyes widened, as did their mouths, but no sound came out, because the aimed guns suggested complete silence and obedience. To emphasize this, Leon waved his gun left and right—no, no—and shook his head and raised a finger to his lips. They got the message.

The couple who'd seen them started nudging those nearest. Within seconds, all eyes were on Leon and Carlota.

In a low voice he said, "If you don't do anything rash, you won't get hurt."

In response he got a few nods.

"Sit down, all of you," Carlota ordered.

They complied. They were medics and doubtless knew what gun-wound trauma could do and had no desire to end up on the pathologist's slab.

While Carlota covered the medics with her gun, Leon walked past them and peered through the round window in the far door.

He was looking into the OR. There were two surgeons and a nurse standing around two operating tables, with a naked young Japanese woman on one; and on the other was a man with a bared chest, a surgical sheet draped down from his waist and covering groin, legs and feet. The bastards were preserving a degree of modesty for the recipient not afforded to the live donor. The young woman had to be Akemi.

He opened the door and heard classical music blaring. Both surgeons seemed engrossed in it.

The surgeon standing beside Akemi was waving his arms as if conducting the orchestra, and then he called across to the other surgeon, "Time for her to die." He lifted a metal rod from the nearby tray and leaned over the unconscious Akemi. He placed the rod against her temple.

Holding his automatic two-handed, Leon aimed and fired.

The surgeon screamed as his hand burst into blood and bone and splattered the side of Akemi's face. The metal rod clattered to the floor.

The nurse shrieked.

The other surgeon shouted, "Oh, no!"

Nursing the bloody shattered hand, the medic yelled, "What have you done? You've ruined my life! I'm a surgeon!"

"No!" Leon snapped, walking toward the operating tables, gun leveled on both surgeons and the nurse. "You're a butcher!"

The other surgeon stumbled unsteadily round the anesthetized man. "You shot my brother! We're twins—"

"Well, let's make you a matching pair!" Leon fired again.

The second bullet shattered that surgeon's hand. The man wailed in despair and backed away, bumping into the nurse.

Leon was close enough now to properly identify Akemi on the operating table. She was still breathing shallowly. Much of her left side was bruised: upper arm, forearm and hip. Otherwise, she seemed unharmed. Then he noticed the girl's amputated finger stump. He went very cold; he had a fair idea who was responsible for that mutilation.

Over his shoulder, he called, "Carlota, come in and cover up Akemi—and see if you can rouse her."

Carlota stood halfway in the doorway, still watching the eight medics. "What about these guys?"

"Give them the day off!"

Carlota turned and barked, "Go on, scram! All operations are canceled for today!" Then she hurried into the OR and ran to the side of Akemi. She snatched the surgical sheet off the intended recipient and draped it over the Japanese girl, then attempted to get her to sit up.

Akemi's eyelids fluttered, shut, partly opened, and she moaned.

The recipient lay still, unaware.

"Who are you?" the surgeon he'd first shot demanded, tears trailing down the sides of his face.

"Your nemesis," Leon replied. He eyed the nurse who stood rigid in shock. "Nurse, get some bandages, whatever, and tend to your surgeons' hands before they bleed to death!"

Given something practical to do, the nurse quickly emerged from her shocked state and nodded. She then moved with surprising alacrity, ransacking a couple of drawers on a unit against the wall and started attending to the two surgeons.

Akemi moaned again, her eyes flickering half-open. "Oh, Ethan, Ethan..."

"What about Ethan?" Carlota whispered gently.

"They—they butchered him..."

Leon clenched his teeth. No point in hunting for him right now, then.

"What about Reed Carter?" Carlota persisted.

Akemi groaned and her eyes widened. "He—he betrayed us—left for—for I can't remember..." She screwed-up her eyes and tears flowed.

"Never mind," Carlota said. "Rest now. You're safe."

Keeping an eye on the two surgeons, Leon removed his cellphone and speed-dialed Laurent.

"Yes?" A ton of Gallic anxiety in that one word.

"We've got Akemi," Leon said, "and she's alive."

"Thank God!" Laurent exclaimed. "And Ethan Ward?"

"We reckon he's dead. Sorry. You'd better call the police and an ambulance. Direct them here." He gave the address.

Leon closed that call and then phoned Hiroki.

"You have news, Santos-san?"

"Akemi's safe."

"Thank you, my friend... Is she—is she hurt?"

"Only a bruise or two, nothing serious."

"When can I see her?"

"Soon." Leon gave him the address. "The police will be here by the time you arrive. I'll tell them to expect you."

"Thank you again."

"*De nada*." He closed the call.

———

LEON AND CARLOTA directed the two surgeons and the nurse into the Prep Room, which was now deserted. They sat the twins on a bench and tied them up with bandages from the OR drawers the nurse had used, then tethered the nurse separately to a radiator against a wall.

"That should keep you till the police get here," Leon said.

Carlota returned to the OR and planned to stay with Akemi until help arrived.

Leon found a white medic's coat in a locker and put it on. They'd been lucky so far; he didn't want to spoil it now. He said, "Won't be long," and left.

He kept his automatic in the voluminous pocket and strode confidently down the corridor.

A tall nurse with the name-tag *Mª. Inés Jara* walked past. She didn't stop to chat. He recalled that the two surgeons didn't have name-tags. It wouldn't do to sew up a body only to discover the tag was dropped inside, he supposed. He returned to the store room. Okudara and his pal hadn't moved.

Leon ripped off the tape from their mouths, bringing tears to both, and then stood over Okudara. "I want a name and a place."

"Go to hell!" Okudara spat at Leon, but his aim was off; it splatted the toe of his shoe.

"I'm not playing games," Leon said. "I want you to talk!"

"No chance," Okudara said.

Leon wiped his toe-cap on Okudara's thigh. "Hiroki Kuroda will be pleasantly surprised to find you're a captive here—and responsible for his daughter's ordeal."

"You can't scare me with threats like that."

"He won't be pleased to learn you amputated her finger," Leon said.

Okudara shuffled his ass on the floor, briefly glancing at his pants pocket. "You can't prove it was me."

"She will talk soon."

"Her word against mine!"

Leon lunged down, slamming a fist into Okudara's crotch, which disturbed the other guy he was tied to, and they banged their heads together, and in the same motion he tapped Okudara's pants pocket and extracted a handkerchief wrapped around the part of a little finger. "All the proof I need, don't you think?"

"So? Kuroda would not risk breaking the law to hurt me."

Leon shrugged. "Alright, have it your way." It wasn't easy to get them both to stand since they were secured back-to-back; it was almost farcical, but they managed it eventually.

He pushed them toward the Prep Room, one walking forward, the other backward. Now he didn't care if any staff accosted them. His gun would dissuade anyone.

Once there, he dumped the pair onto the floor of the Prep Room.

He pointed to the bandaged bloody hands of the two surgeons. "That's just for a start," he said.

"You wouldn't dare! The police would arrest you!"

Leon turned Okudara round, pressed him down on the floor and grabbed Okudara's right hand, He pushed Okudara's hand onto the floor, and the guy attached to him swore and groaned; Leon ignored him.

He stood on Okudara's damaged wrist. "I can finish what Hiroki Kuroda started with his shuriken!"

Okudara whimpered. "No, no, alright, I'll talk. He—"

"Who?"

"Dr. Godsafe. He's the fixer I deal with."

Leon pressed harder. "Where can I find this ungodly bastard?"

"V–Venice."

PART THREE

MUSIC IS GONE

Chapter 15

Music Buff

The Black Foundation Administration Offices, Venice, Italy

"I think disrupting that WHIT team will have set back any WHO investigation." Reed Carter's resonant voice set up a faint echo in the large room. Standing in front of Aiden Black's impressive desk, his hands in his pockets, he was pleased with himself. He grinned self-confidently, displaying his gleaming white teeth, which contrasted with his dark African-American complexion; not as dark as Mr. Black's, however.

Black leaned forward, elbows on his desk, fingers steepled. "Sadly, while you were flying here, I had word from Córdoba and it isn't good news."

"Really?" Carter's tone softened; sounding no longer so certain. "Not good?"

"That's right."

"Didn't the operations on my two colleagues go to plan, then?"

"Actually, the whole clinic has been exposed. A police raid has closed it down and virtually all the members of staff were arrested!"

Carter gaped. "How can that be?" He ran a hand

through his tousled hair. "Everything was running smoothly when I left."

"Your little decoy ploy didn't account for a private detective tracking down the missing team and discovering the clinic despite its innocuous cover."

"Private detective? What's a PI got to do with us?"

"I wondered that myself. I asked for clarification. It seems the father of your colleague Akemi Kuroda has connections. He's ex-Yakuza."

"Shit. I didn't know that." Reed recalled Akemi espousing knowledge of the Japanese underworld. And he'd even made fun of her. "What about her and Ward?"

"She was rescued before they could perform the op."

"A pity. And Ward?"

"His heart's snug in Abdel Yasir Fuad's chest. It was a good match; both about the same age, as well. Fuad was transferred from the clinic to the recovery house about an hour before the raid."

Reed let out a sigh of relief. "So it wasn't all bad news, was it? You got a hefty payment from the Arab businessman —and his eternal gratitude."

Black slammed a fist on his desk. "Not all bad? For God's sake, we've lost thousands of dollars' worth of equipment, not to mention the skilled staff!"

"Yes, I see."

"Do you really? After that mess in Massachusetts five years back when we had to grease a lot of palms, we had to rebuild new transplant centers, and it took time and money. Then the Chinese pandemic virtually closed down all our business. For over two years Covid-19 has constrained worldwide legal transplant operations, not just ours. Hundreds of people on the waiting lists have already died. There's a massive demand for organs—from the rich of all shades— and now we've lost a fucking entire clinic in Córdoba!"

"Yes, I understand..."

"I don't think you do. One or more of those under arrest will inevitably point the finger here!"

"Surely not, sir. Your generous salaries ensure loyalty."

———

Spain

THEY SHOULDN'T NEED their passports, since they were passing from one Schengen country to another in the EU, but they took them anyway. Leon was ambivalent about it. Yes, the Schengen agreement made it easier for travelers throughout Europe, but that ease had its cost: free-roaming criminals and illegal immigrants. They had left their firearms with Hiroki as they couldn't risk them being discovered in the airport.

"We haven't packed enough clothing to go gallivanting," Carlota said. "We were only supposed to spend a couple of days in Córdoba."

"We're not gallivanting," Leon corrected. "This isn't recreation, my dear, it's hunting."

She kissed him. "I like it when you put on your serious face. Sends shivers down my spine."

He hugged her and traced his fingers down her spine. "This isn't getting the packing done, is it?"

"There's time for that, don't fret, my hunter." And there was; time for everything.

"Have you been to Venice before?" she asked when they returned to the task of packing their clothes.

"Yes—once or twice. On occasion incognito, too."

"You must tell me more."

"When I'm old and gray…"

She opened her mouth to respond and he laughed gently. "Don't be tempted, young lady!"

After booking their flights, Leon contacted Rose Lo Verde who would arrange replacement weapons and accommodation.

"Who is she?" Carlota wanted to know.

"She used to work for AISI: Italy's internal intelligence organization. Now she heads a personal security firm."

"You worked together when you were incognito?"

"A few times..."

"Is she attractive?"

"She's Italian, my dear."

She playfully slapped his shoulder. "You can be a brute sometimes, you know that?"

"That's because you bring out the animal in me, no?"

The packing did get done—eventually.

They flew from Córdoba to Madrid and from there caught an Iberia flight to Marco Polo airport, Italy, which was on the mainland.

———

Venice, Italy

EXITING the airport terminal on the ground floor, they were in time to board the train which took them to Venice's Mestre station and then across the Liberty Bridge to Santa Lucia station, the terminus. Carlota was excited by this final part of their journey, gaping out the window as the ancient city on water—La Serenissima—approached.

At the terminus they were met by Rose.

She stood on tiptoe to peck his cheek and then he introduced Carlota.

"*Buon giorno. Come sta?*"

"*Hola,*" Carlota replied, adding with a smile, "*Molto bene.*" She laughed. "A bit of Spanish crept in there!"

"We can speak English, I think," Rose said. "My Spanish is not so good."

Rose was the same height as Carlota. Unusually, her hair was russet-colored; it was long, falling to her narrow shoulders. Her bosom was prominent but not overly so. She had thick full ripe lips and her big reddish-brown eyes shone with sincerity. Carlota liked her at once. Rose wore a fashionable black-and-white jacket and figure-hugging white pants and black stilettos. Carlota felt dowdy beside her; partly she blamed Leon, for she had packed so little variety of clothing, not in her wildest dreams expecting to visit Italy!

They made their way to the landing stage. Carlota's face lit up at seeing all the varieties of waterborne craft.

"Here's our water taxi," Rose said, pointing at a speed-boat approaching, the driver at the wheel in the bow of the vessel. Rose waved to him and he drew alongside.

After they boarded the boat with her, sitting on the cushioned benches aft, she said, "I have booked you into the hotel Palazzo Canova—it overlooks the Grand Canal."

"Thanks—that's central," Leon said. "Ideal. I can show Carlota the sights."

Carlota was already staring at the profusion of buildings, the ornate architecture on both sides of the wide canal, water lapping at the edges. "I must go in a gondola!" she cried excit-edly as they passed one.

"That can be arranged."

The taxi driver took it steadily. The air draft from the water was cooling as they motored. On their right was a domed church. They motored under the first bridge, Ponte degli Scalzi, and Carlota was fascinated at the steepness of the arch for the pedestrians to negotiate. "You need crampons for that!" she joked. A slightly narrower canal veered off to their left.

Rose pointed to a building further along also on their left. "That's the Palazzo Vendramin Calergi. The composer Richard Wagner died there in 1883."

"Rose is a music buff," Leon explained. "If you're a lover of art or music then this is the city for you."

"I am. It is." Carlota clapped her hands. "The canal, it seems to go on forever!" she said enthused as they passed the Baroque façade of San Stae and its richly decorated statues on their right.

And then they were motoring under the exquisite and

distinctive Rialto Bridge and heading to the right-hand bank. "Riva del Vin—your hotel's here," Rose explained.

The water taxi came alongside a small jetty and they disembarked.

They strolled through a passage and entered the hotel foyer.

"I'll leave you to register," Rose said. She checked her wristwatch. "I'll meet you both in St. Mark's Square at 4pm and I'll bring your package then."

They registered and took the elevator to their room, which was attractively furnished and possessed tasteful colored accents.

As promised, the room did indeed overlook the Grand Canal, with its own balcony.

"This is fabulous!" Carlota squealed, dumping her case on the bed and rushing to the French doors and swinging them open.

He stopped behind her, wrapped his arms round her. "There's no place like it, dearest."

She swirled round, head to one side. "What package is Rose delivering?"

"Guns. I packed the empty holsters."

She shuddered in his arms. "Do you think we will have to use them?"

"I would hope not. It depends on the opposition, doesn't it?"

On that somber note they unpacked. Their choice of clothing was limited. Carlota complained she had nothing to wear.

"I'm happy to see you wearing nothing," he replied.

She threw a pillow at him.

They tussled on the bed for a while then got undressed, intending to have a shower, but that objective was put on hold while they made love. Carlota rode him, affectionately gripping his love-handles, until they were both sated.

Afterwards, the shower was welcome, refreshing and invigorating, though not a patch on the hammam, she'd said.

He put on a malachite green embroidered guayabera short sleeve shirt with its traditional four pockets, black chinos, and his lightweight suede jacket—ever mindful of concealing a weapon.

She wore bright red high-waist wide-leg pants that tightly fitted her curves, a coffee brown leather zipper front Moto jacket, which would hide her shoulder holster, and a white stretch bandeau that revealed a tantalizing glimpse of décolletage when the jacket's stand collar was open.

———

Lazzaretto Piccolo, Laguna Veneto, Italy

DR. GODSAFE hesitantly entered the clinic's office and immediately Black knew he was going to be gravely disappointed yet again. "Tell me, Doctor."

Godsafe's sunken glacial blue eyes were evasive. "I regret to inform you that the news is still bad, sir." When he spoke, some words whistled due to the gap in his front teeth. "We haven't found a match for Byron."

Black leaned forward in his chair and rested his elbows on the desk and put his head in his hands. "I don't believe it," he murmured.

Two weeks ago the boy's symptoms had grown worse. A barrage of tests followed. The prognosis was that his son Byron had a hitherto undisclosed heart defect. The clinic's resident physician Doctor Caruso referred to it as arrhythmogenic right ventricular dysplasia. "ARVD for short," he said. "It's rare, which is no comfort, I know. The heart's right ventricle is replaced by fibrous tissue which means the ventricle doesn't dilate and contract as it should. The result is the heart can't pump the blood adequately and that explains the abnormal heart rhythm we detected."

"Is it serious?"

"Yes, there's a real risk of sudden cardiac arrest..."

"Death?"

"I'm sorry."

"Can medication help?" Black had asked.

"No, sir. I fear he hasn't got long...The fibrous tissue is building up..."

"How long?"

"Weeks, our tests suggest. It might be a month or two—but not more..."

"So," Black concluded, "you're telling me my son needs a replacement heart, is that it?"

"It is short notice, sir. And as you know the waiting list is long." The doctor was unaware that the clinic deftly side-stepped the official transplant waiting lists. "But a transplant is the only way your son will live to see his next birthday."

"He's only sixteen!"

"It is very sad, sir."

"Thank you, Doctor Caruso." When the physician had retreated, Black had phoned his fixer.

"Dr. Godsafe, I need you to find me a young man under twenty who is healthy and fit. I need you to harvest his heart."

"Sir?"

Black explained, ending, "Can you give it your highest priority?"

"I'm sorry to learn about Byron, sir. Yes, of course, I will begin my search right away. It may take a little time to find a precise match—we don't want any risk of failure."

"No, quite. Just find our donor."

And now, two weeks had passed and he still had not found anyone suitable. Time was running out for Byron.

CHAPTER 16

FOUR LETTERS

AT 3:45PM THEY WALKED INTO ST. MARK'S SQUARE and Carlota marveled at the view. "You can see it on the screen but it can never do the place justice, no?"

Leon agreed. "It does tend to take your breath away. It's not only photogenic but a magnet for artists."

At one end was the distinctive campanile of the Basilica which dominates the skyline almost anywhere in the city. On one side of the square were the landing stages and the berthed gondolas, and beyond the open expanse of the St. Mark's Canal and the large island of Giudecca and the smaller San Giorgio Maggiore with its Palladio church and campanile.

"It's magical, all of it!" Carlota exclaimed.

He indicated a table and four chairs outside a busy restaurant. "We'll wait here for Rose."

"Is this prearranged?"

He shook his head. "She'll find us, don't worry. A lot of people-watching goes on here." He gestured vaguely at clusters of people strolling by, chatting yet with one eye on the seated patrons on each side of the square. "She won't be out of place searching the tables."

A waiter approached.

Leon ordered two macchiato coffees. "It's a mite early for alcohol."

"Macchiato is fine by me." She hardly looked at him, so intent on the folk sauntering past.

The coffees came together with two small glasses of water. It was strong, and full of taste.

As the clock chimed the hour, they were hailed by a familiar voice.

"There you are!" Rose said, striding up to them, a slightly bulging shoulder-bag under her arm.

"Cappuccino?" he suggested as she sat next to Carlota. "Not grappa?"

"You're right; it is too early for alcohol. A Cappuccino would be lovely, Leon. You haven't forgotten."

Leon signaled the waiter and ordered the beverage.

Within a minute, the waiter brought the coffee and added the check slip to the earlier one tucked under Leon's saucer.

"How's Pietro?" Leon asked. "I heard he's a government minister now."

"Yes, he's done really well. He's a deputy to the Minister of Health. The work takes him to Rome frequently, alas."

"That's a pity—I mean, you don't get to see him much," Carlota said.

Rose nodded. "Since he entered the political arena, it has not been easy, I must admit." She made a vague hand motion. "But we work through it, somehow." She gazed into the middle distance, as if reflecting on her past.

————

Eight years ago, in fact...

For hours Rose had walked through the night, her thoughts tumbling, high heels echoing and disturbing the stray cats and the odd rat but nothing else. Only the rosy aurora igniting the domes of St. Mark's lifted her dark mood out of bleak despondency: Venice is renowned for the quality of its light, as countless painters flocking to the canals testify.

Abandoned to all save the pigeons in the early hours of dawn, the piazza sent a warm shimmer down her spine as she remembered the good times they'd had listening to the competing bands of the Quadri, Lavena and Florian restaurants.

Now, though, with a shake of her russet-colored hair she sent those treacherous memories scuttling away and leaned her elbows on the ornate metal rail. From the vantage point of this bridge she watched an early-morning merchant steer his boat-load of bottled beer, soft drinks, boxes of chocolate bars and mail through the waters of Canale di Cannaregio.

Not for the first time she marveled at the uncaring way the world went on even though her own world was spiralling out of control. Suicide was never an option and, besides, the water was not inviting. It was probably a lot cleaner when Lord Byron swam these canals.

This unique place redolent with history and gorgeous art seemed to put her troubles into some kind of perspective and, despite the aching heart, she was grateful her melancholia had lifted.

Hard as it was, she *had* decided while she paced the city. She would meet Pietro, her husband, and pick over the bones of their dead marriage.

She seldom came to this sestiere, the historic ghetto. Pietro chose it because it was rarely crammed with tourists like the rest of Venice.

Their marriage was crumbling—like the city, she supposed. La Serenissima has lasted a thousand years—their marriage a mere ten.

Although she worked in intelligence, her hobby when she could indulge it was freelance writing, specifically articles on music in Vivaldi's city. She had made a point of attending Pietro Lo Verde's latest master-class; the program notes told her he was six years older than her. The students were performing the *Four Seasons* in Chiesa di San Samuele. The two male guys were okay, but she thought the girl student was excellent—until Pietro stood up and played the same piece. A fusion took place, between man and violin. He was simply the music. She fell in love with him at that moment, his dark good looks rapt by the music, thick brows furrowed in concentration, dark eyes half-closed, black lashes flickering. During her interview afterwards, he was fascinated by her distant ancestors who were Scots; she was proud of that link.

One thing led to another and, after a whirlwind romance, they got married. For the first three years they were blissfully happy. Unfortunately, he was bitten by the political bug and moved away from his music. She argued with him about it. Even his mother was not pleased, which was saying something. An Italian man's mother is the first woman in his life and the sooner his wife learns that, the better for all concerned.

She could see that politics was eating him up. He thrived on the cut and thrust and the deals and Machiavellian machinations.

Her intelligence job mostly involved working behind a desk and the hours were not too onerous, unless there was a scare on. So she was still able to keep her hand in with writing. But she wasn't a workaholic like Pietro.

She confronted him about it but Pietro simply shrugged. "Politics is a way of life, my love. We strive to help those who need us."

"I need you here at home!" she said, aware she sounded selfish and needy.

Infuriatingly, he said, "It is a calling, my love. I cannot ignore it."

She fumed and raged, exhausting her considerable assortment of Italian expletives on him.

He just laughed and fought through her flailing arms and embraced her, every time, saying between kisses, "I *love* you so much, my Scottish firebrand, and most especially when you are annoyed with me!"

———

AN INVOLUNTARY SOUND emerged from her mouth and her throat briefly constricted.

Now, seeing him sitting alone outside the café in Campo di Ghetto Nuovo, she realized he had her at his mercy, and the awful melancholia threatened to return.

On the wall to the left were seven bas-relief memorials to the Venetian Holocaust victims: "your memories are our only graves", the poignant engravings ended.

Two old men in black wearing yarmulkes sat on a nearby bench, chatting away, while at their feet roamed three ginger cats lazily eyeing the pigeons that boldly walked within easy reach of a single pounce. They, at least, were oblivious to their fate.

Pietro's thoughts must have been miles away. He noticed her shadow cross the table top, started out of his reverie and looked up. He stood and smiled, his hand offered in greeting. "Rose, I'm glad you could come."

She was too, but she wasn't going to say so.

She studiously ignored his hand though she dearly wanted to touch him.

His eyes, usually so vital and deep brown that she could lose herself in them, now seemed abstracted. It gave her no satisfaction to think that he, like her, hadn't slept last night.

He held a plastic chair for her. "Cappuccino?"

"*Si*," she said, sitting opposite, wanting something stronger to get her through this ordeal.

She noted the black leather briefcase resting against the table-leg and her heart sank. He would get his pound of flesh, she thought. It was so unlike him, to be vindictive. Yet he had to hit out, because his male pride was hurt. Very Latin! It was so unfair. She had strayed only once. And she was about to pay. Well, her and Alessandro.

He beckoned the motherly woman who owned the café and ordered two Cappuccinos and *grappa*, and she was grateful. The grappa may be an after-dinner drink, but they had enjoyed the ritual, having one with their coffee. It's the little things that make a marriage.

————

THE POLITICAL EVENT of the year had been held at Hotel des Bains. Their home was in a peeling building of faded elegance in Fondamente Nuovo overlooking the Laguna Morta, with a view of the island of San Michele with its poplar trees rising above the walled cemetery. There, Igor Stravinsky and Luigi Nono, among other notables, were buried. It was both fascinating and somber to see the funereal gondolas transporting the dead there. For convenience and a need to be pampered by hotel staff, she'd booked a room on the Lido. And why not, since Pietro was off campaigning, as usual.

That was her first mistake.

Her second was to start a conversation with Alessandro Zuccarelli, the "Minister for Families," as the press dubbed him, drawing attention to the fact that Alessandro had abandoned the Church for politics. He was gracious enough to consent to a private interview in his room. She should have known better, but it was a scoop, something rare for part-time freelancers like her, so she went along and while they sipped champagne he spoke warmly about family values being eroded by commercialism and the modern age in general.

Alessandro was charming and overly attentive but she kept saying "no." Finally, though, the champagne tumbled her inhibitions. She should have known better. But she succumbed to Alessandro's charms, which were considerable, and afterwards felt empty, rotten, and disgusted with herself and him. The angst ate away at her. She couldn't understand how anyone could cheat on their marriage. Depends on the marriage, she supposed. Hers was far from perfect, what with Pietro burning his office midnight oil for his ideals and his needy people. But his seemingly perpetual absences hadn't driven her into the arms of another man. Her foolhardiness had done that.

Sometimes, she now thought, you're so busy taking life for granted you don't know what you are putting at risk until it's lost.

Then the love letters came. Four of them. She was convinced Alessandro was a frustrated poet. His handwritten missives pleaded with her to leave Pietro. He wanted her to set up home in Verona and be his mistress. The first letter was flattering and the poetry in each was quite good, but the prose got rather sad and desperate. She didn't know why she kept the letters—perhaps she had considered finding some way of using them to knock sense into Pietro, to show him that he was at risk of losing her. She didn't think that she was actually taken with the poetry itself.

Pietro found the four letters. The word "Love" is made from four letters. As are swear words. So is "lost." Pietro had looked quite lost and devastated when he showed her Alessandro's letters. She knew then that she had truly lost him. Her work in intelligence suffered and she was reprimanded twice.

Pietro had said, "Your countryman Robert Burns, he wrote something about a minister who kissed a fiddler's wife, no?" She was impressed that he was able to remember that and said something about being clever but pointless. Their words grew angrier and seriously deteriorated after that. Need a body cry? Yes, indeed.

You can't argue with your heart, she realized. She truly didn't want "Ae Fond Kiss" of Burns—farewell forever—but the decision wasn't hers to make now.

As he stormed from the house he called back, "We'll discuss this at the café in Campo di Ghetto Nuovo tomorrow morning!"

———

THE COFFEE WAS DELICIOUS. And the grappa gave her the strength to concede. Farewell forever.

"You win, Pietro," she said resignedly as they left the Euro coins in payment on the table. "I'll grant a divorce. Just return the letters."

With the briefcase tucked under his arm, he walked alongside her. Infuriatingly, he didn't acknowledge that she'd given in to him. Instead, he said, "I'm sorry we're meeting like this, grabbing precious minutes before I leave for Murano." He was ever the politician now, his violin forsaken for his voters. Perhaps that's where they went wrong—they let the music leave their lives.

"I've got a meeting with the workers at the Glass Factories," he explained. "Every vote counts, you know." This was a new Pietro; he rarely explained his business arrangements.

"It's alright. I understand. Business comes first." That was a little bitchy, but she couldn't call it back.

They sauntered across the square and over a bridge. "Divorce," he said, "it seems drastic, don't you think?"

So he had been listening.

A couple of oarsmen were practicing their rowing technique in their gondola on the tranquil Rio Degli Ormesini.

"Last night—I thought..."

"That was just me in a fit of temper," he said.

They turned left into Calle Larga and she sensed her foolish hopes rising. Maybe a scandal could be averted. Scandal was an acceptable part of politics in Italy, not least Venice's corruption cases. Selfishly, she did not want to be dragged through the courts, newspapers and television newsreels, with people criticizing her hair, her clothes, her sense, even her smile—she did it to herself every day, but that didn't give the media circus the right.

"Separation, then, is that what you want?" she asked.

"Perhaps that would be for the best."

The Gothic church of Madonna dell'Orto loomed ahead; it was eye-wateringly beautiful with its richly decorated and ornate campanile. Beautiful things often draw tears, she thought, rubbing moisture off her lids. The vaporetto landing stage was named after the church. She loved their city's exotic-sounding names that tripped over the tongue: Sant'Alvise, San Marcuola, Sacca Fisola.

They were the only passengers at the landing stage. Pietro validated his ticket at the ACTV machine.

To their right across the gray water was San Michele, its dark cypresses pushing above the high terracotta walls. Further still was Murano, to the left of the island cemetery.

Bury our marriage here? she wondered morbidly. Forget separation. Bury it.

The sky was clear, a uniform blue to flatter the city's buildings—in complete contrast to last week when they'd both dashed through puddles futilely to avoid the rain and laughed at getting drenched.

As if by magic, tourists had appeared dressed in yellow rain-capes and coats, supplied by enterprising vendors.

But that was before he found those four letters.

Pietro released a sigh. "Alessandro and I go back a long way, to school, if you must know. His love letters give me the chance to show him to all and sundry for the hypocrite he is."

"But this is Italy. Politicians aren't supposed to be whiter-than-white! You're the exception, I know..."

He rummaged in his briefcase and brandished those damning sheets of paper. "Hah! Usually there are double standards, yes, but not where it comes to family. Alessandro stood in parliament and preached to all of us, selling family values!"

"But, Pietro," she said softly, "you won't only be hurting him."

"What do you mean?"

"When this goes public, his wife and two children will suffer."

"He should have considered that. They're not my responsibility!"

"And me. I'll be hurt."

"You?" His tone was deep, anger lurking beneath the surface. "In what way?"

She turned to watch an airliner climb over the lagoon. If only she could fly away now, but she couldn't. "When you're away, wrapped up in your work, Pietro, you don't seem to give me a thought. You're always busy building the next vote-catching campaign. When was the last time we ate out or shared an evening together? Each absence cuts a piece of my heart from me." She felt her hand pressing against her chest and dropped it to her side; enough of histrionics.

"You hurt me," he said, wafting the papers, "with these —with him!"

She faced him again. She would not plead. "Don't you realize, your work is like a mistress. It takes you away from me." It sounded so selfish, put like that, but what's the point of a marriage if you're never together, never sharing anything?

"But I trusted you, Rose!"

Those plaintive words pricked her heart, and rightly so.

His face was getting blurred. Tears, of all things, even though she had vowed she wouldn't cry. "That one night I stayed with Alessandro because he was there—and yet again you were not." She wasn't trying to shift the blame, which rested wholly with her and her actions. These days, so many people don't consider the consequences of their actions—and it seemed that she was no better.

"You don't love him?" he demanded.

She laughed, on the verge, possibly. "Love him? It was a stupid mistake that I'll always regret... That's all!"

"Then why protect him?"

"I don't care about him. But I don't want to have anything to do with his political downfall or the pain his family will suffer."

He lowered his briefcase to the landing stage floor. "Perhaps you should have thought of that before it began between you two."

"Perhaps I should," she conceded. "But I truly don't want his family to suffer."

When he looked at her his eyes shone, the lower rims glistening. "Neither do I," he said, his voice notably calmer.

"What did you say?" Her heart was hammering, but not like last night when they'd been shouting and shouting.

"I don't want to hurt you, Rose. I am deeply sorry that my work shuts you out of my life." He touched his chest expressively, the letters crumpling against his jacket. "I ache; to see you upset like this." He pounded his chest, the letters crinkling, and gazed across the water.

"I'm so sorry, Pietro. I will still love you, no matter what you decide."

Then his eyes found hers and they were moist too. "And I love you, Rose." He swung round and used the back of his hand to erase the damp unmanly signs.

Abruptly Pietro ripped the letters into shreds and flung them across the water. They didn't go far but that didn't matter. A few pieces floated for a brief time and then were gone.

The vaporetto was approaching the landing stage.

Someone said that music begins where language falls silent. From an open window they both heard the exquisite intonation of a violin playing the Adagio from Mozart's G major Concerto.

Pietro cocked his head to one side, listening, and then he smiled fleetingly and picked up his briefcase and turned to her, gently gripping her upper arm. "I think my business in Murano is not as important as I thought," he said, leading her away, back into their city.

It was perhaps a tenuous hope, but maybe their marriage could endure like La Serenissima, after all.

And it *had* endured, though the demands on Pietro's time increased over the years until he finally was promoted to the post of Deputy Health Minister.

She valued those years after the Alessandro debacle and realized that until Pietro's political career took a downward curve—as inevitably all political careers did—she must accept the status quo.

She vowed never to cheat on him; from time to time she did wonder if he was faithful, but did not dare question him on the subject

At times she was lonely, but tried to emulate Pietro and get lost in her work. But it wasn't working, the marriage. These last couple of years it had been disintegrating.

She glanced at Leon and smiled wanly. She'd forgotten how much she'd enjoyed his company. It was good to see him again. It was good that he had Carlota with him. She was very attractive and clearly besotted with him, which was understandable.

Enough reverie, she scolded herself.

Chapter 17

Glorified Pimp

Rose moved their coffee cups to one side and then lifted a brown-paper parcel out of her shoulder-bag and plonked it on the table. "Here's your package."

"You had no difficulty?" Leon asked.

"No. I have good contacts and suppliers." She looked around.

"Nobody can overhear us in this crowd," he stated to calm her nerves.

True enough, the hubbub of so many patrons eating and drinking nearby, not to mention the constant stream of couples and groups walking by, all militated against eavesdropping.

"What do you want to know?" she asked.

"We're interested in speaking to a Dr. Godsafe. He's supposed to be an expert in intensive care."

"Supposed to be, huh?" She produced her cellphone, swiped a few apps with healthcare logos and then glanced at Leon. "I got the apps off of Pietro's phone; Blue Tooth is so handy, isn't it?

"Indeed," he said and raised a puzzled eyebrow at Carlota.

Carlota whispered, "I'll tell you about it later."

Rose's finger hovered over one of the apps and then she

keyed in the name. "Elijah Godsafe," she said. "Age thirty-two. American. From Savannah, Georgia. It says he works for the Black Foundation Clinic. The clinic's accredited—Pietro was responsible in some small way in helping it get established, as I recall. Strangely, it doesn't say where Dr. Godsafe is living, but I can soon obtain an address from other sources."

"Please do," Leon urged. "That would be most helpful."

"Bear with me." Rose manipulated her smartphone a little more and came up with an address and gave it to Leon. "Can you tell me what he's done?"

Leon smiled. "You don't want to know."

"I see. Should I question Pietro about him next time we phone?"

"I'd rather not get your husband involved, Rose. It might taint his career."

"Ah, his career... So Godsafe is dirty, is he?"

"Highly likely, but don't quote me yet. I'll let you know after we've spoken to him."

"Fair enough." She stood, pocketed her phone. "Well, I must dash, I've got a client's deadline to meet! Keep in touch, as you said."

"I promise." They hugged briefly, a kiss on each cheek in platonic Mediterranean fashion, and she waved at Carlota, said "*Ciao!*" and departed.

Carlota fingered the brown-paper parcel. "She doesn't seem too happy."

"Oh?"

"In her private life, I mean."

"You can tell?"

Carlota nodded. "When she was gazing into space, I studied her face. She was reliving a painful period in her life. And it hasn't gone away."

He grinned. "You're in the wrong business, dear."

"Oh, what should I be doing?"

"Fortune telling?"

She chuckled. "Talking about fortune—how much is our hotel costing? It's on a prime site."

"It isn't cheap," he said. "I've never told you how I obtained riches beyond our dreams, did I?"

"No, though you hinted more than once."

"Well, one day I'll tell you. So be assured there's no need to be concerned about the cost of the hotel. You're worth it."

"All these promises—one day this, one day that. I hope I live to hear them all fulfilled!"

———

ONCE THEY WERE BACK in their hotel room, Leon unwrapped the brown-paper parcel. Rose had managed to meet his specifications as to size, stopping power and weight. The Beretta Model 84 weighed a mere twenty-three ounces and was only six and a half inches long, suitable for concealing on Carlota's person. Its magazine held thirteen rounds.

To fill his shoulder holster he'd opted for a Bernardelli P-018, its magazine holding fifteen 9mm parabellum cartridges. The slightly smaller and lighter Tanfoglio TA90 snugly fitted his ankle-holster; it too held fifteen 9mm parabellum cartridges. Rose had also supplied a spare clip of cartridges for each weapon. Between them they should have enough fire-power to deal with a crop of organ harvesters, he reckoned. And they each had a silencer that would fit.

"Now we're properly equipped to pay a call on Dr. Godsafe," Leon announced.

Leon had hired a motorboat, a Galeon Galia 700 Sundeck. "Difficult to get around otherwise," he explained.

He motored to Canale della Misericordia and drew alongside the steps to a small alleyway called Corte Lovo.

Carlota tied up the boat and they stepped ashore, climbing the shallow stone steps into what appeared to be a paved courtyard. On the left hung washing, items in blue, green and brown. There was a profusion of pots crammed with lush green bushes and plants. The buildings on both sides rose to four stories. Old gray plaster had crumbled on a good portion of the walls, revealing bare ancient brickwork. There were five doorways. Each door gave her the impression of being unwelcoming, unprepossessing, and ancient; four of them were wood; three were green, their paint peeling off; one was varnished wood; and the fifth was rusting metal. Each door accessed several apartments. On the right-hand side of the rusting door was a metal box with four doorbells attached. The fourth button showed a label: *Dr. Godsafe*.

Leon pressed that button.

A speaker responded, metallic, hardly human: "Who is it?"

"Leon Cazador, a friend of Pietro Lo Verde!"

"What do you want?"

"I have vital information regarding the operation in Córdoba." It was a long shot, but worth a try. He had alternative options to use if that drew a blank. "I'd appreciate it if you would speak to me and my assistant, Miss Friday."

Carlota smirked.

"Ah, Córdoba, eh? Very well. Alas, you cannot stay long. I'm suffering from Long Covid."

"I'm sorry to hear that. I promise we won't take too much of your time, Doctor."

The lock of the door automatically clicked and buzzed open.

Leon cautiously entered, followed by Carlota. The contrast with the dilapidated outside was stark. Both he and Carlota were familiar with this, however; it was typical of Mediterranean dwellings. The vestibule was tiled in green and cream. Everywhere was immaculate. A set of pigeon-holes for four apartments hung on the left-hand wall. Two bicycles hung on the wall on the right, secured by chains and padlocks. Directly ahead was a broad flight of marble stairs with an ornate iron balustrade. There was no elevator. A lightbulb illuminated the place; it was probably on permanently as the skylight high above admitted only weak sunlight through its grimy panes.

They climbed the marble stairs, their steps echoing, and finally arrived at the door marked *Dr. Godsafe.*

Leon pressed the bell-push.

"Just a minute!" a raspy voice echoed from inside.

It sounded like three separate bolts were opened and then the door swung wide to reveal a man who was thirty-two according to Rose's search, though he could be mistaken for someone ten years older. He was tall and tended to stoop a little. His glacial blue eyes were sunken; no telling whether they were like that all the time or as a result of his illness. He had unruly eyebrows and a florid complexion and a receding chin.

He didn't offer his hand, but instead scratched his head of untamed tawny brown hair that covered his ears.

"This way, please," he beckoned, adding, "shut the front door, will you?" He spoke with a slight whistle as a result of a gap between the front teeth. He walked bow legged ahead of them down a narrow passage. Carlota shut the door and brought up the rear of the little procession.

Godsafe turned left into a room.

Tapestries hung on two walls—depictions of ancient scenes in Venice.

The air was chilled—typical of these old buildings with their thick walls—even though it was hot outside.

Godsafe sat on a wing-back armchair and pulled a tartan rug over his legs. On a small round table at his side was a box of paper tissues and a glass of plain liquid—maybe water, maybe vodka. "Take a seat, the pair of you," he said.

There was a sofa draped with a leopard-print blanket. They sat.

"What's your connection with Pietro?" Godsafe asked.

"I've known him for years," Leon replied.

"And his wife," Carlota added pointedly.

Godsafe hunched his shoulders and rubbed his hands together, as if cold. "Pietro's been very useful helping Mr.

Black. Without his *considerable* aid the Foundation would have been stillborn, I reckon." He chuckled. "And I have the documents to prove it."

"Yes, that's my understanding," Leon said. He wondered if Rose knew how considerable Pietro's aid had been. He somehow doubted it.

Clearing his throat, Godsafe said, "What have you to tell me about the Córdoba operation?"

"It has been closed down by the authorities," Carlota said.

The doctor broke into a fit of coughing, grabbed the glass of liquid and drank half of it. "That's most unfortunate," he said and licked his lips. "It means the other clinics will have to take up the slack." He looked at the ceiling—its corners harbored countless cobwebs. "I suppose we've forfeited the donated organs when this happened?"

"Yes, it seems so," Carlota confirmed.

"There are going to be plenty of clients who will be dissatisfied. Mr. Black is not going to be pleased."

"It is unfortunate," Leon echoed.

Godsafe shook his head. "I can't understand why nobody has told me yet. I will have to do a lot of rescheduling. I should have been told at once."

"An oversight, perhaps?" Leon suggested.

"Not everything in Córdoba is clear yet," Carlota chipped in. "We're still getting feedback."

Godsafe gave a raspy chuckle. "The twins have been troublesome as well, I suppose?"

"You could put it that way, Doctor," Carlota said. "What do you know about the twins?"

"They're a law unto themselves. I supply them with material on time, always, and they then frequently botch the procedure and I have to source fresh material!" He exhaled heavily and hunched his shoulders. "To prevent too many blockages in the supply-chain, we've had a compound built for donors." He chuckled and then coughed again. He wiped his mouth with a tissue and stuffed it down the side of his armchair. "It's more like a holiday camp—dining hall, cinema, play area for the kids, dormitories, plenty of board games and playing cards, and even an exercise yard." He tapped the side of his broad nose; a dribble of mucous trailed to his mouth; he licked it clean. "And we give them medical checks. They don't know why they're there, of course. That would be too upsetting..."

Leon reflected that in truth Godsafe was a glorified pimp.

"It must be a constant worry," Carlota confided.

"It is." He leaned forward in his chair, tapped his nose again. "The irony is Mr. Black of all people has been having problems getting a good match for his son, Byron."

"Now that is ironic," Leon said.

Godsafe rasped a cackle again and smiled crookedly. "At last, I've got a match. I arranged the harvest from the young boy barely an hour ago; in Verona. So it's not far. The heart's on the road as we speak." He embarked on a paroxysm of coughing.

Leon stood. "We've taken enough of your time, Doctor." They didn't shake hands. "We can see ourselves out."

Godsafe continued coughing and waved them off.

———

As THE PAIR got into the motorboat, Carlota asked, "Why do you want to get into the clinic? Can't we just tell the authorities and they'll raid the place?"

"That will take time and a lot of paperwork. We can't do anything about the victims who have been killed for their organs. My main concern is that they might have on tap a number of live donors like Akemi in that damned 'holiday camp' compound."

"That doesn't bear thinking about. Where to now, then?"

"An old acquaintance," he said mysteriously, veering the boat to the right into the so-called Canale della Fondamente, though Leon couldn't see where the canal ended and the Laguna Morta began.

On their journey, he gave Carlota a brief history lesson about several of the outlying islands.

Far over on their left was the island of Murano, almost directly ahead was the cemetery island, and beyond that was Lazzaretto Vecchio, a small island to the right of Murano. The concept of a lazaret began in 1485, when a devastating plague outbreak hit Venice and killed even the doge.

In response to the deadly pestilence, Venice's government built a public hospital on Lazzaretto Vecchio to isolate the infectious and curb the disease's spread. In 1486 the small island of Sottile—named because it was shaped like a small waist—was used as an additional hospital to house more plague victims. This smaller hospital island was renamed Lazzaretto Piccolo; in 1632 it was abandoned. In recent years archaeological work has undergone to exhume bodies on the two main lazzaret islands, Lazzaretto Vecchio and Lazzaretto Nuovo. However, Aiden Black purchased Lazzaretto Piccolo in 2014 and requested the help of the Italian health service in the form of the deputy Health Minister, Pietro Lo Verde—whose slogan was "Green by name, green by politics!"

Leon steered the motorboat to the jetty of Fondamente Nuovo, a private landing stage, and Carlota jumped ashore and tied the painter to a stanchion.

"You're sure this is the place?" she asked as Leon stepped onto the jetty, which was wet due to constantly passing waterborne traffic sending bow-waves to lap over the lip.

"Yes. As he's a creature of habit, he's not due for another half-hour." He pointed to the vacant stanchion next to theirs. "He parks his boat there."

She nodded. "Now what?"

"We go up and wait." He led the way, onto a solid stone jetty, and then ascended steps that had two half-landings. A lingering dank smell permeating the place.

Then he reached a timeworn wooden door with a brass fish knocker; there was no bell.

Leon used his lock-pick to gain entry and Carlota shut the door after them.

They'd entered a utility area with a washing machine, a tumble dryer, a stainless steel kitchen sink, several cupboards and a closet.

A heavy door at the other end opened onto a large lounge with tiled floor; it was sparsely furnished: a fifty-five inch television screen, a music center, speakers, a couple of two-seater sofas, a cocktail cabinet crammed with a colorful collection of liquor bottles, and a wall display cabinet with various awards, trophies and assorted books in Italian and English. In a corner stood a violin on its stand, its wood highly polished. Another sturdy door at the far side of the room doubtless accessed the front of the building and stairs down to the adjoining street.

To the right was the dining room with a mahogany table with chairs that would accommodate six at a sitting. On one wall was a display cabinet with colored blue and gold glass items, probably from Murano, and on another wall a long sideboard with a runner on its surface, possibly acting as a counter where food is placed prior to serving. A door at the far end of the dining room opened onto a bedroom which had two single beds separated by a nightstand. The bedroom's decoration had a woman's touch. On the dressing table he saw a framed photograph of Rose and Pietro taken several years ago: they were smiling.

Carlota picked it up. "I don't think they are smiling now," she said.

Leon cocked an eyebrow at her.

"Rose does not live here anymore. No woman does."

"Go on, tell me."

"There is not a hint of perfume. Only the musk of a man's eau de toilette."

Leon checked the bathroom: sure enough, there was only evidence of a man's toiletries.

"You never cease to amaze me," he said, smiling.

"That way, I keep my man, no?"

"I'm yours for as long as you can put up with me," he said. He took her arm. "Let's take in the view." He led her to the door on the left which opened onto a small balcony, barely big enough for two metal chairs and a little matching table. It overlooked the jetty area. He could see their motorboat. Plenty of craft wended their way over the lagoon.

Then he spotted the distinctive white-and-green livery of an approaching speedboat. "He's coming," Leon said. "Let's take a seat."

They both sat on the sofa that faced the door they'd entered earlier. A key was inserted in the lock.

Leon sat with one leg resting on the other, ankle on thigh, within easy reach of his gun. Carlota was on the other end, with legs primly together.

Pietro entered carrying a briefcase and started on seeing them, his dark eyes widening. "Who let you in?"

"Nobody." Leon flashed a smile. "Is that any way to greet an old acquaintance?"

Pietro's long lashes flickered. "Sorry, Leon, it was a shock. After all these years." He closed the door after him.

"Who is the lovely lady with you?" Pietro wanted to know.

"My—"

"Girl Friday," she supplied. "Carlota."

Eyeing her up and down, Pietro said, "You're a bit young for him, aren't you?"

"It isn't cradle-snatching, you know," she riposted. "I'm a grown-up with her own mind."

"Sorry, I shouldn't have said that." He glared at Leon. "You haven't explained..."

"I was in the city and thought I'd look you up." Leon waved a hand at the door, shrugged. "Sorry about gaining entry—old habits, you know?"

"Rose isn't here," Pietro said.

"I know. She told me she's working in her office to meet a customer's deadline."

"Then... you actually want to see *me*?" He strode over to the other sofa and dumped his briefcase on it. He took off his jacket, flung it over the back of the sofa. "Do you want a drink?" He gestured at the cocktail cabinet.

"Thanks, but no. At my age I need to cut back." Leon also wanted his hands free—just in case.

Pietro eyed Carlota.

"I'll have tonic water," she said.

"Fine." Pietro walked to the cabinet. "Don't mind if I indulge, Leon?"

Leon offered a smile. "Hey, it's your home."

Pietro poured two fingers of Johnny Walker Black on ice in a tumbler and then opened a small can of tonic water and poured it into another glass. He came over, handed Carlota her drink and then sat opposite them both, sipping his whisky. "You know that Rose has left me?"

Leon said, "We guessed, but it is not my concern."

"I guessed it was, since you two were an item..."

"That was some five years before she met you; she was nineteen, starting a career in Intelligence then."

Pietro darted a glance at Carlota as she drank. "See? He likes them young—he must've been sixteen years older than her."

"He will always be sixteen years older than her, won't he?" Carlota replied logically. "Some women prefer older men, Mr. Lo Verde. You know, they're more mature, even wiser."

He raised his glass. "Touché!"

Leon lowered his leg, leaned forward. "I was pleased for her when she fell in love with you. Your music captivated her, I believe. One of her strengths was her love of music." Leon nodded at the violin. "Do you still play?"

Pietro looked askance at the instrument. "The music's gone. Has been gone for a long while. Now, tell me, why do you want to see me after all this time?"

"Your involvement with the Black Foundation. When did it begin?"

"Involvement?" He swilled the liquid in his glass, the ice cubes clinking.

"You know, when did you start getting kickbacks from the Foundation. From Mr. Aiden Black."

"I resent your insinuation, Leon! Everything between us is above board."

Leon sighed. "I would dearly like to think so, but sadly that's not what Dr. Godsafe told us."

"Godsafe? He—he's... Anyway, what business is it of yours?" He took a large gulp, finished the liquid contents.

Carlota said, "The Foundation performs organ transplants, doesn't it?"

Pietro stood and went to the cabinet and refilled his glass. "Yes, that's one of its roles." He returned to the sofa. "It does research as well. Advanced, state-of-the art stuff; you wouldn't believe what they're working on. In a couple of years they will revolutionize transplant surgery."

Leon said: "That's good to hear if it reduces the queues for transplant organs."

Another gulp. "It is, isn't it?" Pietro smiled weakly.

Sighing, Leon went on, "What is not so good to hear is that the majority of Mr. Black's donors are not willing participants. They have been murdered for their organs."

Pietro stood abruptly, spilling a little drink. "That's absurd! Melodramatic tosh!"

Leon shook his head. "We've just come from Córdoba where the police have arrested and charged a good number of employees of the Black Foundation. The charges involve illegal organ harvesting and transplanting of those organs."

"I don't believe it! What evidence have—"

"The corpses are evidence enough. And then of course there are the twin surgeons."

"Oh, Roland and Yves Dubois! They're still working in Córdoba?"

"They're in jail, to be precise," Carlota said.

"They're both pretty sick," Leon added, "playing that damned music while operating on a patient!"

Pietro smirked. "The Odd Twins we in the ministry call them."

Leon stood up to face Pietro. "I fear your days at the ministry are numbered."

"Why? I've done nothing wrong."

"Godsafe has documentary proof you were paid by Black to engineer the building and creation of his clinic on Lazzaretto Piccolo. Damning evidence, in fact."

Shaking his head, Pietro turned and returned to the sofa he'd impulsively vacated. He put the glass on the seat's arm and reached for his briefcase. "I have adequate proof that not only is Godsafe lying but he is the one implicated." He unzipped the briefcase and plunged his hand inside.

He dropped the briefcase to the floor and pointed what appeared to be a Beretta Model 92 at them both. Had Rose supplied him with that, or had he come by it from someone in the criminal fraternity? "I will not let you ruin my career!"

"Have you ever shot anyone?" Leon asked calmly.

"No, of course not!"

"Then I advise against attempting it now. It can be messy and will only lead to misery."

"I don't know how you got that pimp Godsafe to give you evidence, but I can assure you he won't live to testify. We have people to shut down disloyal employees."

"Ah, so now it's 'we', is it?" Carlota observed, putting her glass on the sofa's arm.

"What do you plan doing with us?" Leon asked reasonably enough. He didn't believe Pietro was capable of cold-bloodedly killing two people. But if he became too stressed, the gun might accidentally go off with unforeseen but dire consequences.

All of a sudden Pietro reached out, grabbed Carlota's upper arm and pulled her to her feet, placing the gun's snout against her temple. "She's coming with me!"

"No I'm not!" she snapped.

"No, you'd better go with him, love," Leon said gently. "I'll be right behind you."

"I'm sorry, Leon," Pietro said, "but I only need one hostage till I'm safe." He fired his Beretta and Carlota screamed as Leon pivoted and fell to the tiled floor and lay still.

"You killed him!" she wept.

"Do as I say," he snapped, yanking her arm, "or I'll shoot you right here!"

He reached the door, opened it and pushed Carlota through, and slammed the door behind them, the sound echoing.

Chapter 18

Obeying Orders

Searing hot pain lanced through Leon as he rolled over and got to his knees. In a split second he had perceived in Pietro's eyes his intention and, knowing he could not reach his gun in time or cover the distance between them, he turned sideways on to the man, offering a thinner target like duelists of old.

He tugged his shirt from his waist. Blood seeped from the love-handle at his left side. It was a bloody graze; that was all; the slug hadn't even penetrated the fat.

Playing dead had probably stopped Pietro crazily emptying his gun into me, he thought.

He stood, surprised to find he was a little giddy. Mild body trauma, he guessed; the dizziness was certainly not due to blood-loss. It was not the first time he'd been shot, but the shock was always going to be considerable. This time he admitted that the shock was not so much from the minor wound as from the realization he'd been wrong: Pietro could be a cold-blooded killer. It stood to reason, he supposed. While he and Carlota—and Godsafe—lived, Pietro's career was going only one place: down the tubes.

Withdrawing his pistol, he hurried to the door, swung it open.

He passed through the utility area and descended the

steps that led to the jetty; halfway down he spotted Carlota's automatic: she'd either dropped it or Pietro had relieved her of it. He shoved the weapon in his jacket pocket.

The Galeon Galia motorboat was still where Carlota had moored it.

He holstered his gun and shielded his eyes against the glare of the sun and could see Pietro's white-and-green vessel pounding the waves, steering into the lagoon.

Leon untied the painter and jumped into the motorboat and then wished he hadn't been so precipitate as his wound reminded him to go easy. Breathing steadily, he switched on the Suzuki engine and it roared as he steered at pace into the lagoon to give chase.

There was a strong breeze, which was welcome under the hot sun. The water was choppy, the boat bouncing over the waves, spray splattering his face.

He'd gone a good distance when he spotted Carlota dive from the rear of Pietro's speedboat.

Leon increased the revs to close on Carlota.

Then he saw Pietro wheel his boat round in a wide arc, trailing a frothing white wake. He was going after Carlota.

She swam with the crawl stroke, but it wasn't easy fully clothed in this swell.

Pietro started firing his pistol at her! The bullets made small splashes to her left. She continued her stroke undeterred.

The gap was closing between Leon, Carlota and Pietro.

Leon pulled his automatic from its holster and started firing over the windshield, not expecting to hit Pietro, but the shots might deter him or send him scurrying away. After all, Leon had lived under fire; he was willing to bet Pietro hadn't.

But no, Pietro kept on coming, shooting wildly.

Carlota was about ten yards ahead when one of Leon's shots hit the fuel tank of Pietro's boat and it ignited immediately, exploding with a tremendous bright blue and orange flash. Pieces of superstructure flew everywhere as the loud detonation spread across the lagoon.

As gravity claimed the debris and it splashed into the lagoon, Leon set the motor to idle and leaned over to offer Carlota his hand.

"So you *are* alive!" she exclaimed, grinning.

He grabbed her hand. "Talk of my death is exaggerated," he said.

"You scared me back there, I can tell you!"

"Sorry, my love, but I wanted him thinking I was dead." He hauled her onboard.

"I'll forgive you—though it didn't do my heart any favors!

Water slewed from her and she sank onto a bench seat and gasped in air. "I wondered who was chasing him!" She shivered but he didn't think it could be from cold as the sun was bright and hot.

"Are you alright?" he asked, taking off his jacket, putting it over her shoulders.

"Yes, I'm okay." And then anxiety crossed her brow. "He *did* shoot you," she breathed in concern.

He looked down at his side. His shirt tail still hung out, a bloody patch on it. "Oh, it's just a flesh wound. It's stopped bleeding."

"Okay." Her brow creasing, she palpated the pockets of his jacket. "You need to go on," she said. "To the clinic on Lazzaretto Piccolo." She removed his jacket from her shoulders and fumbled in the pockets, removed her automatic. "Glad you found it." She checked its magazine and then slid it in her shoulder holster. She removed her own wet jacket and spread it out to dry on the other part of the bench seat, and gave him his jacket which he put back on.

"You're wet," he observed. She wasn't wearing a bra under her clinging white bandeau.

"I can see why you're a private eye." She grinned. "Don't worry, I'm not going to catch my death. The sun and the warm breeze will soon dry me."

"Hope not—catch death, I mean." He revved the boat forward.

She stood and moved to his side. "We all die, eventually, darling."

He hugged her with one arm while steering. "Let us not hasten the inevitable, eh?"

As they passed the burnt-out shell of Pietro's boat, they saw no sign of the man, only pieces of flotsam. "Probably fish food by now."

She nodded. The sun shone on her bare wet shoulders. "Toward the end," she said, "he was rambling about taking too many wrong turns in his career and he regretted alienating Rose, but he was becoming less lucid by the minute. I reckoned he was at the end of his tether. So I jumped ship while he concentrated on steering the boat!"

———

THEY WERE GETTING close to the island now. Leon spotted a heavily laden boat ploughing and bouncing through the waves about a hundred yards ahead of them. "Look, there's a supply boat going to Piccolo!"

"That might give us access," Carlota suggested.

"Agreed. We'll follow them in and see." He steered a slightly aslant course, running parallel with the wake of the supply boat.

Eventually, the supply boat berthed alongside a long jetty. Far on the right was a small marina with about a dozen boats of various sizes and class. Perhaps they were moored for staff recreation.

Leon noticed that two white Fiat Ducato vans were waiting to one side of the jetty.

"I'm going alongside. Cover up your holster," Leon said.

Carlota slipped on her jacket; it wasn't completely dry, but at least it hadn't shrunk. She let it hang open.

He steered the boat to gently bump against a half-tire that acted as a fender, and then cut the engine.

They stepped onto the jetty and fastened the boat to a bollard. "Follow my lead," he whispered. He tucked the blood-stained shirt tail into his waist-band and fished in his back pants pocket for his billfold, extracting a business card in the name of Simon Santos, insurance investigator.

Leon checked his jacket and could hardly detect the blood stain on the side. "Stand slightly in front of me to hide the stain, will you?"

"Sure—though I suspect they won't be looking much at you." She grinned suggestively, her jacket flapping open, revealing the almost transparent wet bandeau yet concealing the shoulder holster.

They approached the vans which had been turned; their rear doors were now open. The two drivers and the boatmen were carrying produce from the boat to the vans, while a man with a clipboard checked the items.

"*Mi scusi*," Leon said to the clipboard man.

"*Si?*" Clipboard glanced at Leon and then seemed to have eyes only for Carlota.

Leon continued in Italian: "I have been advised by the health ministry to investigate certain financial claims made by Mr. Black." He showed his business card.

"So?" Clipboard shrugged, eyeing Leon. "What is it to me?"

"Tell me, where are you taking this produce?"

Clipboard rolled his eyes; officials! He pointed to the van on the left. "That one goes to the clinic. Vital medicines, equipment and food of course."

"Of course," echoed Carlota.

He again studied Carlota appreciatively and his tone softened. He gestured with the clipboard to the van on the right. "This one is going to the compound and it contains in the main only food."

Leon said, "That is ideal."

Clipboard's face twisted in confusion. "How so?"

Leon explained, "There are two serious claims to be resolved. The first one is regarding the compound you speak of. Have you room in your van for us both? We should go there first, to the compound."

Clipboard said, "If you can wait until we're loaded?"

"Yes, we can wait."

"Should I assist you with the loading?" Carlota offered.

Scrutinizing her enthusiastically, Clipboard rasped a hand on his bristled chin and nodded. "That would help— I'll direct you to the appropriate van as you unload."

———

BY THE TIME the two vans were fully loaded and the emptied supply boat had cast off from the jetty, Carlota and Clipboard were on friendly terms—he was named Stefano.

Stefano ordered the second driver to go with the clinic van while he would drive to the compound then, after unloading, come on to the clinic. There were three seats in the cab so it wasn't cramped; Carlota sat next to Stefano, the better to conceal Leon's wounded side.

Stefano drove the van inland from the jetty. The road snaked round large rock outcrops and was potholed but on the whole not too bad. Fifteen minutes later, the van approached the compound.

There was a watchtower on the right-hand side of the metal gates. A sentry armed with a rifle manned the tower and another was at the gate, his Beretta AS70 rifle slung on his shoulder. They must have been expecting the van because he was already swinging open the gates. A fence ran from the gates on each side with razor wire strung along its top. Leon almost swore under his breath; if sentries were armed, they had to be willing to use their weapons on intruders—or escapees.

The gate sentry ambled to the driver's side. "Hey, Stefano, how come you're driving?"

Stefano laughed. "I fancied a change!"

Fancied Carlota, more like, Leon mused.

The sentry mopped his brow. "Being stuck in a cab is better than this gate sentry duty any day."

"It sure is!"

"And," the sentry persisted, "who's this with you?"

"Insurance guys. To see Rossi. Is he in his office?"

"Yeah, where else would he be? Doesn't do any *real* work." The sentry waved Stefano through and started closing the gates.

"I'll drop you off at the office block," Stefano said.

Shortly, he braked. "Here it is." There were several single story buildings, all with small windows and iron grilles over them. Stefano pointed to a block on the left. "I'll be unloading at the kitchens there. Next to the admin block. If you finish your business before I leave, I can give you a lift to the clinic."

Carlota laid a hand on his forearm. "That's good of you." She glanced at Leon then back to Stefano. "It's difficult to say how long the business will take."

"Well, you know where I'll be," Stefano said.

"Thanks." Leon opened the door and got out. Followed by Carlota. Stefano winked at her and she shut the door.

They waved off Stefano and walked slowly to the office door with its label *L. Rossi, Supervisor*.

Leon turned to scan the compound.

The gate sentry was looking beyond the compound, as was the man in the tower. There was nobody else in the area.

"Time for a revolution, I think," he said. He withdrew his pistol and screwed on the silencer. Carlota did the same.

He opened the door.

There was only one person in the room, sitting behind his desk, boots on its surface, eyes closed, smoking a cigar. He was overweight, his belly overlapping his leather belt. He had a double chin and a cauliflower right ear. The desk name-plate matched that of the door; no doubt to reassure him of his identity. Near the desk was a coat-stand and hanging from it was a peaked cap and a holster with a revolver inserted.

Rossi opened his eyes; they were submerged in puffy flesh. "You're supposed to knock!" he barked.

Carlota shut the door behind them and Leon raised his pistol, aiming it at Rossi.

"What's the meaning of this? Who are you? How dare you?"

"The meaning of life," Carlota said, "it's always questions, questions, questions."

Rossi reached for the telephone.

Leon fired a single shot, it hardly made a sound, but it made a mess of the receiver. "Don't."

Rossi raised his hands, the cigar dangling from dry lips.

Carlota went over to the wall telephone outlet and unplugged the cable, crushed the connector underfoot.

Rossi slowly lowered a hand and removed the cigar from his mouth and put it in an ashtray, and then licked his lips. "What—what do you want?"

"Tell me," Leon began, "why are you keeping people here in the compound?"

Sweat sprouted on Rossi's forehead. "Orders from Dr. Godsafe at the clinic. I'm just obeying his orders, that's all."

"How original," murmured Carlota.

"Where is the barracks?" Leon asked.

"Barracks?"

"Where do your sentries sleep and spend their off-duty time?"

"Oh, the administration block, you mean. There's a bar-lounge, a games room, a shower-block."

"How many sentries are there in the compound right now?"

Rossi wiped his brow with the back of his hand, briefly studied a wall chart behind his desk. "One on the gate, one on the tower at all times." He pointed to the chart. "Twelve men."

That meant a lot of killing. "Other staff—kitchens, store-keepers, cleaners?"

"Ten all told. We run a tight ship," he ended with a misplaced hint of pride.

Leon nodded. "Well, we've holed your ship below the waterline and it's about to sink."

Rossi's complexion paled and his eyes darted to the coat-stand.

"Again I say don't."

Rossi sat deflated, which was an achievement for one of his considerable bulk.

Leon took the revolver out of its holster and shoved it in his jacket pocket. "This is what I want you to do," he said to the supervisor.

CHAPTER 19

FISCAL CONCERNS

THE SUPERVISOR STRODE OUT OF HIS OFFICE AND stood in the doorway. He cupped his hands round his mouth and shouted, "Bono, Morelli, report to my office at once!"

"What, and leave our post?" demanded the gate sentry.

"Don't argue, Bono. At once!"

Standing to one side of the doorway, his pistol aimed at Rossi, Leon said, "Well done."

Rossi scowled and returned to sit at his desk.

Minutes later the two sentries rushed to the doorway and entered.

Carlota stepped behind them, her pistol raised. "Lower your weapons!" she ordered.

Rossi said, "Do as she says!"

Leon grabbed the two rifles. They were not carrying side-arms.

"Don't bother asking!" Rossi barked at the two men. Then he looked at Leon. "Now what?"

"We go over to the administration block," Leon said.

The short journey was tense. Rossi led the way, looking left and right, perhaps hoping an off-duty guard might accost his captors. If so, he was out of luck: not a soul appeared. The sun beat down on them and reflected heat back from the hard stony ground.

Finally, Rossi stopped at the administration building, next to the kitchens where Stefano's van was still parked.

"Open the door—slowly," Leon instructed.

Rossi was correct. There were ten men in the dormitory, some sitting on armchairs reading newspapers or paperbacks, others playing cards at a table, and a couple sound asleep in their beds. At the far end of the dormitory was the armory cupboard, with the rifles chained behind iron bars. Easy. Too easy?

Alarm showed in the faces of the few men who had noticed them enter.

"Everybody pay attention!" Leon shouted, waving his pistol for effect.

Those asleep were abruptly shaken awake; all heads turned to face the newcomers.

"Supervisor?" queried a dark tanned man with curly hair.

Rossi raised a hand in acknowledgement and shrugged his shoulders helplessly.

Carlota gently shoved Bono and Morelli forward to join the others.

"We are closing down this compound," Leon told them. "Your services are no longer required!"

Some murmured, a couple exclaimed, and Curly chipped in with "What about our back-pay?"

Leon sighed. "You can stay and face arrest and a lengthy jail sentence, or you can make arrangements to leave this island. The choice is yours. And whatever choice you make, be assured there will be *no* back-pay!"

"What about the people in the clinic?" said Curly, the man who had fiscal concerns.

"Don't go near the clinic or attempt to alert them. Save your own miserable skins while you can!"

Almost as one they scurried to their beds, ransacked their nightstand cabinets, packed several small items in holdalls and donned their jackets. One or two gazed wistfully at the armory, but without any dissent every one of them headed for the door.

"Wait!" Leon called. "Who has the key to those rifles?"

The oldest man among them held up a hand, the keyring dangling from an index finger.

"Leave that with me," Leon ordered. The man threw it and Leon caught it.

"Bono has the key for the gate," Carlota advised them. "Just leave and keep on going!"

Curly, their spokesman hesitated.

"If you return, you will be shot," Leon stated matter-of-factly.

They all exited the door and Leon watched them hurry in the direction of the gates.

Only Rossi was left with Leon and Carlota.

"That plan worked," Carlota observed.

"Loss of face," admitted Rossi.

"True," Leon allowed. "But no bloodshed."

"Yes. For that I am grateful," Rossi said with feeling.

"Now," said Leon, "for the inmates—the donors."

"*Donors?*" queried Rossi.

Carlota stared at him. "You really don't know what they're doing at the clinic?"

He shook his head. "My job is to look after the inmates. I was told the clinic is researching viruses, common colds, that sort of thing and needs these volunteers." He hunched his shoulders. "That's important—after the pandemic. We need to be more prepared."

"You'd better stay with us," she said.

They holstered their weapons, left the administration block and stopped outside the kitchens beside the parked Ducato van. There was a strong smell of cabbage and pasta as the door opened and Stefano walked toward them.

Stefano grinned. "Ready to go to the clinic?" he offered. Then he noticed Rossi. "Supervisor, is there something wrong? You don't look well."

Rossi grimaced.

"You're right," Carlota said. "He took a turn for the worse while we were talking. We think he should go to the clinic straight away."

"There's room in the back—and two folding seats."

"Ideal," Leon said. "Carlota, you'd better accompany Supervisor Rossi in the back. I'll go in the front with Stefano."

Stefano shut the door on Carlota and Rossi and jumped into the cab. He switched on the engine and drove to the gates. "Eh?" He stared and glanced around. "Where are the sentry guys?"

"The Supervisor has re-arranged their duties," Leon improvised. "He feels there is little need for them now."

"But the gates, they're wide open!"

Leon released a sigh of regret and withdrew his pistol, pressed it into Stefano's side. "And they will stay that way. Be a good fellow and simply drive us to the clinic, will you? And no more questions."

"But–?"

"You'll get more answers than you'd like shortly, I assure you."

"Okay, okay. It's obvious you aren't insurance guys, anyway."

"I suppose we are in a way. Actuaries. Calculate the mortality rate of individuals. Notably evil people..."

"Eh?"

"No matter." Leon slid his pistol into its shoulder-holster. "I'm putting the gun away if that makes you feel better."

Stefano wiped a sleeve against his forehead. "It does. Thanks."

———

STEFANO DROVE to the entrance gate of the clinic. Unlike the compound, this gate was imposing and ornate. On each side was a pillar of carved sandstone, a black and gold painted metal gate; a push-button and voice box was on the left-hand gatepost. A CCTV camera pointed down from the right-hand gatepost.

Leaning out the van's window, Stefano pressed the buzzer.

"Hey, Stefano, it's you!" a voice crackled over the intercom.

"Yeah, it's me."

"We were told to expect you. You've got two guys with you, right?"

"Actually, it's a man and a woman," he said, giving Leon a lopsided smile. "Oh, and the compound supervisor is in the back. He isn't feeling too good."

"Right. Stand by."

The gates automatically swung open.

Stefano drove in and through the wing-mirror Leon watched the gates close.

As Stefano drove along the wide access road, Leon said, "Are there any armed sentries here?"

"I haven't seen any." Stefano shrugged. "But I usually drive to the rear of the complex to deliver the goods, never the front door."

"Are all the different sections of the clinic complex connected?"

"I wouldn't know. I reckon so."

"We'll take a chance, then. No point in announcing our arrival too soon."

"The security detail knows you've come in," Stefano pointed out.

"Are the security people armed?"

"I—yes," Stefano said, "I've seen them. Wearing side-arms."

"Alright. Drop us off at the usual place you unload."

"That'll be the store-room entrance."

A matter of minutes later, Stefano turned onto a side-road from the main driveway and finally braked on the blacktop outside a delivery area large enough to accommodate several vans at once. A stack of empty wooden pallets was piled to one side. There was a concrete mezzanine, about three feet high, for goods to be discharged from the rear of small trucks and vans. Back from this was the delivery door which was rolled up; thick wide plastic blinds hung from the ceiling of the entrance, doubtless to minimize the intrusion of dust.

Leon opened the passenger door. "Are you staying or going?" he asked.

"I'll stay in the cab, if it's alright with you. If there's going to be any shooting, I'd prefer not to get involved."

"See you soon, then." Leon strode to the rear of the van and opened the doors. Carlota clambered out, followed by Rossi.

Leon led the way to the delivery entrance and climbed onto the concrete mezzanine, then offered a hand to Carlota. Rossi made his own way up.

They passed through the plastic dust curtain.

It was a small warehouse, with a concrete floor and on two sides stacks of boxes and crates, all labeled. Right now Leon wasn't interested in their contents.

At the far end was an office and to the right a door labeled *Access to Clinic Staff Only* in Italian.

"That's us. Today," Carlota said and opened the door.

Cautiously, they moved down a long corridor lit by fluorescent lights. Partway along one of the lights flickered. The others were undimmed.

Doors, again labeled. He doubted if anybody could get lost here.

"Where are we going?" Rossi queried in a hushed voice.

"Just satisfying my curiosity," Leon said. "Wondering if there are any more live donors about."

They came to a door marked *Laboratory. No Unauthorized Admittance.*

Carlota reached for the door-handle.

"No, that can wait," Leon said. "Right now we're interested in operating theaters, preparation rooms, more than lab work."

"Okay."

Further along they came to a door marked *Operating Room 2*. A red light shone. An operation was in progress.

———

WITHIN THE LABORATORY, Professor Yu Wei pored over computer readouts, his dark eyes speed-reading. Along one wall were a dozen cages containing macaque monkeys and piglets. Three of the monkeys were in the advanced stage of pregnancy.

"Andros, these results are exceptional!" Yu's normally flat features were animated.

The Greek scientist bobbed his head vigorously. "I know, Professor. Your immune injections have helped immensely."

"They have, haven't they?"

Initially, they had put stem cells into days-old monkeys and they had integrated very well with the monkey tissues. Now, they had gone beyond that. In those wombs was a living creature, potentially part-human, part-monkey. He feared it wouldn't survive to term, but they'd come a long way already; he was hopeful.

"I'm looking forward to seeing what these mothers give birth to!" Yu stated.

"Next stage, the pigs?" Andros suggested.

"Yes, preliminary tests have been good." They would attempt similar tests on the embryos of those piglets next. Yu rubbed his hands together. "You know, it's only a matter of time before we will be able to grow human organs in these animals!"

Andros laughed. "You could be in line for a Nobel prize, Professor, if you can dramatically reduce the years people spend on a waiting list for transplants."

Professor Yu chuckled. "I know. The pigs and monkeys might not be so agreeable about it, though." He had long ago dismissed any of the concerns that had been expressed about the development of human/non-human chimeras. That was for the philosophers. He was a pragmatist.

————

THE CHINESE SURGEON'S black pebble eyes glinted under the operating table lighting. Speaking through his surgical mask in his high-pitched voice he said, "I'm about to crack the chest." He lifted the hand-held sternum saw, placing its blade on the exposed area and began cutting the breastbone down the center. "Music to my ears!" he exclaimed.

Leon stepped forward, shaking his head. "Not to mine!"

The surgeon stopped, lifted the saw blade away from the half-incised sternum. "What are you doing here? This is an operating theater!" He peered at the nurse next to him. "Sister Li Jing, get them all out of here!"

The sister moved toward Leon and then stopped as Leon drew his pistol. "Dr. Gho, he—he has a gun!"

Carlota and Rossi stood in the doorway. Carlota also pointed an automatic.

Leon called to Rossi. "Go over and check the corpse. See if he was one of your inmates."

Tentatively, Rossi went to the side of the corpse. He covered his mouth with a hand and stared at the dead man's face. Then he nodded.

"You're sure?" Carlota asked.

Rossi removed his hand and supported himself against the operating table. "Yes, he was one of our people. He was sent here yesterday. He was supposed to come here for virus tests..."

"Instead of which he's going to donate his heart—unwillingly, I suspect—to that living client over there!" Leon gestured at the other operating table, where an obese middle-aged man lay.

"You have no right to be here!" the theater sister shouted.

Gho screamed, "You're going to kill our client with all your germs if you don't get out!"

Rossi stared at the corpse of the donor, shaking his head in disbelief. "I didn't know, honest to God, I didn't know..."

"You're spoiling my fun!" Gho exclaimed. In a sudden vicious movement, he lashed sideways with the sternum saw, slashing Rossi's throat wide open.

Arterial blood spurted in a fountain as Rossi collapsed to the floor.

CHAPTER 20

BLACK HEART

"DAMNED FOOL!" LEON BELLOWED AND SHOT GHO in the head.

The other surgeon stood with his hands raised in surrender and the rest of the theater staff did the same.

Leon spotted a door labeled *store room*. "Everybody in there!"

Hesitantly, they shuffled into the store room; there was barely space for all of them. Shelving and equipment trolleys took up considerable area. Leon shut the door on them, turned the lock on the door and then heaved a cabinet against the door for extra insurance. A fist or two started banging on the door. He ignored the sound and went over to check on the compound supervisor.

Rossi had stopped jerking. He was surrounded by his lifeblood.

"Come on," Leon said, "let's see what else is going on in this place."

They passed another OR: fully lit, with staff congregated around two operating tables, but only one of which was occupied. The person appeared to be a naked young male, having not long reached puberty. His chest had been opened in readiness. "Another poor donor," Leon said. He noticed a preservation transport box similar to those he'd seen in Córdoba.

"But where's the recipient?" Carlota asked.

"Maybe she or he has had a heart attack?" Leon shrugged.

Carlota said nothing.

And they walked on.

They passed two more operating theaters, both empty, their lights extinguished. There was a ninety-degree dogleg in the corridor and they followed it until they came to the doors of private wards, all of them with round windows for observation.

Leon moved up to one and saw a young woman attached to an IV and a machine performing her breathing function. He went in and checked the chart at the foot of her bed: Eleni Demopoulos, aged 15. Below this was another notation: *Charity Case*. A recent recipient—or an expectant one? He gently lifted the sheet that covered her: she was naked and there was a sutured incision down between her young breasts. Recipient, then.

They left and went to another ward door.

He looked through the window. This one was occupied also—a young man of black complexion, sleeping.

Opening the door, Leon stepped inside with Carlota following.

The chart identified him as Byron Black, aged 16.

"I think he's waiting for a new heart," Leon said.

"Godsafe said as much, remember?"

"I remember. Let's see who else we can find, hmm?"

Together they walked along the corridor until they came to a door at the end. Writing on the pebble-glass stated: *Clinic Director: Mr. Aiden Black.*

Without hesitation, Leon opened the door.

A man of dark complexion sat at his desk, his hands clasped together on the desk surface, as if praying. He must have heard the door open for he raised his head, eyes widening in surprise. "Who are you?" he demanded. "You don't have permission..."

Leon drew his automatic. "This gives me all the permission I need, Mr. Black."

"What do you want?"

"I want you and me to have a chat with your son," Leon said.

"If he sees your gun, he might have a serious heart attack."

"I won't show him it, don't worry," Leon reassured. "Shall we go?"

Reluctantly, Black nodded and stood up. His gaze scanned the office, as if he wanted to remember its every feature. As though he did not intend to return.

"Lead on," Leon told Black, slipping his gun into its holster. "And don't try anything. I can pull out my gun and shoot you in the blink of an eye. Don't let it be your last eye-blink."

"Okay." Obediently, Black exited his office and moved along the corridor, Leon and Carlota following.

A doctor and a couple of nurses passed in the other direction, fleetingly greeting Black, and hurried on, seemingly unconcerned about the presence of Leon and Carlota: the Director had guests, so what?

Black stopped outside the door of the private ward they'd been inside earlier. Byron Black's. He opened the door and entered and Leon and Carlota were directly behind him.

A nurse was finishing writing up notes on the chart on a clipboard and now fastened it to the foot of the bed. "Oh, Mr. Black, I wasn't expecting you yet." She tilted her head at Leon and Carlota and raised an eyebrow.

Black cleared his throat. "That's alright. They're with me. Are all preparations made?"

"Yes. We will take Byron down in thirty minutes."

"So he hasn't had his injection yet?"

"No, sir. That will be done in the OR."

"Of course, I do recall now." He touched her elbow, leaned in to her. "Can you leave us for a short while?"

"Yes, certainly, sir."

She left.

"Who's this, Pa?" Byron asked. He had a golden brown complexion and his father's high forehead, broad nose, and thick lips. His dark brown hair was brushed straight back. His chestnut eyes showed no concern about the impending operation.

Black said: "This man wants to put a stop to my work, son. He doesn't want you to have the transplant."

Leon drew his automatic, held it down by the side of his thigh.

"He's got a gun!" Byron exclaimed.

Black glared at Leon. "You promised!"

Leon shrugged. "Sorry, at times I think a hand-gun is part of me."

"Are you alright, Byron?" Black asked as he walked to the bedside and gripped his son's hand. Then he swiveled round to face Leon. "You can't in all conscience stop it—it will be the waste of a good heart! They're waiting in the OR now."

"Your pimp Dr. Godsafe had a boy killed for that heart," Leon said.

"Pa, what's he saying?"

"Stuff and nonsense, son!"

"Pa, what did he mean?"

"This is my son," Black snapped. "He will die without this transplant. He's innocent!"

Leon exhaled heavily. "So was the dead boy."

Byron yanked his hand from his father's grip and shunted to the other side of the bed. "What have you done, Pa?"

"It's the only way, don't you see?" Black pleaded. "The defect is too far gone. You'll never survive if you go on the waiting list..."

Abruptly, Byron folded his arms across his chest. "I don't want it!"

"No, no, no!" Black screamed. Tears trailed down his face.

"Yes, Pa! I couldn't live knowing a boy was killed so I could live."

Leon said, "Your son has more scruples than you, it seems."

Black leaned on the bed, attempted to reach across it with a hand, to hold his son. "Oh, Byron, Byron..."

The boy slid out the other side of the bed. "You'd better go, Pa. Cancel the op! Keep the heart on ice. That's what you do, isn't it?"

"You don't know what you're saying, son. The prognosis..."

"I'm done talking, Pa." Tears glistened on Byron's cheeks. "Go."

Shoulders slumped, Black moved away from the bed. He looked at his son and said, "You know, I'd give anything to save you..."

"Go, Pa. Just go..."

Black opened the door and strode into the corridor.

Leon shoved the gun in his shoulder-holster and turned to Carlota. "Stay with Byron, will you?"

"Will do," she said.

———

PROFESSOR YU WEI STARTED, lowered the computer sheets he'd been perusing. "Did you hear that?" he asked Andros.

"What—a car back-firing?"

"That was a gunshot."

"A gun here? Highly unlikely, Professor."

"I know what a gun sounds like," Yu stated firmly. "From experience, I can assure you." He'd witnessed a good number of executions of criminals, after all. "Stay here."

"No, I will come with you, Professor. You'll see, it is nothing."

They exited the laboratory fearfully, but thankfully there was nobody in the corridor as far as the dog-leg.

Both walked along the corridor until they came to OR2; the operating light still flashed red. Yu peered through the round window in the door and stepped back, his mouth gaping wide in shock.

"What is it, Professor?"

"Bodies..." Breathing in deeply, Yu opened the door and hastened to the nearest body. It was a civilian he'd never seen before, his throat viciously cut, and he was lying in a pool of blood. He looked at the donor body. The cut through the sternum had been interrupted. Yu recognized the man on the other side of the donor's body: "Dr. Gho..."

"Professor!" Andros exclaimed. "The store room!"

Now Yu heard it, the banging.

The pair rushed over to the store room. Together they hauled the cabinet clear and turned the lock.

The medics tumbled out, all of them pale-faced.

"Dr. Kwan!" Yu exclaimed. "What happened?"

"A man came in with a gun," Kwan said.

"No, two men and a woman," corrected the theater sister.

"Yes," Kwan said. "Gho snapped! He killed one of the men, so the other one shot him, just like that!"

"It was horrible!" the sister said.

"Do you know why?" Yu asked.

Kwan shook his head.

Yu feared the worst. "The killer could be an agent for our Ministry of State Security—working in the External Security and Anti-Reconnaissance Division..."

"But he was European," countered Kwan.

Yu nodded. "They would hire a mercenary, a trained assassin. That would give the MSS deniability."

"What do we do?" Kwan pleaded. "The assassin might still be in the clinic!"

"Put all your research notes on a memory stick," Yu told

him. "I'm doing the same. Then we must leave by the back door—the delivery area."

"And go where?" queried the sister anxiously.

"We must commandeer the boats in the marina," Yu declared.

Kwan gripped Yu's arm. "We can be useful to other regimes. Maybe the Saudis would welcome us, no?"

"We will worry about that once we are clear. Now, go!"

———

Leon followed Black down the corridor the way they had come. "Where are you going?" Leon asked.

"Back to the office. I have an OR waiting for me to tell them the news. I need to cancel the op."

"Okay."

They reached the office and they both sat; Black slumped behind his desk. He appeared drawn, his complexion more gray than ebony now. Lethargically, he clicked on the intercom. "Nurse, hold the OR ready but for now keep the heart on ice. It will be used for another lucky recipient soon, I'm sure."

"Yes, sir. But—but what about your son?"

Black moved fast. He opened the desk drawer and took out a revolver: a short-barreled Astra 357.

Defensively, Leon wrapped his fingers around the butt of his automatic and drew the gun.

"My son can have *my* heart!" Black bawled and shot himself through the mouth. The muzzle blast was considerable due to the powerful cartridge.

The nurse on the intercom shrieked.

Leon shoved his automatic back in its holster.

Brain dead. That's the proof they required for a donor's organs to be viable for extraction.

A doctor and a nurse rushed in.

"What happened?" the doctor demanded.

Remaining seated, Leon indicated the revolver still

gripped in the dead man's hand. "He shot himself—but left explicit instructions about his son."

Sobbing, the nurse said, "Yes! Oh God, I heard him say that!"

With surprising calm, the doctor said to the nurse, "It's highly likely his father's a good match, anyway. We can do the necessary tests while we prep." The nurse gave the impression of still being in shock. "Get the staff. We need a gurney here now!"

With an effort the nurse pulled herself together and wiped her eyes. She rushed out.

The doctor turned to Leon. "Will you be a witness—to make this legal?"

"Yes." Leon stood. "I'm available to talk to the police in due course. But right now I think I'd better break the news to Mr. Black's son." He was glad Carlota was there with the young man.

———

IT FELT STRANGE, returning to the Lo Verde apartment, particularly only accompanied by Rose. Carlota had tactfully decided to stay at their hotel. Leon noticed a couple of dried drops of his own blood on the tiled floor where he'd fallen— a long time ago, it seemed.

Rose sat on the opposite sofa, her face drawn, almost haggard. Her eyes were red-rimmed. He suspected she had no more tears to shed.

"I'm sorry it ended this way," he said.

She stared into space. "I wonder how it would have been different if I hadn't..."

"Hadn't what?"

Her gaze evaded his eyes. "Oh, nothing. Thinking aloud."

"Pietro chose his path. Nobody forced him to become a crooked politician."

She chewed her lip. "He started with such strong ideals!"

"I'm sure many politicians begin the same way, wanting to make a difference. But allegiances, political complexities creep in and policies are watered down, the powerful or the vociferous are pandered to, and before you know it, those precious ideals are irretrievably compromised." It sounded trite and of no comfort at all.

She stood up, walked toward him. Her eyes were moist. "I must ask you—about her, Carlota..."

He stood also and put a hand on her shoulder. "Don't go there, Rose. We had a good time—in the past. Look to the future."

He glanced at the violin in the corner. "Let music back into your life."

———

CARLOTA AND LEON attended a musical evening performed by a string quartet in the ancient church Chiesa di San Samuele. The program consisted of, among other pieces, Massenet's *Meditation*, Sarasate's *Carmen Fantasy* and Tartini's *Devil's Trill*. Carlota was convinced that the latter was inappropriate for a church, though she enjoyed it.

At the end applause erupted.

Rose Lo Verde chose that moment to step into the aisle and walked to the dais. She was carrying Pietro's violin.

The soloist lowered his old violin to his seat and bowed to her. "Signora Lo Verde, it is an honor to have you in the audience," he opined.

"My husband was your mentor. I think he would have liked you to have this." She solemnly presented him with the violin.

"You are too kind," the violinist stated and accepted the gift.

As the applause broke out again, Leon turned to Carlota. "You know, I can't understand how anybody can live without music."

"You mean like the Taliban and their ilk banning it?"

"Yes, precisely. Music transcends borders and even goes beyond national languages. It is truly international. It speaks to your soul, it talks to your heart."

Carlota nodded. "Truly, Leon, those who ban people from listening to music are heartless."

Afterword

Rose Lo Verde discovered that her husband had amassed a considerable fortune; however, it was frozen pending official enquiries as to its provenance. She continued with her private security business. However, she became a modest patron of music in the city and was well known for her soirées.

Akemi Kuroda stayed with the World Health Investigation Team and eventually became a team leader. She was stationed in Geneva but was called upon to travel widely.

When the police raided the administration building of the Black Foundation overlooking the Grand Canal, Reed Carter's body was found in Mr. Aiden Black's office. Curiously, his little finger was missing.

Government investigators landed on the island of Piccolo found twenty-six "donors" in the compound; they were well fed and unharmed.

Armando Salinas resigned from the FBI and established a private investigation business in Charleston, South Carolina.

Sister Cristina of the Order of the Missionary Sisters of the Mother of Christ continued to do good work at St. Paul's hostel for the homeless in Charleston, South Carolina. From time to time, much against the wishes of the Abbess, she teamed up with Armando Salinas, Private Eye to resolve the occasional mystery or crime.

Dr. Godsafe never got to buy his dream home in Savannah. He died from complications following a bout of pneumonia. He had no next-of-kin. His sequestered funds stayed where they were.

Byron Adriano Black survived the impromptu heart transplant operation.

International investigation began to unravel the many properties and businesses of the late Aiden Black and his Foundation. Lawyers were going to have a field day.

In October 2022 Mr. Kenneth Carswell, aged 58, died from a massive heart-attack. He was grateful to have enjoyed six years additional life. He bequeathed his entire wealth, about $3,000,000 to Save the Children.

In November 2022 an earth tremor off the coast of Greece caused a freak tidal wave which sank entirely the small island of Piccolo; minor flooding occurred in Venice, notably in St. Mark's Square, not dissimilar to the familiar acqua alta phenomenon.

GLOSSARY

Spanish unless stated otherwise

- AISI—*Agenzia informazioni e sicurezza interna;* Italy's Internal Intelligence and Security Agency
- Calle—street in Spanish and Italian
- CESID—*Centro Superior de Informacion de la Defensa* which later [2001] became the CNI (*Centro Nacional de Inteligencia*).
- Daigashi—second under-boss of a Yakuza syndicate (Japanese)
- Doge—Venetian head of state (historic; the last was appointed in the eighteenth century)
- Giri—a debt or obligation (Japanese)
- Kai—a suffix denoting association or society, often used in gang names (Japanese)
- Leche frita—"fried milk": cold-milk pudding encased in a warm fried shell of egg and flour.
- Mizu shobai—"water business"—nightclubs, bars, restaurants (Japanese).
- Polígonos—industrial estate
- Yubitsume—Yakuza ritual act of slicing off the little finger at the joint to atone for a mistake (Japanese).

IF YOU LIKE THIS YOU MAY ALSO ENJOY: THE SQUAD

BY JEFFREY J MARIOTTE

SOMETIMES BRUTAL, SOMETIMES BLOODY, THIS STRAIGHT-LACED POLICE PROCEDURAL WILL HAVE YOU TURNING PAGES AT LIGHTNING SPEED.

Phoenix, Arizona Detective Russ Temple has a new case—two burned corpses in a house apparently victimized by arson. But before he can make headway, he's tasked with forming a brand-new squad within the department's Violent Crimes Bureau.

The Major Crimes Squad is to handle headline-making cases that the city wants closed—and fast. They'll also be expected to track down and bring in the worst of the worst as Temple quickly learns when they're newly-formed squad is handed its first high-priority case—the days-old death of the mayor's son from a fentanyl overdose.

Investigating these two cases pits the Major Crimes Squad against drug dealers, an outlaw motorcycle gang, and the newest—and most dangerous—face of organized crime in the city. From saguaro-studded hillsides to the sun-splashed streets of Phoenix, no criminal is safe from their reach.

But that notoriety has a downside, for each squad member is a target now, too...

AVAILABLE SEPTEMBER 2022

ABOUT THE AUTHOR

Nik Morton has sold over 100 short stories, edited periodicals and contributed to magazine articles, chaired writers' circles, run writing workshops, and judged competitions. He has edited many books and was sub-editor of the monthly magazine *Portsmouth Post* (2003-2007) and Editor in Chief of a U.S. Publisher (2011-2013). He has had 32 books published—including 3 books in the psychic spy *Tana Standish* series and 8 westerns—and co-written 4 books in the *Floreskand* fantasy series. His *Write a Western in 30 Days – with plenty of bullet points!* is a best-seller. With his wife Jennifer, Nik lived in Spain for several years (2003-2019). They have since returned to England, residing in Northumberland—near their daughter Hannah, son-in-law Harry and grandchildren Darius and Suri.